MW01126392

SEAL'S
PROMISE

SHARON HAMILTON

Copyright © 2014 by Sharon Hamilton

All rights reserved. Without limiting the rights under copyright reserved above, no part of this publication may be reproduced, stored in or introduced into a retrieval system, or transmitted, in any form, or by any means (electronic, mechanical, photocopying, recording, or otherwise) without the prior written permission of the copyright owner of this book.

This is a work of fiction. Names, characters, places, brands, media, and incidents are either the product of the author's imagination or are used fictitiously. In many cases, liberties and intentional inaccuracies have been taken with rank, description of duties, locations and aspects of the SEAL community.

ISBN: 1503038424
ISBN 13: 9781503038424

AUTHOR'S NOTE

I always dedicate my SEAL Brotherhood books to the brave men and women who defend our shores and keep us safe. Without their sacrifice, and that of their families—because a warrior's fight always includes his or her family—I wouldn't have the freedom and opportunity to make a living writing these stories. They sometimes pay the ultimate price so we can debate, argue, go have coffee with friends, raise our children and see them have children of their own.

One of my favorite homages to warriors resides on many memorials, including one I saw honoring the fallen of WWII on an island in the Pacific:

> "When you go home
> Tell them of us, and say
> For your tomorrow,
> We gave our today."

These are my stories created out of my own imagination. Anything that is inaccurately portrayed is either my mistake, or done intentionally to disguise something I might have overheard over a beer or in the corner of one of the hangouts along the Coronado Strand.

Wounded Warriors is the one charity I give to on a regular basis. I encourage you to get involved and tell them thank you:

https://support.woundedwarriorproject.org.

SEAL BROTHERHOOD SERIES
Accidental SEAL (Book 1)
Fallen SEAL Legacy (Book 2)
SEAL Under Covers (Book 3)
SEAL The Deal (Book 4)
Cruisin' For A SEAL (Book 5)
SEAL My Destiny (Book 6)
SEAL Of My Heart (Book 7)

BAD BOYS OF SEAL TEAM 3
SEAL's Promise (Book 1)
SEAL My Home (Book 2)
SEAL's Code (Book 3)

BAND OF BACHELORS
Lucas (Book 1)
Alex (Book 2)

TRUE BLUE SEALS
True Navy Blue (prequel to Zak)
Zak (Book 1)

NOVELLAS
SEAL Encounter
SEAL Endeavor
True Navy Blue (prequel to Zak)
Fredo's Secret
Nashville SEAL

So he'd screwed up, been a bad influence on the groom. *So what else is new?* With a past of foster care home rejections and "repositioning" he was used to being on probation. It felt normal. Not until he got into BUD/S did he feel like he'd found home. A real home. Guys who finally shared his intensity for life and irreverence for batshit rules that everyone else thought applied to him. The SEAL's ethos was the only set of rules he wanted to live by. And the beginning pretty much said it all:

> *In times of war or uncertainty there is a special breed of warrior ready to answer our Nation's call. A common man with uncommon desire to succeed.*
> *…I am that man.*

He didn't have to be a perfect man, and hell, there were very few on the Teams. He was good enough. He'd never be perfect anyway, and who would want to be? No, he was that guy who wouldn't give up. That was all it was. Not ringing the bell. No matter what.

He thought about it while he watched Shannon's white dress fill the aisle as she began her stately walk along the burgundy carpet to her willing but completely shitfaced groom. Her father was proud, as any father would be, to have such a radiant daughter, pink and soft in all the right places. She possessed the steady gait of a fearless warrior princess, and the purposeful way she advanced, like she was intent on a plan she was going to fully execute, was just like any SEAL. Her eyes nailed Frankie, who didn't have a clue what he was getting himself into.

That made T.J. smile and check out his shoes. She was the kind of woman who would call the shots, run the household, run Frankie, manage the hell out of his schedule and get her future soccer players up on time and off to everything moms did with a house full of hellions. He saw lots of them in their future for some reason. Kids with snotty noses and hair a bit too long. Band-Aids and skinned knees. All the things he never had as a child.

But he'd watched those kids play through chain-link fences. Watched their parents cheer. Watched the juice breaks and the encouragement he never got from a single coach or foster mom. He was never noticed. Never special.

And that was just fine.

CHAPTER 2

Shannon felt the pressure of everyone's eyes on her back. She tried not to think about her maid of honor, Cindy, who had pummeled her with questions about the mysterious, bad-boy best man she hated, T.J. Talbot.

That man had done his best to break them up, Shannon thought, and now was working hard to ruin her wedding. He'd exposed Frankie to the seedier side of life. Nothing they experimented with in the bedroom had ever been Frankie's idea. It was always something T.J. had described to him.

Fuck T.J.

Yet, she knew that by marrying Frankie, tradition said she was, in fact, marrying all the SEALs on Team 3.

To hell with that!

Thank God she'd never have to sleep with any of the rest of them. Knowing they were so possessive about each other, made her a little bit jealous.

Frankie was listing to one side. T.J.'s strong arm propped him up, which was the biggest fuckbomb of all time.

Stop it, Shannon. She'd picked up their language, their mannerisms, as if they'd been wet paint and she was rolling through them naked. She not only thought in swear words, she was starting to say them. They rolled off her tongue as though she'd always talked and thought that way.

Yeah, and that was T.J.'s fault, too.

She could see the little Cheshire cat smile he was giving her, not that she would give him the satisfaction of knowing he was even a piece of cat litter stuck on the bottom of her shoe. Frankie was going to be all hers. She'd extricate him from his Brotherhood and give him back to them when she was good and ready. Screw the wives who told her she would always come second when it came to the Brotherhood. They didn't know their men. She didn't want a normal plain vanilla relationship with Frankie. He was fuckin' addicted to her, and that was exactly the way she liked it.

There you go again. On your wedding day, and before you get to the altar and kiss your betrothed, you've sworn—what? Maybe three or four times? And had unclean thoughts?

Yeah, even ladies in white wedding dresses had dirty thoughts.

She knew that was normal.

Come on, Frankie. Stand up straight. She saw the glassy eyes and knew T.J. had caused it. Her Frankie was drunker than he had a right to be. From the unearthly glow in his blue eyes it was probably tequila, which he couldn't hold well at all.

Not like she could. Oh yes, there was that song about dropping your clothes for margaritas. That was her. But Frankie was having a hard time standing up, let alone being conscious for the wedding. And it wasn't because all the blood had rushed to his groin, either. That would have been funny. She'd have been happy about that one.

She shot a quick *fuck-why-did-you-do-that?* look at T.J. His smile broadened, and she saw him move his arm when she stood about a foot away from the man she'd chosen for the rest of her life.

The moment T.J. released his hold on Frankie, the groom fell, almost toppling her as well. Her veil was ripped from her hair, her bodice pulled down—maybe too far down for a second or two. And accompanied by the screams of everyone, especially the two mothers in the front pew of the church. Frankie did a face-plant onto what was luckily plush carpeting.

She adjusted the detachable beaded bodice to make sure she was decent first, and then had difficulty turning in Frankie's direction, thanks to her long dress of chiffon and layers of voile. Feeling like her feet were stuck in mud, she turned slowly. T.J. was leaning down to get Frankie, and she caught a hint of his aftershave, nearly brushing her lips across his cheekbone as he stood.

Three big SEALs helped Frankie up. His face bright red, sweat pouring down his forehead, and his shame preceded what Shannon knew would be a huge bender, perhaps one that would eclipse their wedding night. He'd messed up her wedding. He'd tried so hard not to. He'd told her every day he hoped everything came off the way she wanted. Perfect. Like she was perfect, he'd said. Did he suffer from premonitions?

Fuck perfect.

So…there was her fifth swear word and unclean thought. She had another one as she grabbed his arm and hoisted him to her side, which made a few people in the audience titter. T.J. was chuckling just loud enough for her to hear that too.

This is not happening. She knew she would wake up any minute. This must be the nightmare wedding from a bad movie. This wasn't *her* wedding day. The day she'd dreamt about her whole life. The one where she'd be the star of the show.

After the vows were said and the rings exchanged, the two of them walked down the aisle, both relieved to have survived the ceremony without further bloodshed. Frankie led her straight to the bar, which she thought was a great idea.

He'd stopped to tell someone in the last row he wasn't even drunk, which was such an obvious lie. It was a classless further slight to her not-so-perfect wedding. Like maybe God was responsible for all this.

It could be her fault, scaring the shit out of him and making him need to get so drunk he passed out. It would be a cold day in hell before she'd admit it publicly, though. She knew Frankie was scared to death to displease her. In her heart of hearts, she knew she was fully responsible. But no one would ever know.

No one. Ever.

What she loved about Frankie was his soft heart and how easy-going he was. That, and the fact that she would be the center of his universe, regardless of what her girlfriends warned her about the Brotherhood. He would be a kind and devoted husband and some day father. She could count on him to be there for her. She loved exciting and surprising him. He would support her in everything she wanted to do without question.

T.J. came up behind her. She could smell him before he put his palm on her shoulder, matching the other palm on Frankie's shoulder while they stood waiting to get poison into their systems quick. The bartender had dropped the first glass he'd filled with ice for her Tom Collins, so the jitters were spreading. But not to T.J. He was rock-solid, steady and undistracted, and she hated every muscle and sinew of his body. Every drop of his blood. Every cell. She hated all of him for being so calm and light-hearted about her disaster of a wedding.

Not that he'd ever know. She did her best to give him a triumphant, smile. Then she took Frankie's double scotch and downed it before he could get his hands on it. With the liquor on her lips and a glow spreading down her chest, she didn't care how they looked at her. She was a bride on a mission. Her day. Her time, and they better fucking play her game or she'd take them both on.

T.J. gave her an appreciative return glance. Frankie was still trying to figure out what had happened as he told the confused bartender to give him the scotch he didn't get the first time.

"Okay. I'm good. Good now. Time to face my audience," she said and wafted off as if she was wearing a dress of white potato chips. She'd deal with Frankie after he found the courage to look at her. Until then, she didn't want to be anywhere near him or his fuckin' devil of a best friend.

Okay, so that was number six.

T.J. was enraptured. The bride was storming across the wooden floor of the fellowship hall, bloody entrails of his heart guts, if there was such a thing, caught in the hem of her dress. No woman had ever made him feel that way before. He was completely powerless to focus on anything else until she was out of sight.

"Glad that's fuckin' over," Frankie said with a croak, and then coughed.

That brought T.J. to life, but he found it hard to talk.

"I'm never going through that again. Something happens to her, someone else wants to have a big wedding, the answer is no, and if that means I stay a bachelor my whole life, so be it," Frankie said.

"You're not a fuckin' bachelor. Too late for that, man. You'd be a widower. Not a bachelor."

"Whatever the fuck they call it."

"You know, Frankie, I wonder if you realize what you've just done?"

"I don't catch your drift."

"You've committed yourself to one woman. You really sure this is a good thing?"

Now, why are you even talking about that? Oh yeah, to cover up the fact that the bride is the object of your fantasies. Right now that fantasy involves a number of very unholy images. And you're standing next to the only man on the planet who has any right to have such fantasies. This is the guy you'd lay your life down for without a second thought…Oh, thank God, there is Miss Fresh Face walking through the door and aiming for me, just in time.

"Hi, T.J. I thought I'd find you hanging around the bar," Cindy said.

God, she was a welcome sight. She was the drink of water that wouldn't save his life, but would definitely make the next few minutes possible. He was almost ready to ask her if she would suck his dick and be quick about it.

"Cindy, you're lookin' mighty fine," Frankie said, eyeing her. "I was getting a lecture from my best man, asking if I knew what kind of shit I was getting myself into, and you walk back into the room, and now we can talk about something really important."

Cindy giggled. She stood on tiptoes and gave Frankie a lip-lock. "And don't you forget it. I'd have spent my life with you, Frankie, and you wouldn't have had to walk down any aisle or dress up like a penguin." She whispered soft things to Frankie, and T.J. could see he liked it.

Until Shannon showed up. Of course, Shannon would blame T.J. If she'd look at him, that is. She was shooting daggers at Cindy. Frankie removed his palm from Cindy's ass and was, once again, red in the face.

This was not turning out to be one of Frankie's better days.

CHAPTER 3

It was days before T.J. could get Frankie away to enjoy a beer at the Scupper.

"You ever think about settling down?"

T.J. returned a glare he knew Frankie would feel deep in his gut. "Don't ever ask me that fuckin' question again, Frankie." He watched some lovelies who strutted in with unbelievably tight cutoff jeans and knotted tee shirts that showed a good portion of smooth, flat abdomen—just his favorite kind of eye candy. All the girls who wanted to make it with a SEAL did this on Friday and Saturday nights. One of them snagged T.J.'s appreciative smile and gave him a wink.

Perfect.

Frankie watched where T.J. had focused and shook his head. "I don't know where you get all the energy, Talbot. Keeping stories straight, promising to call them and then—"

"What stories? Why the hell would you tell them stories? It goes like this, Frankie, 'Hon, you wanna screw?' Doesn't involve a lot of talking, Frankie. And then if they want to talk too much, you kiss them until they shut up."

Frankie giggled like he always did when T.J. revealed some of his philosophy on women and the other finer things in life. "I always let them talk." Frankie shrugged his shoulders. "I'm interested in what they have to say. Don't you want to know them a little bit first, T.J.?"

"Well, that tells me you're not a very good kisser."

"Fuck you, T.J. How do you know how I kiss? Shannon thinks I kiss real good. She loves it."

"I'll bet."

"I'm not shitting you, man. We get it on, T.J. You should try it. Staying monogamous. Sexy as hell knowing someone is waiting for me at home, and I get to fondle her all night long. And she'll still want to be there in the morning."

"Not for me."

"But I love her, T.J. You'd do it too if you married someone like my Shannon."

T.J. shook his head and raised a finger. "No. Never like Shannon. I'd have to work too hard."

"That's what you do when you love somebody, T.J. Shannon and I have a perfect love. I've never wanted to be so devoted to anyone, well, except for you, of course—"

"Shut the fuck up. Trying to make me jealous? I don't go for guys, Frankie."

"Yeah, but I love you, man. I wish you could have what Shannon and I have."

"You mean you do whatever she wants and have no will of your own."

"No, see, that's what you got wrong. I *want* to please her. She gets so excited sometimes, like a little girl. I feel so lucky every time I look at her. This beautiful, smart, sexy woman is mine and mine alone. I tell you, T.J., you're missing something. One night stands are boring, man. This is where it's at."

"Good for you, asshole." T.J. raised his beer, "To love, then."

"And family," Frankie added.

T.J. nearly spit out his beer "Family? You're not seriously gonna make me drink to family, are you? You remember who you're talking to?"

"Not *your* family, T.J. My family. I'm going to have a baby. Shannon and I made a baby together."

T.J. wanted to slap him. His insides turned to molten lead. He bit down so hard, grinding his molars he almost bit his own tongue. Procreation was a dirty word. He was halfway convinced he'd go get himself fixed so he never had to deal with that situation. His biggest fear was getting a girl pregnant, perhaps creating another fatherless soul, or having to marry someone you really didn't want to just to do the right thing.

And now Frankie was willingly walking into that buzz saw.

"I can't believe it. You ready to be a father, Frankie?"

"Hell yeah. And you know what? You're about to be a godfather."

"Not me."

"Yes, Shannon and I talked about it, and you're going to be the baby's godfather. We want you to do us this honor."

"You sure Shannon okayed this?" T.J. wanted to say no, but he knew it would hurt Frankie perhaps more than anything else he could do or say.

"She knows you're like a brother, T.J. She knows you would do anything for me, even die for me, you know? Who else could be that baby's godfather?"

"Anyone but me." T.J. had said, but in the end he'd agreed. He remembered the wedding and how nervous Frankie had been, so worried about ruining Shannon's perfect day. And now he was going to be a father.

But he knew Frankie, unlike T.J.'s own father, would never abandon his child. Frankie would be there to make sure that child had everything possible. And he'd do it out of love. He wouldn't farm an infant to some hellhole in another state, allowing him to be raised by sadists and mean women and their asshole husbands. Or raised in an institution like juvenile hall. Left like a leaf floating on the current of a river of no return. Nobody could call himself a man and do that to a child. Unforgiveable.

Six months later, T.J. was thinking about Frankie's wedding day while he and the rest of SEAL Team 3 sat in a bombed-out building, waiting for nightfall so they could proceed to the rendezvous. The target hadn't been where they were told he would be.

In fact, this was the third time in as many days that the intel had been inaccurate, which wasn't a good sign. Each day, they were sent further out into the rural parts of the city of Goan. There hadn't been a shot fired, but the eyes of the people they'd seen were hard.

T.J. had tried warming up to their new interpreter. Not everyone on the team trusted him. He was no Jackie Daniels, the interpreter they'd used during their last deployment, who had literally saved their lives. This guy was shifty, didn't look him in the eyes when T.J. spoke to him, and that spooked the hell out of him. The terp was edgier than he'd seen kids on speed in juvie.

The unease was beginning to rub off, even before the terp told him in clipped English. "Something's not good here."

Well if that wasn't the fuckin' understatement of the year. "So tell me the *good* news, Sherlock." T.J. preferred using the name more similar to his Pashtu common name, a word no one, even the few of them well-schooled on the language, could pronounce. He was hoping for something slightly positive to compensate for the hairs standing out on the back of his neck, the ache he was getting in his shoulders from crouching quickly to take cover. The terp was doing it ten times more, eyeing corners and turning around to check for follows.

"No good news, boss. All bad here. Must be very, very careful."

T.J. heard several of their platoon swear openly and wished not so many had heard him. He decided to lessen the load on Frankie, who had been uncommonly quiet, as if he had a premonition. He'd thought Frankie was scared the day he married Shannon. That was a joke now.

"You remember that day when you passed out, Frankie? Your face is at least as red as that day."

"That's because it's fuckin' hot, man. Can't wait for midnight."

"I think it was because of all the tequila we drank. And everyone in their Sunday finest."

"That was a fuckin' nightmare of a day, except for the fact I married the girl of my dreams."

"That you did, my man." T.J. leaned to the left to peer out of the hole in the rubble. He couldn't shake the uneasy feeling about this place. He didn't like the howling wind, the way everyone avoided being anywhere close to them, like they were lepers. Sand was getting into everything. He was getting a huge blister where one of his socks had a hole, these boots unforgiving.

An RPG hit barely six feet from them, exploding out a cloud of rubble, sending all of them into the air. While pebbles and body parts rained down on them, T.J. saw they'd lost at least two men—and Frankie was hit. He checked himself and discovered he still had twenty and didn't hurt anywhere, and then he went to tend Frankie. He'd landed on his back, blood pouring from his mouth. T.J.'s gut tightened but he worked to hide the concern he felt for his best friend.

"Shit, Frankie. You bite your tongue?"

"No, man. Got hit in the back. Can't feel my legs, T.J. What the fuck?" Frankie brought his hands out from behind him. He'd been sitting on them. His fingers were dripping with his own blood.

T.J. rolled Frankie to the side, far enough to see a metal piece imbedded in Frankie's lower spine. The blood was bubbling, watered down by what T.J. assumed was spinal fluid. Fredo was radioing for extraction. T.J. swung around so he could hold Frankie's head up slightly while he checked for combatants.

"Got Marines on their way, gents," Kyle yelled out over the cries of their CIA embed, who had been hit as well. T.J. shared a look with his LPO, something he knew Kyle had seen many times before. His Team leader's tight jaw and unwavering eye contact commanded him he'd better hold it together for Frankie. That's when he understood Kyle knew Frankie wasn't going to make it, but they had to convince Frankie he would.

Sonofabitch. He took a deep breath and barked, "Frankie, getting you home. Bird is coming now. Hang tight. I'm going to go see if I can help out some of the others."

"No. Don't go. I don't want to die alone, man."

"Frankie, you're not going to die."

"T.J., you're a fuckin' bad liar. Always have been."

"Shut up, Frankie. I gotta stop the sound effects or they'll know right where to send the next one, and we'll all buy it."

"Trust me, they know. They're looking to get themselves a turkey. Why mess with a sparrow?"

T.J. knew Frankie was telling the truth. It still sucked.

It was happening more and more, light injuries requiring evacuation, and then the combatants went after the helo and got everyone. Of course, that was if the SEALs or a sniper on the chopper didn't pick them off first. But fifty percent of the time it worked, which was much worse than it used to be.

"T.J., please hang here for a minute while I finish this mission." Frankie's eyes were kind, tears running down his cheeks. "If there was ever anyone in the whole world I would want to take care of my Shannon, could ever see her fuckin' besides me, it would be you."

"Frankie, stop it. I'm not going to fuck Shannon."

"Your loss, you dumb shit. She's going to be a widow, and someone needs to watch over her and the baby. I want you to raise my little girl, T.J. I want you to beat up the first asshole who tries to get in her pants. I want you to hold Shannon's hand while she's in labor. And I'll be right there with you, man. Just not in this body."

"Frankie, stop it. This isn't helping your situation." T.J. could hear the chopper approaching, but he knew it wasn't what Frankie needed right now. Frankie needed a miracle, and T.J. couldn't do anything but watch his friend die. He wanted to hug the big dufus who he'd joked and played around with, slap him in the face and tell him to wake up, that the play was too realistic and was creeping him out. Take the man for a beer and laugh about scaring each other. He wanted to be anywhere but here, doing this thing right now, and not being able to say the things he'd never gotten to say to Frankie. Because if he lost it, Frankie would too. "Hear that? That's the sound of home, and apple pie, and you getting well and telling her all those things yourself."

"Love you, man. Do it, T.J. You promised. You're our little girl's godfather, man. You promised, man." Frankie's lethargic gaze showed nothing but love. T.J. never had a real brother, that he knew of, and now he was losing the only man in the world who had been more than a real brother to him.

"Do what?"

"*Promise* me. Promise me you'll take care of Shannon and the kid."

"Fuck me."

"*Do it*, goddamn you!"

T.J. nodded, gripping Frankie's hand, which didn't grip back. His blue eyes were as glazed as they had been on his wedding day. Except this time he wasn't going to wake up. He was already on his way to his next mission—in heaven.

CHAPTER 4

Shannon wasn't supposed to, but she was painting the baby's room. They'd been told the little one, due in three months, would be a girl. Frankie had been thrilled, and it warmed Shannon, remembering that Skype call that day when she relayed the news. She'd chosen the name Courtney, and hoped Frankie would like it as much as she did. He hadn't called her last night at their scheduled time. But that wasn't unusual.

The baby was getting very active, so she made a mental note not to hobble up and down the ladder so much. Although she was steady on her feet, she didn't want to risk a fall.

The doorbell rang and she put down her light pink roller of paint, wiped her hands on an old paint-smudged hand towel and barefooted it over to the front door. Standing with the backdrop of a sunny, blue-sky San Diego day were a man and a woman in white Navy uniforms. The officer removed his hat and tucked it under his arm.

With a lump in her throat and heart pounding, she barely heard the news, delivered with unwavering eyes filled with compassion. It was a difficult job for them, she could see. It wasn't a job she'd want, or be able to do as well as they did. But she was thankful they were polished and professional.

She inhaled at first, ready to explode with tears on the exhale, but there was the baby to think of. Any upset she was feeling would affect Courtney, and that was, thankfully, her primary concern.

She thought about Frankie, the way he didn't like sand in his eyes, never told any of his buddies he hated the beach, the worst part of the wet and sandy they all had to endure during BUD/S. And yet, that's where he died, in a sand hole somewhere far away from her and her loving arms.

Her eyes stung and her lower lip quivered. The hole in her chest seemed bottomless, but as she let her breath out and mentally calmed herself she slowly came back to present day, this day she would always remember, and asked if they'd like to come in for a glass of water. They accepted, and entered her little bungalow. She puttered around in her bare feet, getting three tall glasses of ice water, filled to the brim with ice as she was lately fond of doing so she could crunch the tension of Frankie's deployment between her molars.

They did look a little uncomfortable. They answered questions, but didn't volunteer anything. She knew they'd done this many times before. The questions were probably the same, *How did he die? Did he suffer? Was he alone when he died? Who was with him?*

The answer to that last one was like a slap across the face.

"We understand your husband's best friend, Special Operator T.J. Talbot, was with him when he died."

"I'm sorry, but I'm Frankie's best friend. No one loves him as much as I do." She wasn't going to start using the past tense until she had to.

"Yes, ma'am," the gentleman said. "We understand that. However, SO Talbot was with him at the end. He did not die alone, ma'am."

The baby started kicking again, and she worried that her emotions had pumped adrenaline into her daughter's system. She took a long drink of water and closed her eyes, willing calm. If she weren't pregnant she'd be moaning and huddled in a heap on the ground, pouring her heart out. But with little Courtney in her belly, she wasn't going to take that chance. Somehow, it wasn't what she wanted to do, anyway. Her daughter was a strong reminder that life went on. It sucked, but it went on.

Just not with Frankie.

They rose to go when the conversation dwindled off into nowhere, and she began paying more attention to the pink nail polish on her toes. She was wearing pink every day now. Pink pajamas, the ones she could still wear, pink bed sheets (until Frankie came home), pink nail polish, and she even managed to put a hot pink extension in the side of her hair as if a little bit of Courtney was coming through.

The woman gave her a card to the Navy counseling group. Shannon already knew she'd go see Libby's dad, who had helped a lot of the SEALs with their emotional issues, not to mention the marital strains they experienced. And death. They'd all lost someone they loved. There wasn't anyone in the community who didn't know someone who hadn't come home. Today it was her turn.

"Mom. He's gone," she said into the phone before the Navy messengers of death had pulled from the curb outside, escaping to do another mission.

"What do you mean gone? I thought he was—Oh, my God, Shannon. No!" her mother said in a voice strained and brittle.

"Yes. They just left."

"I'll be on the next plane."

"No thanks, Mom. Give me a day or two, please. I've got friends here who can help. You come out soon, though. Give me time to be alone, but please don't think I don't appreciate what you want to do. I do. I need to do this first part alone and with a few of the other wives here. You have Dad."

"Don't be ridiculous. It's what a mother does. I'm still coming."

"No. Really. I need to be alone."

Shannon knew her mother was a little hurt, but would recover. Next she called Frankie's parents, who were out. She left a message without saying it was bad news. Only that she needed to talk to them right away. Important. Involving Frankie. It was the last phone call she had to make.

She put the glasses—the ice cubes hadn't melted yet—into the dishwasher, added soap and turned it on. The paint towels she tossed into the washing machine. She rinsed out the brush roller, the paint in the sink looking like the strawberry-flavored milk she'd loved so much as a child. She tapped the lid onto the paint can. Arched back to give herself a good reverse stretch and looked at the pink glow in the room, the walls she would finish soon, but probably not tomorrow.

Tomorrow she'd go get that white crib she liked with the dust ruffle in pink camo. She'd put up pictures of animals and buy fuzzy teddy bears and maybe a frilly dress or two. A headband with a bow on it. Some pink ruffled socks and Mary Janes.

The phone rang in the late afternoon, waking her. Gloria, Frankie's mom, was calling.

"We've been notified as well. I'm so sorry, Shannon. I can only imagine what you must be feeling."

"Oh, Gloria. He was your boy. I can't imagine how it must feel to lose the boy you raised, the boy who turned out to be a fine and loving man." She wiped the tears from her eyes, giving Gloria time to compose herself.

"We'll get through this, Shannon. We'll do it together. Your baby will want for nothing, sweetheart. Of that you can be sure."

"I know it, Mom." Using the term "Mom" must have touched Gloria, and she sobbed, handing the phone over to Shannon's father-in-law.

"Hey, sweetheart. Only thing I'm thinking about is that Frankie was doing what he always wanted to do. And doing it with the guys he loved so much, his brothers, Shannon. God help me, I'd rather go out that way. Not stuck in a nursing home that smells of piss or alone in a hospital ward. They told us T.J. held him at the very end."

There was T.J. again, inserting himself in her life. Her second thought was more compassionate as she realized he was grieving, too. How would he show his grief? How would he deal with it? He had no family, at least no one who wanted him, anyhow. Which was one of the things Frankie could never understand. How anyone could throw away a little boy's life like that?

T.J. was hard as nails because he'd had to leave behind his childhood before he was old enough to know how else to deal with it. She had to admit she felt a tinge of sorrow for him. A carefully guarded tinge, wrapped in camo duct tape. Something private, dark and never to be revealed to anyone.

They said their good-byes and she returned to face the house again, where she and Frankie had been so happy. There was still so much to look forward to, but all those bright sunny days now seemed like a burden. Everything she'd planned for her and Frankie was suddenly over. Why hadn't she thought about that before? It just never occurred to her that he wouldn't come home. Things like that always happened to other people, not to her.

It still felt like Frankie would walk in any minute, telling her it had been a joke, T.J.'s idea of funny. But no, even T.J. wouldn't play this trick on her. The walls were bare and unfinished. The room smelled of paint, but had a nice warm feel to it, although empty.

But her belly, unlike her heart, was full of life.

It wasn't fair. But that was the way it was.

CHAPTER 5

T.J. processed out Frankie's things and signed the paperwork, taking ownership of his buddy's personal property. Part of him was angry with Frankie for leaving him with all his shit to have to deal with. He cursed under his breath at what an asshole he was to have even that thought.

Wasn't like Frankie had rejected him, like had happened to him so many times over the years. Frankie had touched a part of him that had been vacant and hollow and had filled it with admiration, respect, and trust.

He remembered those days in the group homes when a couple would come by to look at the "older" orphans, and they were made to shower and dress up in the one set of pants and shirt and tight black shoes handed down from some more fortunate boarder at the home. He'd stand in line like all the other boys, looking at them. Probably smirking. Which is why he was never chosen. He saw the other boys react, trying to look sweet and adoptable. And even though a tiny part of him felt the same way, he knew he showed that he didn't care, because that's what he told himself.

Screw them all. If your own parents didn't want you, who cared about anyone else?

Nah, it wasn't fair to blame Frankie for that, but T.J.'s anger still wasn't satisfied. Besides, Frankie made the request he was forced to honor, giving him such a fuckin' impossible task, to bring these things that had been important to Frankie, and hand them over to Shannon, who hated the ground T.J. walked on. Might even blame him for being the one who came back. Like T.J. had used up the quota of survivors for the day, thus abandoning his friend.

And he knew exactly how she felt. He felt the same way. He blamed himself for living, blamed himself for causing so much worry on the part of Frankie's widow. He blamed himself for not trusting his sixth sense over there—that funny feeling he got that said things were all fucked up. He'd kept that knowledge to himself this time. Why? Usually he told his LPO about situations he thought were extra dangerous.

But it was as if he had that force of will, he could make sure it wasn't their time. Like so many other close calls, they would always somehow emerge unscathed.

Except on that last deployment he knew deep down it wasn't the truth. They'd been one step behind. Perhaps trying to do a job the Marines should have been doing, not the SEALs. Not that the Marines were expendable, but the SEALs were supposed to do surgical strikes with good intel. He hoped some asshole's head rolled over that one. He hoped never to have to face the man who was responsible for the decision to go in on the third day and not have them pull out. None of them had liked it one bit.

So maybe that's why he didn't say anything now. Why none of them did. The other side had figured out how to kill more SEALs, and now was using that knowledge as a strategy. You wanted to go in confident when it came to high-risk missions. With enough practice and training, things could go wrong and they would still work out. But this one had seemed from the get-go like the wrong fuckin' TV program on the wrong fuckin' channel. Nothing had been right about it. And a man—Frankie Benson—his best friend, and a man who had everything in the world to live for, was gone.

It wasn't fair, but then death was indiscriminate. He knew that, but it didn't make it any easier to take. Frankie was the one who'd gotten the pretty girl, the good grades, made his parents proud, dutifully knocked up his wife right away, which was the way it was supposed to be done.

T.J., on the other hand, had broken a lot of hearts—foster parents and girls he'd known, teachers who'd believed in him, employers, coaches whose teams he'd had to walk off of because he had to work, or because his grades made him ineligible—he broke everyone's heart, and more than once too. He wasn't any better at the second chances than he was at the first. He was the one who should have bought the farm. Not fuckin' Frankie.

Everything fit into his buddy's duffel and one shoebox. That box had a collection of letters from Shannon. Frankie had read some of them to the guys. God, the lady could write damned sexy things, and everyone got revved up whenever

Frankie got a love letter. He'd sit down as soon as those letters came, glued to the paper, that silly, shit-eating grin on his face, pink cheeks like the bottom of the daughter he'd never see, half embarrassed, but incredibly grateful for his life. That was the thing that separated them. Frankie was grateful for his life. T.J. was out to grab as much of it as he could before the bell rang.

T.J. had stitches in his thigh, on his forearm, and a couple of stitches on his left butt cheek he wasn't sure he really needed but was given anyway by an overzealous corpsman. That was the part that itched like hell, and he was halfway of a mind to rip them out with surgical scissors. They were damned annoying, and he hoped they didn't leave a scar he'd forever have to explain.

He swung the duffel over his right shoulder, cradling the shoebox in his left hand while he made his way to the pickup. He tossed the duffel in the second seat of the 4-door truck, and set the shoebox beside him on the bench seat in front.

Looking down, he pretended Frankie was inside that box, maybe done up in miniature like that movie he'd seen as a kid about the guy named Tom Thumb.

"You're gonna have to help me here, Frankie. Shannon doesn't want to see the likes of me. I can't just show up without calling first, but I did sign a paper saying I'd return your stuff to her, so send me a sign, would you? I'm in need of assistance."

He pretended Frankie said something nasty, which he most certainly would have, if the man had been alive.

Fuck! He punched his steering wheel and then pressed his forehead to the top of it, gently banging it against the black leather padding.

This is totally messed up.

In the silence of the truck cab, he thought he heard Frankie laughing at him. *Big, tough SEAL, afraid to talk to a woman.* But she was Frankie's woman, and she was six months pregnant. The facts were stacked against him. She was fragile, so he couldn't tell her off if she took it out on him, which he was sure she would. She'd lost her husband, so she didn't deserve to be treated in any way other than like the lady she most certainly was, so why did he have to be the one to take Frankie's stuff to her? She hated T.J. with everything in her soul because of all the shit he had caused her and her dead husband.

Maybe he should get Lansdowne to have one of the other Team guys return Frankie's belongings. Would it have been any easier to give it to Frankie's parents? That he could probably have done without any trouble at all, but Shannon? Shannon didn't deserve this.

He dialed her number and hoped like hell she wasn't home.

But he wasn't that lucky.

"Hey, Shannon. How're you holding up?" His voice was raspy, and it cracked like a boy of seventeen.

"How do you suppose I'm holding up, T.J.? You calling to say you're sorry or to give me a hard time?"

Her abruptness was her method of keeping her distance from everyone. He'd heard the other wives talk about how they had trouble getting close to her.

"No, even I wouldn't do that."

"Well, the day is young. Give it time. I'm sure you'll figure out a way to be an asshole before you go to bed."

That unfair statement pulled the plug on his anger. It was like the girls in grammar school who would call him names because they knew he wasn't allowed to push them back. Why was it okay for a girl to use verbal violence, but he wasn't allowed to protect himself by making them hurt in return? Some therapist's idea of the right order of the world. Probably a jerk who didn't know his ass from an anthill.

"You're entitled to your opinion. I might add that Frankie didn't share that opinion of me, not that it should make a fuck's difference to you." He was satisfied he'd delivered a slap and not a full-on blow to the chops.

"It doesn't mean shit to me, T.J." She breathed heavily into the phone. "Okay, look, I'm not at my best, so what is it you called about? You must have something in mind."

"I have a box of his things, and the Navy wants me to deliver it to you."

"I'll be gone tomorrow afternoon. Why don't you drop it by the house then, any time after twelve. It should be safe on the porch for a couple of hours until I get home."

"I could meet you where you're going."

"Seriously, T.J. I don't want you anywhere near my OB. I don't want to be reminded that all my husband's things are being handed over to me for their safekeeping or whatever. I'd like not to burst into tears in front of a waiting room filled with a bunch of emotional mothers-to-be and their husbands."

"I get your drift."

"You can leave it on the rocking chair on the front porch."

"I'll do that, then."

"Okay, we're done?"

"I think so."

"Good. Thanks for dropping the stuff off. Should I leave anything for you? Anything in there you want for yourself?"

"God, Shannon, I haven't even looked at anything much. I know about a few letters of yours in there. That's about it."

"No selfies in there?"

"Um, Frankie never took pictures of himself."

"No, asshole. I sent him a few naked selfies. I want those back."

Oh, those. He'd completely forgotten what fun they'd had with Shannon's selfies. Truth was, some of the guys would sneak them from under Frankie's bed and pass them around quarters while he was taking a shower. The last round had happened so fast, and then they were traveling, so T.J. still had the picture of Shannon in his shaving kit and hadn't had the heart to tell Frankie.

He certainly wasn't going to tell Shannon now.

The next day, the streets of San Diego were as charming as they always were, sunny, filled with light peach and white houses, green gardens, and palm trees reaching up into a bright blue, cloudless sky. He usually reveled in the gentle weather, but today he felt almost resentful about it, as if it wasn't right there were so many happy people living in such a happy place when Frankie was dead.

Frankie and Shannon's house was small, which wasn't unusual, since it was an expensive neighborhood. Even a little one was ungodly expensive. They were able to buy it with the deployment bonus he earned, saying he doubted they'd be able to buy anything larger until they moved to the East Coast.

They'd lived here only a few months, but already the colors were crisper, brighter. Maybe someone had painted the outside. The front steps looked like they'd been painted red so recently he was worried that maybe he shouldn't walk on them yet.

As Shannon had told him, there was a white wicker rocker on the little concrete porch, obscured by a delicate metal handrail with boxwood bushes planted in a row in front. The trimmed hedge also bracketed the walkway to the porch.

He swung the duffel bag down on the far side of the chair, so it wouldn't be seen from the street, and placed the box on the seat. He looked inside at the living room through the small glass window embedded in the massive Craftsman-style front door and was satisfied no one was home.

Walking back to his truck, he checked his cell phone for the time. It was one o'clock. He told himself she'd be along anytime now, and he should get going, but he couldn't leave Frankie up there in that box alone and unable to defend himself should a complete stranger decide they wanted the worthless contents of the box.

He sat back and waited. As usually happened, when he thought about Frankie and Shannon, he remembered their wedding day. It had been a pretty incredible day, certainly memorable. As weddings went, he thought it was perfect. It was so much better when things didn't run on time, and all the unexpected things in life showed up at the wrong moments. He lived for those times.

And Shannon had been all tousled and white, delicate and sweet, like the buttery vanilla frosting on the wedding cake. After the ceremony, Frankie had been on serious probation, so was careful when he placed the cake in her mouth, but she still got a blob of frosting on the right corner of her lips. Frankie had kissed it off. The guy was enraptured. It had been good to see. It had been a good day, despite what Shannon might think. His buddy had the sendoff he deserved and the beginnings of a life he'd earned because he was such a good guy. One of the good guys.

It had always made T.J. feel like a better person when he hung around Frankie. He'd never told him that, and this he regretted. Maybe someday he'd tell Frankie's daughter. Probably would never tell Shannon.

An hour went by. He was surprised at himself for being patient, waiting. He didn't mind it. Was going to be his last time with Frankie, in a way. That box was up there, like Frankie was in heaven, and he, T.J., was here sitting in the front seat of a truck. Waiting for what? Well, to be honest, he was waiting for the rest of his life, and eventually for the end of it.

But he knew it wouldn't be for a while. Another one of his sixth senses.

He thought about the promise he'd made Frankie. Wasn't like he'd agreed to go chase Shannon and get her to marry him, which would be the biggest mistake of both their lives. But he'd find a way to secretly help the little girl, and yeah, he'd kick the first guy who tried to get fresh with her. Would be creepy for the kid, though, having an old, gnarled SEAL shadowing her while she was trying to survive high school. Have this dark shadow around every corner, ready to pop out and defend her. She probably wouldn't like that. And in another sixteen or seventeen years his capacity for stealth would be seriously compromised. Hell, he might even be using a cane, like Tyler had to occasionally.

He was sharing this chuckle with Frankie, really feeling him sitting in the box with the little mouse chuckle Tom Thumb would have given him, when Shannon arrived. Before she drove into the garage, she rolled down her window, and he did the same. They were heading in different directions.

"Left everything on the porch. Just wanted to make sure no one messed with it," he said in his softest, most compassionate tone. She did a quick inhale and ripped her eyes from his face, looking out through her dirty windshield.

"Thank you," she said over the top of her steering wheel. But she didn't gun it, like he'd expected. She was thinking, and then she tilted her head. "You want to come in for a drink?" she said, still looking straight ahead.

"I don't think so, Shannon. You'd probably prefer to be alone, and I only came to bring you his things." That got her to look at him, and he could see the red puffiness around her eyes. Part of him wanted to say he was sorry, but that would have earned him a rebuff. She kept watching him, like she expected Frankie to materialize if she stared at him long enough.

It gave him the creeps, so he looked down at his hands in his lap. "Well, I'll be going, then."

As he drove away, he heard her say, faintly, "Thank you."

But it was probably his imagination.

CHAPTER 6

It was just your basic plain brown box. Didn't identify itself as military, except for the sticker on the front. When she picked it up, it was very light. Much lighter than a box holding all the personal effects of a man, her husband, the father of the baby she was carrying should be. She'd expected it to be heavy, like lead or gold bricks. Because the stuff of a man's life was heavy, dense, not simple and lightweight. Not something that could be tipped over to blown away in a gentle wind. It should be heavy enough that, if you threw it, the box would go straight to the bottom of the ocean.

She set the box on the coffee table Frankie's dad had made years ago, when he'd gotten his woodworking tools. She went back outside and got the duffel, which was heavy.

Laundry.

Probably dirty laundry, she thought, like he always lugged home in this same bag she'd seen dozens of times. He'd walk into the house with the Cheshire cat grin and the gentle eagerness she loved about her Frankie, even though he was a piece of work. She suddenly wished she hadn't been so hard on him. On those days, soon as he got home, all he wanted to do was take her to the bedroom, and she usually held out for getting her "stuff" done. Today, her "stuff" wasn't that important.

She sat on the edge of the couch with the duffel bag propped between her knees. This was going to be hard. She'd always been a self-starter. Could handle any crisis, even when everyone else was freaking out. Right now she felt on the edge instead of in the eye of the storm. Things were buffeting and blowing around her, and she wished she could dance in the wind. She wished she could be scared, wished she could be angry, anything but morose. Dead. She felt dead.

Little Courtney stirred, reminding her that she was soon to be a mother. She'd throw everything into raising her. Everything. Her life depended on it. It was the one thing left she'd accomplished with Frankie, one thing they'd shared that would hopefully outlive them both. Courtney would be the best of him and the best of her. It was a miracle the way it had happened. She wanted this baby more than life itself.

She picked up the duffel and lugged it to the laundry room. Near the top his pork pie was laid to rest on Frankie's neatly folded and ironed shirts with his dress uniform underneath. She took the uniform into their bedroom, setting it, the shirts, and the hat on the bed, like he was going to put them on as soon as he got back from wherever he'd been.

Back in the laundry room, she pulled out camo shirts that hadn't been well laundered. Holding them up to her nose to determine if they were clean or not, she was filled with the glorious man-scent that was uniquely Frankie's, and she lost it.

She ran down the hallway to the bedroom. Crashing down onto the mattress, she held the shirt to her chest and cried like she hadn't been able to do before. She let it fly. She told little Courtney it would be over soon and not to worry.

"Some day you'll understand, sweetheart." She closed her eyes and she saw him bending over her, leaning into her body with his hips, reaching for her lips to kiss while he ground into her. He was always tender, caring more about what she was feeling than himself. Unselfish.

"Love you, Shannon, baby doll."

He'd been the only man ever to call her baby doll. "Love you too, Frankie," she whispered, keeping her eyes closed. "Missing you, baby."

Of course, the sobs involuntarily spasming her chest made it impossible to hear his response.

"I'm trying, Frankie. How am I going to do this without you?"

She thought maybe she heard him answer, *"Don't miss me, baby, love me."*

"I do, Frankie. Trust me, if you ever doubted me, I do" A new wave of tears began when she couldn't remember if she told him she loved him during the last Skype call. She wished she'd told him more often. "Courtney will be my witness. I do love you still. You won't ever be gone for me, baby."

She saw his smiling face as she fell asleep.

Over the next few days, Shannon made herself busy by finishing up Courtney's room, finally removing the newspaper and tape from the window. She'd found the crib she wanted on sale and bought it. They were out of the pink camo sheets, bumper and curtains, so she ordered them. The changing table would arrive next week, so she'd paid for that as well.

The doctor had wanted her to come in to discuss some lab work that was spilling outside the ranges of normal. He made some changes to her diet and recommended she drink more water. She hadn't planned to tell him about Frankie's death until he began to stress the importance of having father at the visits.

"I'm a widow as of a few days ago, doc. I'm afraid I'll be bringing my mom at the end. And probably my mother-in-law."

He was moved, of course. With added concern, he asked, "You sleeping well, Shannon?"

"Yessir. I've been fine. Feeling the energy I was hoping I'd feel at this point. Reading my books. Getting the room ready before I get too big."

"Take it easy too. Don't push yourself. You've gone through a terrible experience, one which affects people's bodies in different ways. Get more rest than you think you need. Spend more time with friends. Don't be alone, Shannon."

"I hear you. Not quite yet, but I'll come out of my cave sooner or later. Don't worry about me." All her life, this had always been what she told grownups. No one ever had to worry about Shannon. It had been drummed into her to be self-reliant. She was determined to use that strength to forge a new path, alone, now that Frankie was gone. Last thing in the world she wanted was to depend on her parents or anyone else. She told herself over and over again she was fine. She could do this.

Frankie's favorite place to go on Sundays was Duckies, the frozen yogurt place where a lot of the Team guys hung out. She saw them, with their dark glasses and cargo pants, their canvas slip-ons or rubber sandals made from old tire treads.

She was a dark chocolate girl at heart. But that day she ordered Frankie's favorite, strawberry. He liked the fresh chunks of fruit they put into their cones.

She added a few white chocolate chips and sat at the little yellow-topped table in the corner, out of the wind, and where she could watch people walking down the Strand. She watched young couples, fingers entwined, older couples walking their little dogs, retired Navy, and new recruits. Everyone walked the Strand, looked into shop windows, and simply enjoyed being alive.

That sent a silent tear down her cheek. Maybe the strawberry was too sweet.

A couple of groups of older Team guys were walking back to their cars from a swim at the beach. Their crab-like walk pegged them. The sand going halfway to their knees told her they'd done a timed swim like Frankie used to do. Someone honked. Someone gave the finger to a pickup truck filled with rowdy young guys.

Being part of the things Frankie had liked didn't help. Her thoughts got sadder. She had to dump the rest of her yogurt and put her own sunglasses on so people wouldn't see how hard she'd been crying. She found her car and drove herself home.

Setting out her purchases, she hung two little frilly pink dresses in Courtney's closet. The first two things there. They were small, almost like they'd been made for a doll. But no question about it. They belonged to Courtney.

Days strung together, and soon another month had gone by. SEAL wives and girlfriends were at her house constantly. They held a shower for her, and both Frankie's mom and her own mother came. It was fortunate the two women got along so well, and Shannon knew they'd started phoning each other on a regular basis. One mother helping the other mother. Gloria was right, "We'll all get through this together somehow."

And then one day Shannon laughed again.

CHAPTER 7

T.J. had been spending a lot of time at Gunny's gym. Timmons was practically living there as well. He'd sold his house, moved into an apartment nearby, and become a permanent fixture there.

The older man had dropped a bit of weight, lost most of his potbelly, and was developing definition in his arms. The frog statue, their Team mascot replaced some five times in the past, was braced to the wall. It stood on a glass shelf with a recessed light shining down on it. On that shelf were several pictures, including one of Frankie's smiling face, taken on his wedding day. T.J. looked at that picture every time he came into Gunny's. He recalled the promise he'd made, and the look of the beautiful girl on Frankie's left. He knew time was running out on his conscience, and he'd have to act soon or the mission would be labeled a failure due to abandonment.

Timmons had brought in several of his older friends, and soon a white-haired group was assembled there regularly.

Detective Mayfield had retired from the San Diego P.D. and was now living with Armando's mother, and he and Clark Riverton, another San Diego policeman soon to retire, dropped by for the group. Sanouk called them the "Silver Senior Running Shoe Circle." But there wasn't anything senior about them, other than the fact that T.J. occasionally heard discussions of Viagra and special hair products.

Amornpan, Sanouk's Thai mother, took care of the older gentlemen's club like they were her boys and she was a Southeast Asian lounge singer. She was beautiful and ageless. She was a gracious lady. She made Timmons a better man simply because he walked in and greeted her every day. T.J. doubted they were lovers yet, but their paths were definitely heading in that direction, and the Team Guys talked about it all the time.

Good for him.

T.J. finished early and said his goodbyes. He always gave his final goodbye to Frankie with a kiss to his forefinger and then a point straight at the guy. Increasingly he also pointed one at Shannon. He was more aware that he needed to do the one thing Frankie had asked before he passed over. No matter how uncomfortable it was.

"I know, I know. You asked me to look in on her, watch out for her, and I haven't done that. Sorry, man. But, jeez, you know about the picture I look at every morning in my shaving drawer. You want me to get rid of it? If I give it back to her, she'll have a fit."

He wondered how Shannon was doing. He had a feeling she needed a little silliness in her life and wondered if he could help out with that.

He stopped by a toy store and inquired about playhouses. They happened to have a pink gingerbread house in the back that had been returned last Christmas since it was missing parts.

It was T.J.'s kind of gift. He bought it at a huge discount, threw it in the second seat of his truck, and, without calling Shannon first, headed over to her place.

He pulled out the partially opened carton, trying not to drop pieces. A small plastic bag of screws fell at his feet, and he cursed but picked them up without losing his grip on the wooden panels of the playhouse.

Shannon had already opened the front door when he got there. Her eyebrows were knitted into a frown. She inspected the pieces of wood under his arm and then looked up at him with questions she seemed unable to verbalize.

"Every princess deserves her own house. A playhouse," T.J. said as he lifted his shoulder to draw attention to the play-house pieces.

"Is this a playhouse or a dollhouse?"

"I think it's a playhouse."

"You are aware she won't be able to play with dolls for probably at least two years."

"So, it will wait for her, then. Maybe in the meantime you can use it." He tried to smile, but the blush on her face and the fullness of her belly were too powerfully distracting. She was the most beautiful woman he had ever seen. She was the first pregnant woman he'd been within ten feet of.

Ribbons of jazz came from the house.

"I can just put this in the back yard, if today isn't a good day. I can come back another time to put it together, but I have time to get it done today, if you're willing."

"I hadn't even gotten to thinking about what she would play with once she's walking. You do know they have to be born first, start crawling, and then walk, in order to use an outside playhouse?" Her frown marks were easing, and a small, very tiny smile formed on her lips as she told him nonverbally she appreciated that he'd thought of the baby. He liked that he'd been able to think of something she hadn't yet.

So far so good.

She opened the door, gesturing him inside. He knew where the door to the back yard was, through the master bedroom at the back of the house. Once inside, he saw her unmade bed, the glass of water by the nightstand. A book was lying face down on the table.

"Did I wake you from a nap?" he asked as he walked past the bed.

"No. I was getting a snack and heard your truck pull up." She opened the sliding glass door and allowed him to walk in front of her into the yard.

She'd planted flowers along the edge of the lawn, ones which had not been there when he visited Frankie before their last deployment. The day of the funeral, he hadn't followed the others to her house for the reception, preferring to linger a little longer at the cemetery. He'd had private thoughts he wanted to share with his Team buddy.

The yard looked happier than he remembered. He was glad to see Shannon had maintained everything like before Frankie was gone. He'd seen a number of wives fall to pieces, not that he blamed them. But Shannon had moved forward and seemed steady.

He knew she must be hurting inside, but because of her dislike for him, hid it well. He decided perhaps he could change that a bit. Maybe he could bring her a bit of relief.

He laid out the pieces, putting the screws and washers on a corner of the box it came in. He crosschecked the parts to the manifest and discovered there were several bags of screws missing.

He began tracing his footsteps across the lawn.

"What are you looking for?"

"I think I may have dropped a few things. Any tiny bags of screws or wooden dowels?"

"I'll go look, but I didn't notice any." She disappeared from the screen door, returning a few minutes later carrying a glass of ice water. "Nope. Not a thing." She slipped out through the slider and stepped down onto the concrete patio in her bare feet...with those hot pink toes he was having such a hard time ignoring.

"Here," she said holding out the glass.

"Thanks." He drank the whole thing, a bit of the cooling water sluicing down his neck and into the ribbing at the top of his T-shirt. He took a mouthful of ice and began crunching it as he handed the glass back to her.

Shannon watched him, expressionless, and said nothing.

He put together what he could, and figured he'd find the fasteners for the rest later. A couple of times he put the wrong side out. He cursed at the instructions, and decided they'd probably been translated from Chinese. At one point he discovered there was an important triangular-shaped piece missing, one supposed to hold up parts of the roof. Just gone. He had one side, but not the other. The clerk at the store said everything was there, even though the box was opened, but now he could see the young man had lied.

A couple of times, the angle of two panels he'd screwed together was compromised, and collapsed. If he'd been home, he'd have destroyed the whole thing, kicked it around, bent and broken it further, and tossed it in the garbage. But this was Shannon and Frankie's house, and this was for their baby, and dammit, he was going to get this done.

So much for playing hero. The pieces were so messed up he didn't know where to start. He sat down and concentrated on them, hoping a solution would present itself, like magic.

Fuck it.

When he was about to give up, he heard the sliding glass door pull open again, and this time out walked Frankie's dad, with his tool belt on and a red canvas hand tool caddy in his left hand.

"Shannon said I should come and do a rescue on this mission," Joe Benson said with a beaming smile T.J. found comforting, though he didn't want to admit defeat.

"Yup. I do believe we have a problem, Houston."

"Well I'm good at fixin' problems. Let's see what you got there," Benson said as he squatted down to peer at the roof and corners.

T.J. turned his back to the house and began showing Joe what he'd figured out, but he felt Shannon's eyes on him.

He kind of liked it.

CHAPTER 8

Shannon watched her husband's hard-bodied friend while he worked outside, struggling to wrestle pieces of pink and light green plywood, painted to look like the sides of a gingerbread house. He first read the instructions, and then quietly aligned the pieces, searching for fasteners, which, all too often, seemed to be missing. He looked for holes that weren't drilled.

By now Frankie would have given up, but in the hour that Shannon watched T.J. curse and nearly throw the pieces over the fence, she'd also seen him quell his anger, tell himself he could do it, and then sigh back into it. Until another problem arose.

Unable to bear the sight of his frustration any longer, she called her father-in-law. Joe was a regular guy and was never shy about helping out, especially if it required any carpentry or woodworking. And he was the most patient man she had ever met. Their personalities were total opposites, but standing side by side, though Frankie was nearly a foot taller, she could see they were father and son, no question.

"Be glad to help," he said, and then appeared at her front door within twenty minutes. Just in time, too, because Shannon could smell defeat brewing in the yard.

"He's getting awfully frustrated, Dad. He thinks there are screws missing, and maybe some wooden pegs." She scrunched up her nose.

"Always are, sweetheart. I got plenty," he said as he jiggled his tool kit. "Or they don't put the holes so they align, or give you the wrong sizes. I'm sure we can work it out."

Within two hours the little playhouse was constructed, complete with new trim around the eaves for extra sturdiness, which Joe had recommended. The two men worked well together, and on several occasions T.J. burst out laughing at whatever Joe had said. She heard Frankie's name several times.

It occurred to her that it did Joe good to have another man Frankie's age to share the work on that playhouse, and if Frankie were here, Joe would have been doing this alone. But with T.J. he'd found a kindred spirit.

Or maybe it was the grief that brought them together. Whatever it was, it was working.

Shannon admired their handiwork. The two men were practically slapping each other on the back. Extra holes had to be made, and one piece was hand-cut to fit in where a piece had broken. "You guys want sandwiches?"

"I'm actually starved," T.J. said.

"I am too," said Joe.

"You want to come in or eat outside?" Shannon asked.

The men looked at each other and shrugged. "Whatever's easiest," T.J. answered. "Makes no difference to us."

She threw a wet towel at T.J., which caught him right across the kisser, eliciting a delicious pearly-white grin. She worked to restore her icy demeanor, but broke out in a brief laugh as she commanded, "Clean off the table and I'll bring the food."

Seated around the round glass-top table while they ate, the men continued to discuss their work. "You know, we work well together. No arguing or fighting. Kinda like working with the Team guys, like Frankie." T.J. caught himself, sighed and fell back into his chair. "I'm sorry, Joe. Couldn't seem to help myself."

Shannon had thought the same thing. She'd seen Frankie doing things with his buds on Team 3, but even that held a healthy dose of swearing, jousting and horsing around. The mission was always accomplished, no matter how much irreverence there was. She also knew that Frankie could be sensitive and very stubborn. T.J., for all his bad-boy qualities, had remained more focused on the task once Joe overcame the two key obstacles.

Stop comparing. Not fair.

Why was she doing it, anyway? The baby kicked as she brought the dishes into the kitchen. Joe was right behind her, carrying the rest of them. "You know, it's good to see you laughing again, Shannon," he said as he set things on the counter. He slung an arm around her shoulder and squeezed her to him.

"Thanks, Dad." She hugged him back. Then she placed one of his palms on her belly so he could feel the baby. "She wants to come out and play with you, Grandpa."

Joe was overcome. "Ahhh," he growled and wiped a tear from his eye. "She feels strong, Shannon. She does this a lot?"

"I have no comparison, but yes, I think she's very active now."

"That's the way Frankie was. His mama wasn't getting any sleep in the end." He pinched her nose. "Make sure you rest up, kid. You're going to need it."

T.J. had come from the restroom and was standing in the doorway to the kitchen, bracing himself with one muscled arm pressed against the top of the archway, hips slung at an angle. Though he was a good ten feet away from them, Shannon could see a tinge of envy there, and she picked up that perhaps he was holding himself back.

"You want to feel the baby?" she asked him.

He shook his head with a small shrug.

"Oh, come on, T.J. Get yourself over here." Joe stepped aside and Shannon walked slowly to meet T.J. halfway. Carefully he extended his palm, and she placed it against the lower right side of her belly. The warmth of his hand caused the baby to jump again, and they were rewarded with a kick and what felt like hiccups.

He stared at his hand, and she could see him soften and transform. When he looked up at her, she saw his need and his pain, which mirrored her own.

"Well, I'd best be going," Joe barked, collecting his things.

T.J. took a step back and jammed his hands into his front pockets. "Yeah, I've got things I need to do, too. I'd say we did well, Joe. And Shannon, thanks for lunch and all the ice water." His smile was gentle.

Joe and Shannon hugged, and then T.J. gave her a gentle embrace. Her belly rubbed against his lower abdomen, and she was surprised by a rush of intimacy. She felt T.J. hesitate to pull away. "You got anything else you need, give me a call, okay? I'm not as good as old Joe here with the hammer, but I can figure out most things."

She found herself saying, "Thanks," but felt the exchange was unfinished.

Joe was out the door with T.J. behind him when she decided to call, "T.J., there are a couple of things I think Frankie would want me to give you," she said to his back. She saw him stiffen, saw him share a glance with her father-in-law, and then hesitate, holding the door open.

"Bye, you two," Joe nodded and took off down the walkway with his toolkit.

T.J. closed the door behind him. Shannon suddenly felt awkward and shy about being alone with him. Something had shifted.

"We need to talk," she said, taking his hand and leading him to the living room and the brightly flowered overstuffed couch Frankie always said looked like it belonged in a hippie museum.

She sat an arm's length away from T.J., curling one leg underneath her. It was getting harder and harder to find comfortable positions as her belly grew. Placing her arm along the back of the couch, she rested her head there at an angle and looked up at T.J., who was focused on her eyes and nothing else.

"I've been missing Frankie a lot today," she said, looking away, unable to look at his face as she said it. Her shyness was coupled with a tiny shiver of danger, making her heart beat harder and sending the baby into another acrobatic routine.

"Yeah, me too," he whispered. He placed his hand over hers on the back of the padded couch, and rubbed her fingers. She saw no smile on his honest face. He knew what she was feeling. "Come here, Shannon," he barely whispered, waiting for her to make the next move.

She found herself leaning up against his chest, his arms wrapped around her, as his long fingers massaged the top of her spine and lazily dove into her hair, sending warm ripples from her scalp over the rest of her skin surface. Her arm had wrapped around his body, her other hand rubbing over his shoulder muscles. She was aware of his heat, the smell of him, which was all male, the sound of his breath as his chest rose and fell, the way her cheek felt pressed against the granite of his pecs. She allowed herself to wallow in the muskiness under his chin.

Then he tipped her face up to his, and he kissed her. Need sparked like a match in a dark room. How she'd missed the tender kiss and touch of a man! She'd told herself she needed to learn to live without it for now. But it flared up anyway.

She accepted his lips on hers, accepted his tongue that waited for an invitation before plunging into her mouth. It filled the vacant and hollow places of her loneliness. His moan flamed her passion, opening to him, and drawing him in deep. She was starving for him in every sense of the word. A tiny alarm bell off in the distance was ringing, but she put it out of her mind.

He kept one large, callused palm under her chin, rubbing her lips with his enormous thumb. His eyes were sharp with what she easily recognized as arousal, though he was masking it. He was also showing her a hint of something deeper.

He waited for her to speak, to give him an answer, put a label on what was happening between them. She'd been doing a lot of telling herself this and that, thinking about how she should feel, how she should be holding things in check, especially with the responsibility of carrying Frankie's child.

But she discovered her body ached for T.J. Her own needs were relegated to the place of someday, and became paramount. She missed intimacy with Frankie, the way it was so obvious he loved being with her. She missed the way he enjoyed her body, the way their lives had entangled and grown like two distinctly different vines covering the same trellis.

She laid her cheek against T.J.'s chest again and allowed the rhythm of his breathing to say what she wasn't ready to hear in words. Her own body responded, and their tandem breathing became background music for their hands, which rubbed and explored. His soothing touch on her back, her neck, down her arms. He laced his fingers between hers, kissing their joining, and she found it heightened her arousal.

She leaned back and studied his face again, tracing her fingers over his lips, begging him to speak what he probably wouldn't feel free to say. She knew it was loneliness that drew them together, the shared understanding that they both cherished the precious memory of Frankie as no other two people could.

His lips found hers again, found the spots under her ear and beneath her jaw as she lifted her face to the ceiling, closing her eyes and reveling in the way he explored her neck and the hollow between her shoulder and her upper chest. His thumb breached the crevice between her upper arm and her chest and then warmly squeezed her breast as he moaned into her ear.

Is this the talk she'd wanted to have? Was talking even appropriate? She'd have to slow things down and check her internal roadmap, even though she simply wanted to let go and plunge over the edge.

Other than his hand on her breast, he hadn't touched her in any sexual manner, the kiss being all the signal she needed to know he was willing to go further. But he seemed relieved to find she wanted to separate. Maybe he wanted the talk too. Maybe he regretted advancing on her. In any event, it needed to be addressed.

Her hands remained in his as he leaned against the couch, examining his thumbs brushing over the tops of her knuckles and down her fingers in a slow massage.

"T.J., it feels so strange to be sitting here doing this. We never got along before, when Frankie—"

"Was alive," he finished for her.

"Yes." Her eyes followed as he brought her knuckles to his lips and kissed them again, then spread out her palm and kissed it softly in a deeply personal and intimate kiss.

"I think what I'm saying is that I'm ready to try to move on."

She watched his eyes dart quickly to her face. Perhaps he hadn't gone there yet inside.

"I think I'll always miss him. But life does go on. He'd want that, Shannon. He said that to me at the end. He wanted—" T.J. stood abruptly. "I can't do this," he said as he tunneled his fingers through his hair and released a sigh of exasperation. "I'm sorry, Shannon."

Shannon got up carefully and stood close to him, wrapping her arms around his waist and pressing her face to his strong upper torso. "It's okay. I understand," she whispered to his shirt. She lifted the cotton fabric, exposing enough of his abdomen that she could place her bare palm there, and pressed. "Help me, T.J. Help me to heal."

He paused and took a deep breath. Could it be so hard for him to show her a little softness, a little kindness and affection for the memory of their shared past? Was it asking too much?

"The baby—" he began.

"Will be fine," she finished for him.

CHAPTER 9

T.J. couldn't believe he was walking down the hall of Frankie's little love nest, the floorboards creaking under their weight, the birds chirping outside in accompaniment to the sounds of an ordinary day. Except this wasn't ordinary. Her body was plumped with the evidence of Frankie's love for her and she was leading him to her bedroom—to do what? Make love to her? The pregnant wife of his best friend? A woman who was seven months along? Was this even possible? How would he feel if something happened to the baby?

He was going to need reassurance before he'd get naked with her, but no matter what, he knew it was going to happen. He really hoped he wouldn't feel like a dog afterwards though.

They walked past Courtney's pink bedroom, all set up with white furniture, waiting for the little one to imprint her personality upon it. What a miracle, he thought, how this happened.

In two months another person would live here with Shannon. A little part of Frankie would grow out here in the real world.

The bedroom was rosier now, the afternoon glow deeper and more intense. She closed the door, and then walked around him to the bed. He watched her take off her top, revealing a heavy bra with her breasts huge and bulging behind the restraint of the white lace fabric. She undid the straps and let her breasts fall, deliciously exposed to him, moving with her breathing. The sight of a woman's breasts, so full and ripe with life had never turned him on more. His cock was fully erect, holding his pants out front in that famous tent.

He was mesmerized by her as she slid her elastic-topped pants over her belly and down around her ankles and stepped out of them. Her smooth skin stretched over the growing child made him want to drop to his knees. She was the most beautiful creature on earth, pregnant and ripe with new life, standing before him unashamed of her nakedness. She was showing herself to him in a most intimate act, one no woman had done for him before.

"Are you sure this is okay?" he asked.

"For now, yes. Not for a whole lot longer, though. But yes, having sex during pregnancy is normal and natural." She seemed to welcome the fact he had walked towards her.

She pulled off his T-shirt. He loved that she was undressing him, giving him time to get used to seeing her so big and so round everywhere. Her nipples were hard and enormous. Her belly button was protruding, almost like a little act of defiance. Her shiny hair smelled wonderful, and he felt her warm need as she rubbed her full breasts against his bare chest. She undid the button fly on his jeans and sat on the bed while she lowered his pants to the floor. His erection bounced to attention and hardened further when she wrapped her fingers around his shaft, squeezing and working up and down gently, then squeezing his balls.

She licked his tip and then pressed him through her lips folding her tongue around him. He'd have been content if she could remain there forever, if he could keep watching while she sucked and rolled her tongue over him. Her hands gently squeezed his butt cheeks and he allowed himself to be drawn deep into her mouth and down into her throat.

He'd never seen anything as luscious as her lips working on him, had never experienced anything that drove his own need so fiercely. Her shimmering hair in the afternoon sun and the smooth texture of her shoulders and thighs illuminated in the golden glow of the day moved him to tears. He thought perhaps this was what she had in mind all along. Part of him was relieved.

But that wasn't everything Shannon had in mind. She scooted back on the bed, knees slightly bent, her taut belly rising and falling as she inhaled and looked up to him with smoldering need.

"How do I—" he started.

She smiled and interrupted him. "T.J. Don't tell me you've never had sex before."

Now he felt stupid. "Not with a pregnant woman."

"Thank God I'm the first for you. I wouldn't want to be second or third."

She was toying with him. His cock was getting stiffer and almost pained him. The little challenge to his ego spurred him on.

Holy cow. She wants me to fuck her.

"You sure this is okay?"

"T.J., if you want to stop, I'd understand. I mean," she said as she rolled over on all fours and presented her sweet ass to him, "I wouldn't want you to do anything you don't want to do."

Fuck it. He could see her wet pussy peeking like ripe fruit from between her legs. She allowed her shoulders to fall to the mattress as she rolled her head to the side and looked over her shoulder at him with those eyes full of smoldering need.

He decided he could do this. "Help me," he said.

"First of all you have to assume the position behind me. Can you do that, T.J.?"

Well, hell yes, he could.

He knelt on the bed and allowed his thighs to touch the backs of hers, his cock rooting up the cleft in her smooth behind. His hands were on her ass, rubbing, squeezing and separating the cheeks.

"Touch me," she whispered.

His fingers found her soft lips. He rimmed her opening and played with her folds, but still felt hesitant to penetrate. She moved herself against him, asking for it, but he found himself almost afraid of her need.

He dropped a shoulder and angled himself under her, kissing her sweet folds and massaging her nub with his tongue. Her sweet and sour flavor, musky with need, was an elixir. Her body jumped as he ran his teeth over her clitoris and then sucked her to a peak.

"Oh God, I had no idea I needed this so much," she moaned.

He gently tipped her to her back, putting one knee between her legs and feeling her ride his thigh. Her face was a beautiful painting of softness and lust as she lost herself for him. His thumbs and fingers pinched her nipples, and she arched, moaning. Her sensitivity to his touch anywhere on her body was spurring him on like never before.

"Baby," he whispered as he nestled a kiss under her ear. His erection pressed under and around her belly. "I have something."

"Thank you, because I don't."

He reached for his pants at the foot of the bed, sheathed himself and returned.

"I don't want to hurt you."

"I'll tell you if it hurts, T.J. But right now, I don't want to talk anymore. I want you inside me. No more questions, T.J. No more," she said in her silken voice. She lifted her head off the pillow to plant a long kiss on him, sucking his tongue inside as she rubbed her sex against his thigh. "Please, T.J., I need you inside me."

He didn't want to press down on her abdomen, so was careful to brace himself, which was no problem. Her writhing form beneath him, the touch of her belly against his abdomen was actually a turn-on he hadn't expected. His cock ran the length of her and then found her opening, and he stopped.

He wanted to watch her eyes while he penetrated her. He wanted them to look at each other. This was not his usual way. But this time was different. He wanted the reality of what they were doing to be front and center. It needed to happen in the full light of the day, without the excuse of alcohol and without the intense foreplay and occasional light bondage he usually liked.

He wanted this woman because she was carrying his best friend's child, and because he'd promised to protect, defend and take care of her. He wanted to fulfill his promise, and maybe receive a little redemption in return. He hoped it would change him, perhaps exorcise his demons.

He leaned forward with his forearms at the side of her face, rubbed his thumbs across her lips and her eyelids and kissed them one by one while he crouched and angled himself to push gently inside her. As he did, little by little, he saw it in her eyes, all the pain for the past and the love for the future. All at once. Right there in her eyes. He gave himself to her in every way he could.

He'd never wanted to mate with a woman this way. Bring her pleasure, rock her world and be the man she could depend on. He wanted that. As he rooted, carefully at first, she accepted him deep. He felt no hesitation as he rhythmically drew in and out, changing the speed but pulling the edge off it. He poured intensity into the slow slapping of their bodies, the feel of the smooth surfaces of her skin, the little moans and whimpers of her soul. He wanted her to bring it all on, full force. He wanted to take all of her.

He didn't know what to expect, but gradually her body slipped into a long rolling orgasm that triggered his own. She rolled her shoulders up and to the side so she could look at their joining. He kissed her belly as she ran her fingers through his hair, massaging his temples. He kissed her nipples and she arched backward, her head falling back into the bed. His spurting inside her was prolonged, and he knew she could feel every drop.

Her eyes filled with tears that spilled over onto the vanilla-colored pillows underneath her.

"Everything okay, baby?"

"It couldn't be better," she whispered. "I thought I had no right to this. But he's here."

T.J. wasn't sure he was going to like what she would say next.

"I know he's here. I know this is what he'd want, T.J."

He remembered Frankie saying that very thing, but he also knew he would never be able to tell her that. His hand smoothed over her engorged abdomen again. He loved the feel of the taut skin under his fingertips and palm. He agreed with her, even though he'd believed he had no right to this.

But he also knew he'd belonged here all along.

CHAPTER 10

Right now her body was sensitive everywhere. The changes in her hormone levels, the softening of her bones and toughening up of her nipples in preparation for birthing a baby and giving succor, mixed with the wonderful glow of a new love… not only growing inside her belly, but also in her heart, as she learned to accept the reality that she could expand that heart and open it to include T.J.

She could love Frankie and all that Frankie had meant to her, even including her occasional regrets, and she could love his child. But she found room in there for T.J. as well. Could T.J. be her forever man now? She was certain Frankie would approve. That was important to her.

They didn't speak of it while he helped her into the shower. As he smoothed the lemon shower gel over her body and kissed the back of her neck, he didn't speak of it. As she rubbed gel on his upper chest, down his shoulders, as she smoothed over his stiff cock, over his thighs, as she took him into her mouth, kneeling before him, while he palmed his way down her back to press fingers into her cleft and squeeze her buttocks, they didn't speak of it.

When he took her from behind, pressing her carefully against the tiled surface of a shower stall barely big enough for both of them, as she wanted him more after his release than before they'd started, they didn't speak of it.

Her connection to him was pliable yet solid. Not like rigid bands of steel. It was flexible. The golden threads connecting them grew with every contact of their bodies. The exploration was delicious, and still left her wanting more.

In the mirror she watched him drying her off with one of the white fluffy towels Frankie had bought. He wrapped it around her, put his face next to hers and stared back at her in the reflection. She loved seeing his face next to her own. She wore the blush on her cheeks from his stubble like a badge of honor, and was proud of how they were together, proud of how she felt and how her heart sang.

He was still stargazing at her.

"What?" she said as she turned to face him in the flesh.

"Marry me, Shannon."

"Oh, my gosh, T.J. Don't you think it's too soon?"

"Too soon for what? Look at what we've been doing all afternoon." He stopped her wandering gaze, raising her chin up so he could look at her straight on. "I'm serious as a heart attack, Shannon. Marry me. I won't rest until you do."

She loved his relentless attitude, the sure compassion of his voice, and his confidence in a future she was sure had been planned differently than it was presenting today. And she could see he wouldn't give up until she said yes. This was far from a game for him. He wasn't the same T.J. who had left on deployment two months ago. This was a man she could marry and live with her whole life.

"It would be my honor, T.J." As soon as she said it, fear crept in, but T.J. was overjoyed.

"Get dressed. We're going to go look at wedding rings."

"No. Not today."

"Yes, today. Today we tell everyone. Everyone. Your mom and dad, Joe and Gloria.

"You're so silly. Are you sure?"

"Aren't you sure, Shannon? Because if you're not, best to tell me now. Just get it out there, and I'll walk away." He didn't smile. She could see he wanted the reassurance, but didn't want to make it too obvious.

"T.J., we had time together with Frankie's dad. And now to call them and say we're getting married, well, I don't think it shows Frankie the respect he's owed."

T.J. got pensive. "Maybe you're right. Frankie would want us to wait, to be sure. String it out for a year or two. He'd want us to wait until after the baby was born, maybe have you date a few other frogs to make sure you were making the right choice, that sort of thing." His serious face showed not a hint of humor, but she knew him well enough to know he was just about to bust a gut.

She beamed up at him. "Have all those girls after you, have you dodging the frog hogs and high schoolers, sampling here and there," she said as she reached for his cock and squeezed it. Her hands were on his thigh as she dropped her towel, went up on her tippy toes, and pressed her big belly into him. "All those lithe young bodies moaning under your strength. The girls you could tie up and cuff."

T.J. stepped back out of her reach. "Whoa. Wait a minute. Somebody's been talking out of school."

"What do you think Frankie was doing after you described what you liked to do to your partners? I heard all about it." She stepped to him and took his cock in her palms again. "And I expect—after the baby's born, of course—for you to deliver. I've had a preview. I want the full fuckin' feature."

Holy shit. Did I just say that?

She realized then and there that things were back to normal in her life, if that was ever possible. She was starting to swear again.

Like a sailor.

CHAPTER 11

T.J. noticed a marked change in Shannon when her mother came to visit. The woman was built so solidly, the guys used to call her the Iron Maiden, whispering it so Frankie didn't hear, of course.

With one eyebrow raised, Mrs. Moore examined him like an ugly insect throwback in some nerd's bug collection.

"Nice to see you, T.J. You been helping Shannon do some things around the house?"

He worked not to blush. It was something like that. He was hopefully helping her get her life back, look forward to something. But he could see in Mrs. Moore he'd hit a brick wall. She might have noticed his duffel bag and some clothes strewn across the bed, a surefire indication he'd spent some nights there, but Mrs. Moore was purposely ignoring them.

She kept her eye on him even as he went to the head to take a leak. When he came out, she stopped whispering to her daughter.

"So, T.J. who are you dating these days? Anyone Shannon or Frankie would know?" Her eyes registered the cold blooded demeanor of a lizard.

He checked Shannon's line of sight and saw she wouldn't look at him.

"I have my heart set on the right girl, whenever she'll have me."

Mrs. Moore leaned back and roared. Her brittle laughter tinkled like pieces of shattered glass. "My understanding is that you'll probably have to forage somewhere outside of San Diego. I think you've bedded—"

"Mother, please."

T.J. was glad Shannon had come to his defense, but a sense of unease and dread began to grow. He felt a sense of danger the more time these two women spent together. And he didn't know why.

"I don't think that is very polite, Mother. T.J. has been a great friend, helping Joe build a playhouse for Courtney. You really ought to see it. Very impressive."

Mrs. Moore walked down the hallway to view the backyard from the master bedroom and shouted back, "You make a good carpenter, T.J. At least you could do that if the SEALs don't work out for you."

T.J. angled his head, looking for some sign from Shannon, but she shrugged and gave a puzzled expression in return. Mrs. Moore came back into the room.

"Well, I'm sure you have a lot better things to do than hang around a couple of old married women. I'm taking Shannon shopping. I'd invite you, but I think you'd be pretty miserable."

He placed his palms in his jeans pockets and nodded for a bit before answering. "You're quite right, Mrs. Moore. I'll just get my things."

"Why don't you wait for us?" Shannon posed. Maybe we could have dinner after I drop Mom off at the hotel?"

"And do what? Clean the house? Straighten your closets?" T.J. felt the scab had been picked and he couldn't stop himself. He didn't like that Shannon was excluding him. Mrs. Moore reminded him of some of the foster moms and state officials he'd known. They'd talk civilly but their hearts were black as coal. Being around her made him nervous.

Shannon was frowning when he stuffed the duffel with clothes from the bed. Throwing his shaving kit inside and zipped it up. With the canvas strap slung over his shoulder, he leaned over and gave Shannon a wet kiss on her cheek, daring her to grab him and demonstrate what she'd been showing him for the past several days and nights.

But unfortunately that wasn't to be.

Fuck it. Definitely overdue for a bender.

He was still cursing himself when he met Tyler at the Scupper later that evening. Tyler was trying to be helpful.

"So, she doesn't like you. Shannon didn't like you at first, either."

"Tyler, I'm not going to fuckin' have sex with Mrs. Moore to convince her I'm a nice guy. No, the bitch is made from body parts straight from hell."

"Come on, T.J. Lighten up." Tyler tried to punch him in the arm, but T.J. glared at him.

Tyler had the stones to wait until T.J. softened his eyes first. That was smart. Wait for the angry man to not debase himself and get things under control. Only jump in and call him out when it was getting into emergency mode. T.J. was glad he still had that control.

"I'm falling for her, Tyler."

"Tell me something I don't know."

"Probably isn't wise, but I am."

"So, can you distance yourself?"

"Not and keep my promise to Frankie. I said I'd be there."

"But not in his wife's bed."

"No he even said that too, in the end. Was the hardest thing I've ever heard. The guy knew he was dying and he made me promise—" T.J. didn't want to show tears, so he squinted and looked to the side at the string of muscled men sitting up to the bar watching a basketball game.

"Grief does a lot of things to a man. You should talk to Nick about that one. Kate says Devon has her hands full sometimes at the winery, Sophia's—you know."

"Yeah, I know. I really miss that sonofabitch. Frankie would know what to say to cheer me up. I never realized how much he did for me."

"I gotta ask you, man. What do you think Shannon wants?"

"Well, that's the thing. I thought I knew. But now I'm not so sure. Maybe she was just lonely."

"Hell, you both were lonely. Wouldn't be the first or last time a SEAL widow took up with another SEAL, you know. Maybe even someone she wouldn't have—"

That put T.J. over the edge. He'd been hit with the two by four called *She's only with you because she doesn't have Frankie*, and that smarted more than anything else he'd felt for months.

He wasn't in good shape when Shannon called him. He was walking down the Strand, because he knew he shouldn't be driving. He was so drunk, he couldn't remember where his pickup was, anyway.

"I'll come get you," she whispered. In spite of his sour mood, his unit lurched, making him swear.

"What's the matter?"

"I'm fine," he argued.

"T.J., come on. This is me."

He watched the steady stream of lights from passing traffic and decided he'd not take a chance to cross the road and run to the beach. It was dark. He was drunk and cold. He wanted to go home and fall asleep in his own bed.

"I'm not much good company tonight."

"Don't do this, T.J."

He knew it wasn't wise, but he sat down on one of the concrete bus stop benches, leaned back and crossed his leg. "You think we did this all too fast, Shannon?"

He hated that she took a long time to answer.

"Can we talk about this in person?"

"You don't want to be around me tonight, Shannon."

"I don't want to leave you this way."

"What way?" He knew what she meant but he wouldn't let go. He knew it was so unwise to even talk to her right now. But he couldn't help himself. Just like Frankie and wanting to talk to the girls. He didn't, but he couldn't help himself.

"You're drunk."

"Well, la-dee-fuckin-da."

"You're an asshole."

"Yes, darlin' I am. I'm a fuckin' asshole."

"I'm coming to get you. Tell me where you are."

He reluctantly told her and then fell asleep on the bench. Next thing he knew, he was being shaken by a policeman he'd had a run-in with a time or two. Shannon arrived just in time to place her very pregnant body between the official and T.J. before he could be arrested.

"It's my fault, officer. I was late," Shannon started. "I got held up and didn't get here like I was supposed to."

T.J. groaned at the lie. The policeman helped her get T.J. into her car after some fancy explanations from Shannon.

He knew she was angry with him when she didn't say anything until they got nearly to her house. "So what brought all this on, T.J.?"

"Why didn't you tell your mom?"

"Tell my mom what?"

He couldn't believe he was hearing this. Did she forget already that she'd said she'd marry him? "You didn't tell her about us, Shannon." He saw pity in her eyes, exactly the thing he didn't want to see.

"T.J. We need to talk."

Yeah, holy fucking right we need to talk.

They arrived at the house, and Shannon parked the car in the garage. T.J. was struggling to get out on the passenger side when Shannon was suddenly there to help him up. He tried to push her arms away, but had to be careful, and in the end gave up and just let her guide him.

He loved the smell of her hair, the brush of her belly as she braced him, pressing her left breast into his chest, encouraging him with little words like he was a child. She led him to the living room, pulled his feet up onto the ottoman, covered him with an afghan and removed his shoes. He heard the buzz of a coffee grinder and soon the fresh smell of the black brew.

"You want something to eat, T.J.?"

He couldn't answer that question. His mind was completely blank.

"T.J.?" she asked, her hands on her waist.

"I don't fuckin' know."

She brought him a mug of steaming black coffee, but didn't trust him to hold it on his own. When he reached for it, she held it away from him. "Wait just a minute or two. I don't want you to burn yourself."

None of this was helping his mood. Finally she put the mug to his lips and watched as he slurped it and then pulled his head back when he'd had enough.

"So I gather you've changed your mind." T.J. didn't see any point in belaboring the point. He decided to confront her."

"I didn't say that."

"But you didn't tell your mom what we've been doing the last few days either. That indicates you've had second thoughts, Shannon. Or am I wrong?"

"You're right about one thing. Perhaps this was all too fast." She was studying her hands wringing in her lap. When she looked up at him, he wasn't sure what he saw in her eyes.

"What is it, Shannon? What's changed?"

She hesitated before starting. "Mom overheard one of the wives say you made a promise to Frankie to take care of me and Courtney."

"Yeah, I did. So?" He was getting a very uneasy feeling about her mother's communication.

"So, I have to ask you, T.J., would you even be here in the first place if you hadn't made that promise? Are you doing this for Frankie, or—" she turned and looked away from him.

"Shannon, honey, no." He tried to grab her but upturned the hot coffee and it burned his leg. "God dammit!" he shouted.

They both ran to the kitchen to get towels. The burn on his thigh didn't hurt nearly as bad as the ache in his chest. Before they returned to the couch, he pulled her to him. "Please, believe me. My promise has nothing to do with this. It got me here, but it's not what's keeping me here. Shannon, you have to believe me."

"Then why didn't you tell me? Did you think I wouldn't find out?"

T.J. was starting to lose his patience. He didn't like his honor questioned. "What the hell lies did your mother pour into you?"

Shannon reared up. "How dare you say that? These are my questions."

"Well, everything was fine until she came down here. What kind of infection did that woman lay on you?"

"She's my mother, T.J." Shannon shouted.

"Yeah? Well I had a mother too, for all the good it did me." He wished he could stop, but he couldn't. Something had become uncorked, something raw and ugly and vile.

He could see she was staring into that dark pit that was his past, and it scared her.

"I never had anyone who cared a shit about me until I joined the Navy, until I met Frankie. Family is just—I could never do what my father did to me, abandon my child. I want to be there for you both."

"I understand, but I think we should wait until after the baby's born to make all these permanent decisions."

He cursed to himself. He'd jumped the gun and gotten in the sheets with her first, and impulsively asked her to marry him, which was a huge mistake. If he could have just taken his time, been patient, perhaps she wouldn't be having this reaction.

And then there was that fuckin' big knot in his stomach that said perhaps he wasn't the right man for her after all. He'd made the promise to Frankie, but what if it wasn't what Shannon wanted?

"Look, Shannon, I'm sorry. I want only the best for you and for the baby. And yes, I gave my word. You have to understand I've never done this before. I fuckin' made a promise and I'm going to keep it. I'm just not doing it the right way, obviously. And maybe I never will. I'm not Frankie, and I fuckin' won't replace him."

"Nor could you, T.J."

Her steely tone stabbed him. Anger flared again in his belly. She was right. He never could be the kind of husband and father Frankie was. He was a completely different man. Different kind of man. Didn't matter how much he told himself, the fact remained he would never live up to Frankie's expectations of him. So why try?

"T.J., I care for you deeply. But I still want to cool things off a bit, catch my breath and figure out what I want. I don't want to rush into anything. I need some time."

"Of course." Tired and defeated, he spoke to his shoes. "I'll sleep on the couch."

Shannon agreed quickly and slept in the master bedroom. Alone.

The next morning, he felt the distance between them growing. He didn't want to be the one chasing her. The dull ache in his chest was unbearable and he told her he'd give her some space and return to his little apartment. She casually said she'd call him in a few days.

He forced himself not to call her and tried to focus on anything but how lonely he felt. First, he'd lost Frankie. He felt like he'd lost Shannon. Nothing he used to do to get himself out of his funk appealed to him, either. Worst of all was the feeling he'd let Frankie down.

T.J. was cleaning his equipment at his apartment two days later when he got a call from Tyler.

"I think a little get together is way past due. You free Friday night, stud?" Tyler asked.

"Sure." He was pretty sure this would involve a blind date with someone they thought was perfect for him. And it never worked. "Who the fuck is she Tyler?"

"Kate's sister from Portland. She's a real nice lady. Got two kids. Very level headed, though, and pretty."

"Not really up for this, Tyler. Not really a good idea."

"So, you're gonna sit home and, what, watch TV?"

"That's pretty much what I've been doing, that and some PT."

"So Friday you're coming over for a barbeque. You're coming alone, right?"

"Probably. Haven't seen Shannon in about three days. And I haven't called her."

"Good."

Gretchen was in her early thirties, and an attractive, thoughtful lady, composed in spite of always being surrounded by her own little wolf pack of girls. Though it was far from anything he'd experienced, he found a new affinity for family, for connection. He knew Shannon would do what she needed to do. He couldn't change that.

But he still hoped she'd opt for staying in San Diego. Even if she wanted a separate life from his, he could still be a part of Courtney's life as he'd promised Frankie. He chuckled at the "old, gnarly guy" spying on the probably gorgeous Courtney at her soccer games or dance parties. The one who would take out anyone who as much as touched or looked at her wrong. The guy would be toast. In spite of himself, he cracked a smile.

Kate switched on the TV and all of them watched a news flash about threats coming from groups in the Middle East. They were threatening the lives of servicemen, saying they'd come get them at home.

Tyler and T.J. shook their heads. "Can't wait to hear what Kyle has to said about this. They've gotta be making plans," Tyler said.

"You check out all the new security on base? I'd say hell yeah they're making plans."

The newsflash was over in seconds, and Tyler shut the TV off. "Not like I have to listen to this thing play over and over again all night." He left to check on the barbeque.

"So how you holding up, T.J.?" Gretchen asked him after the girls ran past them to the backyard. Kate had given them ice cream.

"There are days which aren't so good. Most days, I'm okay. Trying not to do anything too stressful, just chilling. We'll get plenty of stress next deployment."

Gretchen nodded. "Does this stuff, like on the news, bother you at all?"

"I'm not going to lie, things are heating up everywhere. But it's our job. It's what we train for."

"Bad guys coming here?" she asked.

"I'm on a need to know basis." He smiled. "They'll tell us what to do when the time comes. Until then, we just live our lives and get ready for the next deployment."

His eyes landed on her pretty face, and he could see how a guy could fall for her. She had a quiet manner, but a wicked sense of humor he'd enjoyed earlier when she was trying to tell a story at dinner over her three daughters who interrupted her constantly. Surviving the public spectacle of her professional basketball player husband running off with a floozy, and surviving it with grace, added one more jewel to her crown. She was a solid woman.

"How you holding up?"

She stiffened. "Funny you should ask me that question. No one ever does."

He didn't get to hear her answer, because Tyler chose that moment to come barging back into the room,

"Okay, so guess what, pilgrims?" Tyler said. "Tomorrow night we're going line dancing."

"Nah, I don't dance," T.J. Said.

"Makes two of us," said Gretchen. "Besides, I'd have to get a sitter, and I don't know anyone down here."

"No problemo. I know a couple of Team guy daughters who would love to babysit. You aren't going to get out of this that easy."

She looked over at T.J. He hoped he didn't look too displeased, but he was mortified and hoped they'd drop the whole thing. He wasn't that lucky, and arrangements were made for him to meet Gretchen, Kate and Tyler at the Norwegian Hall the next night.

T.J. helped clear the table, bringing in the dishes to the very pregnant Kate, kissing her on the cheek. He wouldn't have done that, but the proximity to Shannon had driven off some of the fear he had about hanging around pregnant women. "Thanks, Kate. That was real nice."

"Well, it was Tyler's show. Loves to barbeque. As I recall, you love it too."

"Yes, ma'am."

"So how's Shannon taking things? I heard you were kind of sweet on her for a time."

T.J. was uncomfortable speaking about it with Kate. Women had a way of getting him to say things he didn't want to reveal.

"We're friends. I think she's trying to figure out what she wants."

"I can understand that." Kate dried her hands on a towel, threw it on the counter in front of her and asked him point blank, "And what do you want, T.J?"

It was a good question. He didn't have a clue. Then he thought of something. "I wanna get home from the next deployment with all 20 fingers and toes. And I wanna keep my promise to Frankie."

"You're a good man, T.J. Talbot."

He wished he could agree.

He ran into Joe at the store the next afternoon. "Hey Joe," he said with a warm, friendly smile. His compassion and respect for the older man had increased since their project with the playhouse.

But he was almost afraid to mention anything about he and Shannon drifting apart until Joe shared news he found very disturbing.

"Heard from Shannon's mom. Shannon's up visiting her in the Bay Area. I sure hope she doesn't relocate there, but I guess the Moores wouldn't mind. Said we should come up and visit any time."

What? How could this be?

He'd promised he'd look after Shannon, but now it was more than a promise. He wouldn't be the same without her in his life. He worried Shannon hadn't told him she was leaving town, taking it as further evidence she was planning on moving on, and perhaps without him. His heart sank to the bottom of the ocean.

"Joe, I'm sorry to hear that. We barely had time to get acquainted," he said to Frankie's dad.

Joe smiled. "You looked like you were getting along quite well, to my keen old eyes." T.J. couldn't look at him, so stared at his canvas slip-ons.

"Son—" Joe put one hand on T.J.'s shoulder, waiting until he returned his look. "I was going to tell you this a couple of days ago, but now…well, I guess my timing kinda sucks."

Did T.J. want to know what Joe was about to say to him?

"It was hard losing Frankie. I won't lie. Probably harder on Gloria. Boy, was he the apple of her eye. She lived for that boy growing up. He never wanted for anything. Anything. I used to lie awake at nights, knowing she was dreaming about our son, planning his life, and worrying about all his needs. My job was to wait. Wait until she came back to me. And now she has."

Joe's eyes watered. T.J. nodded, reached over and gave Joe a bear hug. Why had the God of SEALs not given him a father like Joe? Why hadn't he gotten a father at all? And why did Joe and Gloria have to endure the loss of their boy? It should have been him. T.J. should have been the one to not come home. Frankie'd had so much to live for. Especially now.

After the men patted each other's backs, Joe wiped the tear away from one eye with a knuckle. He took a deep breath and continued. "I didn't know I would have to lose my son to get my wife back."

T.J. felt like a dumbass for being so wrapped up in himself he had missed the obvious pain the Bensons were still feeling. He became more aware than ever before how the cycle of life changed everything with each new addition or deletion. Little Courtney was changing Shannon's trajectory. Frankie's exit changed the trajectory of the Bensons' relationship.

And me? What right do I have to expect anything from these people? Frankie had been on loan to him courtesy of the U.S. Navy. Shannon on loan to him through Frankie. No one owed him an explanation. And no one cared, either.

There he was, thinking of himself again, while Mr. Benson stood before him, tears streaming down his face. Maybe he couldn't have Shannon and the child. But there were things he could do.

"Joe, I honestly hope she doesn't move. I'd miss her too. Let's hope she'll come home, to both of us."

The old man's lower lip quivered. He wasn't able to speak, so T.J. grabbed him again and allowed the man to sob in his arms. Several people passed by them in the cereal section of the grocery store, but T.J. didn't care what they thought. Giving Joe the loving arms he'd earned was way more important. They could think they were a gay couple, a couple of reconnected family members, or old friends. It made no difference to him. Letting Joe know he wasn't alone was the most important thing in his life.

The rest would simply have to take care of itself.

That afternoon, T.J. left several messages for Shannon, all unreturned. He met Kate, Gretchen and Tyler at the dance hall. He told himself it was good to move, to feel the rhythm of the music, to concentrate on following the caller's directions. Gretchen was a good partner, and, while he didn't feel a sexual spark, he did feel something for her. He was ashamed to figure out he felt sorry for her. He could tell she liked him, and he wasn't going to be able to give her back anything at all.

The awkwardness intensified during the slow dances. It was so wrong for him to be here. He wanted to be anywhere but trying to play nice, when something was boiling inside him.

Gretchen licked her lips, perhaps expecting he'd kiss her. "Gretchen," he said as he squinted, moving away to a safe distance, "how long are you down here for?"

"I go back in three days." She was smiling, examining his eyes for signs she'd never see. He knew she didn't find it easy to trust men, and who could blame her? He wished she didn't trust him.

Images of that day at Shannon's, fixing the playhouse for the baby, the lovemaking, all of it came back to him. Along with a double dose of self-loathing. Why had he pushed things so fast? Why couldn't he have just kept his fucking hands off her?

"Hey, T.J. You didn't ask me to marry you, did you?"

Her statement stunned him out of the rut his mind had replayed over and over again. He frowned. "Last I checked, no."

"So why the long face? It's only dancing. I'm a good cheap date. I don't require much. I change partners gracefully, and I won't expect you to call the next day. But I get lonely, and I think right now you are, too."

She spoke the truth. He was lonely. Just like Shannon had been lonely and let him have his way with her.

His face was close to Gretchen's and he could have kissed her, saw her even prepare for it, but he began to pull back. Gretchen grabbed his ears and wouldn't let go until she laid a long, wet kiss on him.

But there was only one girl he wanted to kiss, and it wasn't sweet Gretchen. How he wished it was different.

CHAPTER 12

Although her mother had extended the invitation, Shannon was going home to see her dad. She'd never been able to get enough of his love growing up. He'd worked long hours while she was being shuttled back and forth between piano lessons, ice skating, swimming and the Children's Theater, which was her real passion. Her well-run life was her mother's design, and there hardly was time to think about anything else.

Her dad was devoted to her mother. That same attentiveness was what originally attracted her to Frankie, who would be the same kind of husband her dad was. Now without her husband, it made the visit with her dad all that more important.

The neighborhood looked just as she remembered it, except the trees were bigger and the houses seemed smaller. She'd ridden her bike up and down the level streets, where the curbs were all rounded to make that part of town "kid friendly," or so her mother had touted to all her friends.

Her mother had been a social icon, PTA President and deeply involved in all of Shannon's school activities. Mr. Moore's devotion to her mother only widened the gap she felt growing up. Her mother's events and parties made the local society columns, and Shannon was known as "Mrs. Moore's daughter." She felt more like Mrs. Robinson's daughter from The Graduate, even though she didn't suspect her mother of infidelity. But, she thought, her mother could have played that role well.

When she went off to college and then met Frankie, his easy-going manner and devotion made her the center of his universe, and for the first time in her life she didn't have to share the stage with another Diva. Frankie was her ticket out. She'd never laughed so hard or loved being alive so much.

On this trip, she was hoping to extract some of her mother's iron will and bask in her father's love. She knew it would help her heal.

Not yet ready to face them, Shannon drove past her parents' house. One by one, her childhood landmarks came into view. The town was known for having one of the first children's libraries in California. It also had a children's theater around the corner from where Shannon had taken her swimming lessons. On an impulse, Shannon parked and got out.

She remembered the lifeguard instructor with shocking white-blonde hair and brown eyes, the one who always had a thick layer of white zinc oxide on his nose. He wore dark-rimmed sunglasses and had the physique of Michelangelo's David or Adonis. The worst memory was from when she was eight and would always belly flop if he tried to help her do a front dive into the pool. His habit of putting his hand on her tummy right before she launched her dive had flustered her and always landed her in disaster. Did he ever catch on?

She wandered over to the Children's Theater, finding the doors open. Several children and one adult were on stage, with a director sitting three rows up from the stage, barking instructions.

She turned left, sure that the room was still there, and it was. The wardrobe closet was her favorite childhood memory. It had been guarded by Peg, who had worked there for thirty years. Peg, was enormous, but somehow made it up and down the narrow rows of sequins, feathers and silks, remembering every jacket, every pair of pants, every cummerbund, petticoat or pair of wings, and what size child they would fit. Her loving hands and generous hugs turned plain children, petrified to get up on stage, into magical creatures. In their finery, they would parade back and forth, becoming kings and queens, knights and dragons, butterflies and birds and pumpkins, and a host of other things they'd never thought they could be. The imagination and silliness of childhood were allowed to run free in the theater.

Shannon imagined Courtney taking an acting class. She hoped she might get her first kiss from a boy covered in greasepaint, her little heart going pitter-pat, just like she had.

At the end of the first row of costumes Shannon got to her knees. Carefully, on all fours, she crawled under the red petticoats of the can-can dancers and lifted the glittery finery. She was looking for her inscription written in pencil on the wall.

Shannon Loves Richard.

She recognized her handwriting. Sitting under the mass of red petticoats, with her back leaning against the wall, the baby kicking in her belly, she touched the letters she had scrawled. With one hand on her abdomen and the other pressing against her letter to her future self, she felt the distance between where she had been and where she was now.

This place could be good for Courtney. She couldn't wait to tell Courtney all the stories and adventures of her youth, the piano lessons with the teacher who had performed at Carnegie Hall when she was young, but who lovingly placed her gnarled and crippled fingers over Shannon's small ones, asking her gently to stretch wide to reach all the notes her young hands struggled with.

"Grow into your piano hands, Shannon. You must stretch and grow into them." And gnarled and crippled or not, her fingers had felt smooth and soft, her handwriting perfectly formed as she jotted down the lessons with a soft pencil.

Back in those days, it had been pure pleasure to ride her bike with the breeze running through her hair. She'd watch the big houses with the beautiful yards go by one by one. Imagining the stories, the families inside, and wondering what they were doing, she rode almost invisibly down the heavily tree-lined streets of a community of people who cared about their children. Her stories were her future, riding her bike up and down the rounded curves from the sidewalk to the streets and back again, trying to envision a life like the one she was leading now.

But she'd also felt confined here as a child, with her parents' high expectations she could never completely live up to.

Doing it her own way became more important the older she got.

Now, she appreciated the beauty of her childhood. She saw how it enveloped and protected her. She realized that this was the childhood she wanted for her daughter. The two of them together would find that safe, comfortable place.

She was alive and happy now, although a widow, with a child not yet born, living in a place that reminded her of a past she could not have any longer, wondering if it might be wise to move to a place where she could create a future all by herself.

She'd written down the address of a little house three doors down from the home she grew up in. Smallest house on the block, in need of the most repairs. But it would do. Shannon's past would shield her daughter's future.

She needed to do this. She needed to move away from San Diego. She was determined to be self-sufficient, but it made sense to have her parents close by, just in case. When she told herself that moving here would be no big deal, she knew there was a lie hidden in there, but quickly tamped down the feeling. She'd needed the space away from San Diego to make a clear-headed decision, away from the temptations of her body. Now that she'd decided, she was ready to face her parents.

And then she'd tell T.J. what she'd decided.

Her parents were thrilled with the possibility she'd move up north, and wanted her to move in with them, which she declined.

"Oh, honey, it would be so nice to have little Courtney in this house," her mother had said.

Her dad's face was all the encouragement she needed.

"No, not here, but perhaps close by. There's a little house near the theater that's for sale."

They'd discussed it until late in the evening. She walked outside after her parents went to bed and looked up at the star-filled sky. The move wouldn't be like the last time, when she had just graduated from college, an eager young woman off for her first job, a great adventure in a town full of hunky Navy guys. *A safe place to be*, her friends had said. *Lots of sunshine and mild climate. Nights full of stars.*

It had been one of those starry nights when she'd met Frankie. He'd graduated BUD/S and was getting ready to deploy for the first time. She didn't even know what a SEAL was until she'd met him. He was forever with his sidekick, T.J., and her distrust and dislike of him was instantaneous.

Now she knew why. T.J. had wanted to insert himself between her and Frankie. He was protective. Never having anyone to protect him in a system that had failed him miserably, he wanted to take care of Frankie, even if Frankie didn't even know he needed taking care of. He'd fixed him up with girls T.J. liked, but who scared Frankie to death.

Shannon smiled at this. T.J.'d been so tender with her. She owed a lot to Frankie's best friend. Without her intimate afternoons with him, when she explored the depths of her heart and soul, she would never have been able to find the strength to contemplate moving back home. She hoped he would understand. And that one fine day he would have a woman and a home of his own.

His quiet confidence had instilled in her something special, like Frankie had. T.J. had shown her the way to go on, to deal with life on life's terms, that every day was a gift.

He would forever be special to her. And she'd make sure Courtney knew him as her daddy's best friend, but probably not as her mother's lover. Wrap up a few more details, and then she'd go home, sell the house, and get on with her life.

Telling T.J. he would be welcome to come visit, but not share her bed any longer, would be the hardest part. She hoped this gentle warrior would in time forgive her for parting them, even though she didn't have a clear-cut future.

For the first time in her life, she didn't have definite plans. Her plan was simply to live. To raise her daughter. To work hard to be the kind of mother Frankie would have wanted, give back to her parents the kind of love, through Courtney, she wasn't able to show them growing up.

The next day, she went shopping with her mother for things for the new house. They talked over lunch like they had when she had her first department store job when she was still in high school.

Shannon went with her mother to interview a new doctor, a woman doctor this time, who didn't ask where her husband was. She still wore her wedding ring, the simple gold band that was the only thing Frankie had been able to afford. She made diagrams and drew out the furniture she would bring up. She laid out Courtney's nursery. She thought about the vegetables she'd plant, and she interviewed her realtor's gardener. She found a new place to have her car serviced.

T.J.'s messages finally stopped, as if he'd had a premonition about her plans. Day after tomorrow she'd return to begin the packing and moving process. With her parents as co-signers on the loan, there wasn't an issue about her qualifying. The death benefit was more than ample for her down payment. She knew Frankie would approve.

Now if she could figure out a way to tell T.J. without breaking his heart. Would he be able to support her in this decision? Would he understand?

CHAPTER 13

T.J.'s phone rang early the next morning. It was Shannon. "Understand you've gone up north."

"Yes, I came to visit my folks."

He wanted to say something but held his tongue. He wanted to tell her what a bad idea that was, ask her why she had to go way up there when everything she needed was right here in San Diego. But he didn't want to hear what she'd say.

"I'm actually considering staying here. I want you to think about that before we talk further."

So, there it was. Confirmed. His worst nightmare.

"Sounds like you've pretty much made up your mind."

"I think it would be good up here for Courtney and I."

"Where do I fit in that picture?"

"I'm not sure yet. Where do you want to be?"

"Well, I can't move up there. Sounds like you don't want to be here, with me. So that pretty much tells me everything." He thought he was prepared for this conversation, but now realized how inadequate he felt. He wished they were talking face to face, but realized perhaps that was Shannon's plan.

"I've had some time to think, and maybe staying down in San Diego isn't the best for me anymore."

"Why, Shannon? I already said I'd take care of you and the baby. Why are you running away?"

"I'm not, T.J."

"So you just don't want to be around me, right? It's me, then. Why don't you just fuckin' come out and say it?"

"Because that's not the truth."

"Why didn't we talk about this?"

"You don't owe me anything, T.J. I want to do this on my own. Away from the distraction of—"

He hated this. "So, now I'm a distraction?"

"You don't have to take care of me. I want to know I can do it on my own."

"I just have to ask you, Shannon. Is there someone else?"

"No. I wouldn't do that."

"I'm coming up to see you."

"No, don't. That's not a good idea."

"You saying you'll refuse to see me? That what you're saying?"

"Why do you have to be so in charge? Can't you see I just need to process things a little?"

"You know what you're doing to Joe and Gloria Benson?"

"T.J., that's between me and them."

"I'm fuckin' coming up there to talk to you, period."

"Fine." She sighed. "But I won't change my mind. You can't fix this, T.J."

T.J. got permission from Kyle to make a run up to the Bay Area and then took a transport to Moffet Field. He rented a car on the El Camino and rang Shannon.

"Where are you right now?" he asked.

"You're here? Now?"

"What did you think, I was kidding?"

She decided to give him the address of the little house she'd just made an offer on.

Within a half hour T.J.'s hulking frame blocked sunlight coming through the small rounded window in the heavy oak door. He pushed it open with a loud creek that echoed off the bare hardwood floors and stucco walls. The place was similar in style to the home she and Frankie had bought in San Diego, a Spanish style bungalow, but even smaller.

The sight of her as she walked around the corner from the kitchen took his breath away. She'd developed even rosier cheeks, and her belly looked like it had grown dramatically. He found himself gawking and then remembered himself.

As he got close to her he could see her apprehension. He wanted it to be anticipation of a joyful reunion, but that's not what she showed him. With her arms outstretched, palms facing him, she kept him from her, so he leaned over and kissed her on the cheek.

"Missed you," he whispered.

"Thank you, T.J." He could see she was chosing her words carefully. "I've been good. It's been good here." She turned, walking toward a sliding door that led to the backyard off the dining room. He could see the steam from the heat of her fingers as she placed her palm against the glass. "It's small. Only two bedrooms, but I can afford it, with Frankie's benefits."

He stood next to her. The overgrown yard was going to be a lot of work for her. There was a single swing hanging from the branch of a large shade tree. "You're gonna fuckin' do this?" he whispered.

"I think so."

"Doesn't have a playhouse," he mumbled.

That got her to turn towards him. God how he wished she'd take his hand, give him just some little bit of encouragement. It wasn't much, but she smiled. "Maybe you and Joe could bring the one you made up here. Do you think you guys could do that?"

He wanted to say no. He wanted to grab her and drag her butt back to San Diego, stay right next to her until she changed her mind. He told himself he'd let her drift too long. He never should have waited. He'd given her the space, and she'd gone and convinced herself she needed a separate life. And he knew Frankie wouldn't want that. It was eating a hole in his stomach like acid. He couldn't protect her from afar, and he wasn't ready to leave the Teams, even if she wanted him here, which she clearly did not.

"Shannon, I'll do what you want. I promised to take care of you, and if this is really what you want, well, I guess Frankie will have to forgive me."

"But you could still be part of our lives. I wouldn't ever exclude you from Courtney's life. My parents—"

"Fuckin' hate me, Shannon. Well, your mother does, anyway. How long before she'd convince you that I didn't belong anywhere near you and the baby?"

"I won't let that happen. I promise."

He decided he was ready to look at her. With her face upturned, her full lips so kissable, her nostrils flared slightly, warm breath washing over the delicate hairs on her upper lip, he wished he were the man she needed, she wanted. He wanted her in the worst way. He'd only had a taste of what it could be like. Frankie was right, had been right all along. Shannon was the real deal.

And he'd discovered it too late. He'd mucked it up. And now perhaps that chance would never come along again. He touched her cheek with the backs of his fingers, rubbing his thumb over her lips. "All right, honey. If this is what you want, who am I to ask you to change your mind?" He tried to smile, but couldn't.

She moved towards him and lay her head against his chest. As he rubbed the top of her spine, fingers sifting through her hair, he heard her whisper, "Thank you."

He helped her lock up the house. While she called the Realtor, he took her over to her parents. Forced to stay for dinner, he had no appetite and tried not to look at the beautiful woman sitting across the table, who might as well have been on the other side of the world. A week ago, he never would have dreamed he'd be sitting here, actually strategizing her move, offering to help her get all the people she'd need to make that move. His Team buds would help, of course. It would be painless for her, because he'd make sure it was that way. He'd make sure all she had to do was wait out the last weeks of her pregnancy.

Mrs. Moore was actually cordial to him. She hung back at the dinner table to talk with him in private.

"You've surprised me, T.J."

"Yeah, well I surprise myself sometimes," he said as he took the cup of coffee she offered. Shannon and her dad were looking through catalogs in the living room. He could feel her eyes on him.

"I can't imagine any of this is easy for you."

He told himself not to trust her. The sound of compassion in her voice came dangerously close to pity.

"Not up to me."

"Well, you're being a prince, T.J. I know we haven't always seen eye to eye. This is what's best for Shannon. You'll see. She needs to raise her child here, where her home is."

T.J. raised his eyebrows. "Used to be she thought of that house in San Diego as home."

"Things have changed," she said, and she was right.

"They certainly have." He'd be going home, alone.

But then, he was used to that.

Two days later, back in San Diego, T.J. agreed to meet Gretchen at a local ice cream shop. Kate and Tyler were babysitting the girls, who were hoping their Mom had found another guy. Always on the lookout for a new daddy, they weren't very subtle about it.

T.J. knew there was only one woman for him, though. And he also knew Gretchen understood that. Kate's sister was easy to be around, warm of spirit and gentle on the eyes. A man could do far worse, but he knew that wasn't what he was interested in. He was marking time until his life could start in earnest, giving Shannon all the room she needed, keeping a tiny flame of hope that she'd come back to him.

God, it had only been one day but already the waiting was hard. He'd hoped a little fun with Gretchen would distract him. She was easy to be around, and he found he liked making her happy.

On the way home, she asked him to stop. "Can we have a little talk?"

He pulled to a gravel shoulder on the road that wound through the foothills, angled the car toward the bay and turned it off.

"Shoot."

She adjusted herself to face him, bending the knee closest to him, but she stayed on her side of the front seat of his truck. "I meant what I said a couple of nights ago. I'm a good listener, a good friend. I'm not looking for anything long term."

"Gretchen—"

"Hear me out, T.J. What's wrong with a little recreational sex and some cuddling? You might find you like it. We might find a way to heal ourselves somehow."

"I don't think I can be fixed, Gretchen." He didn't want to look at her because he didn't feel worthy of even her friendship. He couldn't believe he was not interested in the "recreational sex" part. How much he had changed. Now the idea of using Gretchen to heal his loneliness or take the edge off his sexual desires made him sick.

He couldn't pretend with her. It wasn't right.

"T.J. look at me," she whispered.

He did. She was pretty, and she was totally willing. He could have kissed her, done far more, and she would have let him.

"Am I so bad to look at, such poor company?" Her smile was sweet, her eyes innocent and he couldn't go there.

She was on him in a flash, her fingers clutching the back of his neck, pulling him into her, her lips ravenous over his. She was going to move onto his lap, but he stopped her, holding her by the upper arms, stiffly.

"I can't, Gretchen. I just can't."

Her nervous laughter wounded him. "And here I thought you were the bad boy. Kate told me all about you, although she was careful to edit."

He smiled at hearing about his reputation.

"Yeah, well don't believe everything you hear. There are some things I'm not especially proud of."

"What about Shannon?" she asked.

"That chapter hasn't been written."

She watched him squirm. "You two dated a little, Tyler says."

"You could call it that."

Gretchen leaned forward, turned his face toward her. T.J. was wary, but he felt she wasn't interested in coming on to him. "Holy cow, you're *sweet* on her, aren't you?"

He tried to smile, but it was awkward. Involuntarily he looked away as his eyes filled with water.

"Oh. My. God. T.J. You've been hiding this. From everyone."

"No one to tell." He was glad Tyler hadn't broken his confidence.

"Does she know?"

There was *that* question. At least it was one he could answer. "Oh, yes, she surely does know."

"When does she come home?" Gretchen asked.

"Home? She hasn't told me. But I guess in the next couple of days. She's probably going to move away."

"Are you going to try to change her mind?"

He considered that statement. Was he going to try? Hadn't he tried already with zero results? "I don't think I can, Gretchen. Not sure that's possible."

"She's nuts. She'd be crazy not to want to come home to you. You've got to go for broke, T.J. You've got to make a stand. Don't let her get away."

"Gretchen, I love your optimism. But haven't you heard that saying, 'You can lead a horse to water…'"

"Is that how you got through BUD/S training? Is that how you do it when you go overseas?"

He had to admit she was right. That wasn't how he did it. They all had a plan. They had missions to accomplish. They didn't sit there and let insurgents and enemies come after them, they took the fight to them. They openly protected the people they were sent to watch over.

"You didn't ring that bell, T.J. Why are you going to ring it now?"

Holy fuck, she was completely right. He'd given up. He shook his head. What a dumb ass he'd been. Slinking around, feeling sorry for himself.

"Gretchen? I think I love you."

She giggled, and it made his heart sing.

"God I wish you could have said that earlier. I might have kept my big mouth shut."

He hugged her, kissing the side of her face. "I think you're the first woman I've told that to who hasn't had sex with me first."

"Then I take that as a compliment, T.J. And if Shannon is nuts enough not to fall into your arms, well, I'm not ashamed to say I wouldn't mind being a welcome distraction. I think I could do make-up sex pretty good, although I've never tried."

"I'll bet you could," he said.

He realized now what he had to do. He had to fight for Shannon. With everything in his being, he had to fight to keep her. Because it *was* a matter of life or death.

CHAPTER 14

Shannon flew back to San Diego, and the heaviness in her chest increasing the closer they got to landing. Joe met her at the airport, asking about her stay with her folks and how they were. She knew it was just small talk, because Joe had called several times while she was gone to inquire about her. She knew her mother had told them Shannon was considering a move back home.

Joe helped her with her bag, bringing it up the shallow steps to the front porch. One of the reasons she liked this house was the way the little concrete steps had been colored red. The concrete had been stained before it was poured, forever committed to that rosy hue. The heavy oak door had a small window in the center of it, covered by Spanish wrought iron detail. She'd loved this door and the way it protected her home inside.

She was surprised it still felt like her home. Or their home. Hers and Frankie's. And the home where T.J. had told her he loved her, the safe place where she'd learned that she could go on.

Joe quietly stayed behind her, allowing her entry, and without stepping inside himself, set her bag down on the wood floor and said his goodbyes, promising to look in on her tomorrow.

"You've gotten much bigger this week. Are you comfortable?" he asked.

"Not quite uncomfortable yet, still able to sleep, thank God. But soon. It will get dicey soon." She decided not to bring up her move.

She listened to the creaking of the floorboards, took in the way the house smelled. A large bouquet of red roses was on the dining table. Her fingers were trembling as she plucked the little card from its holder and read T.J.'s inscription.

Missed you more than I thought possible.
I know we have to talk. But just know that I love you.

She rubbed her forefinger over the words he'd carefully inscribed. This was going to be more difficult than she thought.

The doors to the master bedroom and the baby's room were closed. She smelled cleaning agents and realized someone had gone all-out to prepare for her return to this house, prepared it as though she was going to stay. The windows had been washed. Area rugs had been cleaned, and larger ones freshly vacuumed.

Opening the door to her bedroom, she looked outside at the play house T.J. and Joe had put together only two weeks ago. Someone had planted flowers all around the little house, as if she were staying. And she could just see a tiny table with a miniature tea set inside.

A small wading pool with pink mermaids on it and fresh, clean water filling it, with a child's seahorse life preserver bobbing up and down in the shallow water. Ready for Courtney…in about a year. There was a two-bucket swing set installed at the side of the yard. An old-fashioned bench swing with green canvas canopy sat under her maple tree, with a couple of new flowered pillows on top. Everywhere she looked, a bit of magic had been added, painted, or enhanced by colorful plantings.

She went back inside and felt like she was coming back to a lovely familiar dream. If a house could love the people who lived in it, this one did. Just as Frankie had. Just as T.J.—she had to stop thinking about him, or it would be more difficult to continue with what she'd decided to do.

Pulling her rolling suitcase down the hallway, she unpacked, put the clothes in the washing machine, and turned it on. She took a long shower, washing her hair, getting all the dirt and grime of airports and travel off of her skin.

After rubbing her hair with the fluffy white towels Frankie had bought, she combed it out and secured it with an antique clip, and then slipped on her favorite nightgown, noticing her belly almost didn't fit now. In her bare feet, she made herself a tall glass of ice water with mostly ice. The refrigerator was fully stocked with food. Fresh vegetables and fruit in baggies tucked neatly away. Two steaks marinated in a covered glass dish. Was she looking in on a fictional couple? Or was this part of her life?

She took her glass back down the hallway to Courtney's room. The mysterious welcoming committee had glued her daughter's name to the door in multicolored wooden letters. She brushed over the letters with her fingers, and then opened the door.

A bouquet of light pink roses, short-stemmed, sat on the baby's changing table and permeated the air with their sweet fragrance. Above the table, a framed poster was hung, inscribed with the words,

May you touch dragonflies and stars,
Dance with Fairies and talk to the moon.
May you grow up with love and gracious hearts,
And people who care.
Welcome to the world, little one.
It's been waiting for you. We've been waiting for you.

She walked over to the roses, and touched the letters on the poster. They were hard to read, because her eyes had filled and tears were streaming down her cheeks. She sniffled, overcome by the message T.J. had left for her daughter, the man she had decided to leave for…for what?

She wiped tears from her cheeks with the backs of her hands, then reached up to touch the words again, like she was touching his face, the man she had decided to leave behind, like her pencil scratch in the costume closet at the theater. Except this wasn't a memory. This was real time.

"I thought maybe you'd like it." T.J.'s voice filled the room, wrapping around her, with that warm, familiar cadence, snagging her heart, squeezing tight, and not letting go. "I have to admit, I got some help from Kate and Gretchen. They helped me pick it out."

She turned to find him leaning against the doorway. His long, muscular legs encased in blue jeans above bare feet, a light blue shirt opened to his tanned chest, revealing more muscles than he had a right to. His hips were cocked at an angle, his hands jammed into his front pockets. With his dark hair and blue eyes, the need written all over his face, he was a package she hadn't been prepared for.

"It's beautiful, T.J."

"I could say the same about you."

He didn't come over to her, but his eyes drank up the sight of her like it was the last time he'd see her.

He nodded to her flannel nightie, "I see you're not quite ready to entertain company. Perhaps I should come back another time, then?"

"Don't be silly. You're here."

"Yes, I am, Shannon. I'm here. But where are you?"

She examined her bare toes. She'd had them done in pink again. Her eyes began to tear up. Where was she? It was a good question.

"You can barely fit into that nightgown," he whispered.

"Watch it." She gave him a smirk and was rewarded with a tiny smile.

"But I love how you look, so full. You're the most beautiful woman I've ever seen, Shannon. I mean that."

She rested her hands on her stomach. "Never thought I'd need to be reassured."

"Oh, honey, I intend to remind you every day and all night long." His eyes pierced the veneer of her tough outer shell. She took in a deep breath and then walked over to him. "We should talk."

He reared back a step. "We will. But I've got something to say first, Shannon."

The distance between them felt achingly like the Grand Canyon.

"I love you, Shannon. I love that baby you're carrying. Whatever you're going to tell me next, I just want you to know that before we start." He looked down at his feet and then pleaded with his eyes. "And I've missed you. God, I've missed you."

It was natural to be drawn into his powerful arms, as she stepped in to feel him against her. He was careful. He simply held her tight, massaging the back of her neck at the top of her spine. She could hear his heart beating, strong and true. The sound of his breath surging in and out of his chest cavity washed over her like the soothing sounds of waves at the ocean.

There was something she had been protecting—what was it, anyway?—and now that protection was falling away. She felt herself open up to him again, and discovered the careful, familiar reassurance that all was well. In his arms, all was well.

That's when it hit her. She'd been shielding her heart. As she looked up at him, as his lips found hers, she knew she didn't have to steel herself against the pain of losing again, losing what she so desperately wanted.

He was respectful and chaste with his kiss, allowing her to lead. His hands came up to cup her face as he kissed her again, this time deep, but still tender. "Missed you, baby," he whispered to her lips.

She unwound from him. "Come. We need to talk, T.J." She took his left hand and led him to the living room, and then turned to offer him the couch, before she sat next to him. She became self-conscious of her wet hair, but she saw in his eyes that he loved her just the way she was. It was not conditional.

"Why, why did you do all this, T.J.?"

"That's an easy question to answer. Because I love you. Because I'm all in. I think the more important question is, what are your plans, and do they include me?"

She cocked her head to the side, lowering her gaze, not wanting to look up at him. He took it well. He straightened his back, sitting across from her, the leather couch groaning under his huge frame. He reacted like he'd been given an order, his chest filled, allowing the oxygen of his heavy breathing to calm him. It was what he did when he was nervous.

"I've been trying to sort it all out. Confused, here. I came home with one thing in mind, and now I don't know—"

"Well, Shannon, you're going to have to tell me to pack it up and quit, because not texting me or calling me back, or feeling confused, aren't going to cut it. You're gonna have to tell me to stop loving you, because I'm not going to unless you demand that of me."

"T.J., don't," she pleaded. But what did she really expect him to do? Of course he would react this way.

"Honey, I'm trying to understand. Did I come on too fast, too strong? Did I push you? Or is it that you don't like me, or is there someone else? Because I don't understand why you won't grab that big brass ring, that juice of life we have here, and go for it."

"That's what I'm trying to do. I thought maybe going home, back to where I was raised, would be good for me and for Courtney."

"Away from me, you mean? You want away from me? What have I done to make you want to run away? All I've done is love you, honey. Make me understand, please."

"I thought it would be good to go home, back to a place where I had happy childhood memories."

"So this isn't your home? This place. You and Frankie bought it right before you got married. I heard you say you never wanted to move. Ever."

"That was when Frankie was here with me."

T.J. nodded. "Well, that's true. I'm not Frankie, Shannon. No one will replace Frankie. You'll never find that, honey."

"I don't want to live in the past, T.J."

"Isn't that what going home is all about? *This* was your life. This was Frankie's life. These were the men and women he loved. His community." He looked up at the ceiling. "Oh, God, Shannon, I was hoping maybe I'd gotten it wrong somehow, but now I can see, you're just not that into me. As hard as it is, I know I have to accept that and move on."

He still wasn't leaving. He turned and asked her, "Is there anyone else?"

"No. For heaven's sake, no!"

"Then, can I ask you another question?"

"Fair enough."

"Are you going home or running away?"

He was right. She was running away.

"This place, this community scares me," she had to swallow because her voice wobbled. "Reminds me of what's changed. It's like I'll never be able to escape. I'll never be on my own."

T.J. chuckled at that.

"What's so funny?"

"You don't understand diddly about being alone. I've been alone my whole fuckin' life and never knew I'd missed anything until I found the SEAL family here. Do you know what it's like living in a community of people who would gladly die for you?"

He abruptly stood, walked around the couch and pointed down the hallway to Courtney's room.

"We do that. We make it so there are dragonflies and angels and fairies."

She quickly turned her back to him, weeping softly, but not wanting to show him her tears.

He came back, standing in front of her seated body, now uncomfortable because the baby was kicking up a storm as if wanting to be heard.

"You think it over, Shannon. Say the word, and I won't bother you again."

She was shocked at her own mixture of feelings. She'd been so set on her course, she hadn't prepared herself for the change of heart she was clearly having. Shannon hadn't considered this part, hadn't envisioned it.

He put his hand on the front door handle, and suddenly the importance of his leaving woke her up. Had she been catnapping through life? The door he was offering her could give her the world. And she was giving it up…for what? So she could be independent? She could do it on her own, but was that reason enough to do it on her own?

She knew the answer to that. And she knew she'd fallen for this hero the moment she'd kissed him. And now she was being a complete fool.

His hulking frame filled the whole doorway as he prepared to step outside and out of her life forever.

"Wait, T.J.!" She stood and watched as the force of her shout out triggered a jolt in his neck and shoulders. His back was still turned to her. His hand gripped the door handle so tight she thought he might twist it off.

"Forgive me," she whispered.

When she saw his face, she saw his tears. Of course she'd never seen him cry before. They'd spent most of their time either jousting, angling for position, or sparking off each other. Even when she didn't trust his friendship with Frankie, the passion between them had been strong.

Was she grown up enough for this big, strong man with a heart the size of all San Diego? Was she ready for the next great adventure? Was she ready to keep the memory of Frankie beside her as she made her life with this man, who she now knew loved her so completely she'd never need to feel alone again?

And could she handle it if anything happened to T.J.? Would it be worth the incredible pain of possibly losing him in order to live with him in the here and now?

The answer was yes. He was waiting for that answer. He deserved that answer, she thought as she walked slowly up to him.

"Yes. T.J, I've been a fool. I need your forgiveness. I need your love. I need you."

He gathered her in his arms. "I'm right here, baby. Nothing to forgive. Never going to leave you. Never."

She knew he'd keep his promise until his dying day. And she would too.

CHAPTER 15

T.J. woke up with a start, and then remembered, unlike the last few mornings he'd awakened, all was well. Finally well.

Shannon's warm pregnant body was spooned in front of him. Her hair was all over the pillow, with his nose buried in that space he loved at the base of her skull, the place where her scent was strongest, fine baby hairs tickling his cheeks and sending shivers down his spine. He'd never felt as connected to anyone in his life. His hand smoothed over her giant belly, loving the feel of her ripeness and her motherhood. He couldn't wait to see the baby Frankie had placed there in her tummy, to love that little girl and let her know what a wonderful father she had. He promised to make sure she knew about Frankie. He could feel Frankie's love all around him now.

Shannon stirred. Then she pulled his hand up to her breast, turning her face to his lips, coaxing him to touch her cheeks. "Good morning, sweetheart," he whispered.

Her little moan told him she was sleepily aroused. He didn't want to be too urgent with her, so large with child, but his need was never-ending. He was rewarded when her hand dove down between them, and she gripped his shaft.

"I love how you're ready all the time, T.J."

"Anyone around you would be ready all the time, Shannon. Would be a fuckin' freak of nature not to be, honey." She squeezed him, and he sighed into her ear. "Sorry for the swearing, but sometimes…" She squeezed him again, and he couldn't think straight.

"You can swear all you like to me, T.J., as long as it's in bed. I love it when you tell me you like to fuck me. That's not swearing. It turns me on."

"Thank God. We're both blessed with the potty mouth gene."

"Should I take your cock in my mouth?"

"Um. Would you?"

"I'd love to."

Sure as shit, she slid down the bed, her nipples leaving a tingling sensation when they rubbed along his lower abdomen, and then pertly nestled against his thighs as she took him between her lips and sucked.

He laced his fingers through her mass of brown hair at his chest. He slid one hand down to her cheek and mouth and felt where her lips covered and pleasured him. Her belly nudged its way between his legs when he separated his knees. Warm pregnant Shannon was the most exciting sexual partner he'd ever known. This unexpected pleasure was something that filled all the gaping holes in his soul.

She was moaning, coaxing him harder, and working to make him spill, ravenous with that tongue of hers.

"Baby, love this, baby," he whispered. He pulled the hair from her face so he could see her. "Love watching you going down on me Shannon."

She smiled, pulled her mouth to his tip and sucked as her eyes gave him a sultry smile that ignited the bed sheets. He was so damned lucky. She loved like she lived, with a full heart and spirit. She had some magic he'd never felt before with any other woman, as if being around her would be just plain good for him. That her essence was good for him. Made him a stronger, better man. This gave him more than the erotic pleasure he craved, it gave him life itself.

She took his seed, drawing every drop from him and then asking for more. She was writhing on the bed as he spurted, taking him deep. Her fingers clutched his butt cheeks as she pulled him to her. When he was done, she kissed his thighs and smoothed her hands up his lower abdomen, kissing him all the way to his belly button. Then she snuggled under his chin as he pulled the covers over them both.

He reveled in the warmth between them, the way they just seemed so right for each other. They'd come together like two comets in the sky that should have exploded on impact, but instead fused together and became a brilliant supernova. The bright light of their love was strong, their desire fierce. He'd always known Shannon was like this, but that she could be like this with him, well that was the real miracle.

He rubbed his fingers against her shoulder while he thought about all the dumb things he and Frankie had done together, all the times he had made Shannon furious with him. Frankie always seemed to walk away unscathed, leaving him to battle with Shannon. Now he saw why. He and Shannon were so much alike they were the same side of the same coin. Her intensity was what he craved as sure as he loved that in himself.

He could tell by her breathing she wasn't going to fall asleep.

"What do you want to do today, sweetheart?" he asked.

"Um. This," she said, kissing and flicking a tongue over his nipple.

"You surprise me, sweetheart."

"Didn't anyone ever tell you that a woman has lusty thoughts when she's pregnant? She has certain needs?"

She looked up at him, and yes, he could see it in her eyes.

"Love those needs. You can show them all you like."

She smiled and snuggled her face under his chin. "We won't be able to do this too much longer. But we can for now. I want all I can get while I feel I can."

"I want to be careful too."

"You're careful, T.J. You're the most tender lover I've ever had." She looked up at him again, and he was nearly hard already.

He chuckled. No one had ever told him that.

"What's so funny?"

"I'm not normally known for my tenderness, honey, but with you, it's just the way I love to be."

"Because I'm carrying a baby, T.J. Our baby, little Courtney. We'll love her together. And then maybe later, you can show me some of your other side."

Her eyes called to him again, daring him to summon his strength. He couldn't wait until after the baby, when he could exhaust her and make her bones turn to rubber.

Shannon wanted him to move in right away. She dressed in one of Frankie's big shirts and her drawstring pants and announced she was going to help him move. That day.

"No hurry on all this, Shannon. I can get it. Not like there's a ton of stuff."

"All the better to do it now. And besides, I'm big, or haven't you noticed?" She pulled her shirt up, and damn, every time she showed him her bare tummy with the belly button that had started becoming an *outie* he grew hard. He silently cursed himself, but she had such an enormous effect on him, he could hardly be in the same room with her without getting hard.

T.J. promised he'd get things moved over in the afternoon.

"No. We. Do. It. Now."

"Shannon, honey, my place is—"

"I know. A bachelor pad. You probably never anticipated having to entertain me there."

"I never entertain there period." Even before Frankie had married Shannon, the two of them had little in the way of furniture, using cardboard boxes for tables where they cleaned their weapons while watching the TV set perched atop some fruit crates. They hadn't bothered to buy a couch, chairs, or even a dinette set. But they did have the biggest TV they could afford and a gas-fired barbeque. Frankie's room was bare, since T.J. hadn't had time to get another roommate.

When they got to the complex, T.J. tried one more time to ask her to stay in the truck while he went inside and got his things. The answer was the same.

First thing he noticed was the smell coming from the brown bag left by the front door since he hadn't invested in a garbage can. He'd left remnants of a sandwich and a sour half-quart of milk. He'd not turned on the AC because he had to pay the electric bill, which was not part of the lease. He never left it on, because he never knew when he'd be back home.

Shannon went over to the sliding glass door and opened it, looking for a non-existent screen. She quirked up an eyebrow.

"Football accident. Screen is downstairs in the carport, a little bent."

She walked to his efficiency kitchen. T.J. tried to place his body between her vision and the sink full of dishes.

"Shannon, stop checking me out."

She glanced down at his package. "I wasn't checking you out, but come to think of it, that might not be a very bad idea." She slid over to him and placed her palm warmly against him and smiled. "Nice, T.J. I can see all this turns you on too. Like playing house?"

"Seriously, Shannon, let's just get this stuff out of here and get out. You don't have to look over everything, do you?"

She stepped as close as she could to him, her belly being the obvious impediment. She squeezed and pressed her palm against the hardened ridge of his shaft. "What are you worried about, T.J.? We're all friends here, very good friends."

He was having a hard time liking it, but his groin loved the massage her strong little hand was giving him. Damn, he was filled with such confusing thoughts and feelings. A real mixture of dread and lust. He allowed himself to be led while she had her way with him. He was powerless to stop it.

"Show me your bedroom. Now," she demanded.

If she hadn't been so pregnant, he'd have refused and fucked her on the living room floor, but because she was rubbing that enormous belly against him, showing him her need, he took her hand and pulled her to the bedroom.

He had black sheets and a matching comforter cover. A used dresser from Goodwill stood in the corner. Other than the posters of naked women all over the walls, the room was empty. Some were just pictures of large asses and boobs. He also had a couple of pictures of women bound and trussed with black silk straps across their bulging chests.

She raised her eyebrows. "Seriously kinky, T.J. I had no idea."

"Really, Shannon? Really? You had no fuckin' idea?" He wasn't sure if he was mad or excited by her perusal of the things he liked to see just before he went to bed at night. "Like I said, I don't entertain here."

"No. You probably like the beach, or the back of a pickup, or a motel."

He nodded.

"I happen to like it. Turns me on, kinda." She took off her shirt and slipped off her pants. Naked except for the huge nursing bra trying desperately to hold her breasts inside, with her bulbous tummy swaying underneath her she crawled up on his bed. Her sweet ass waited for him, her sex wet with need.

"Not here," he whispered, fixated on the peach between her legs he so wanted to kiss.

"Here. Am I the first, T.J.?" she asked, peering around her thigh, making sure he couldn't miss her ass. "Am I?"

"Well, yes."

"Oh, that makes me so hot."

"But not here."

"Come to me baby. I need you," she said.

Well, fuck it. He wondered if it was because she was pregnant or if the posters really did turn her on. Didn't matter what she said, he would not be bringing any of these to their bedroom at the new house. He'd done too many unmentionable things to the sight of these posters, and there was no way he would introduce that to their world. He dropped his pants, as she backed up into him. He took hold of her hips and pulled her back onto his shaft, careful to slide in along her wet channel without forcing himself. She seemed to be getting tighter each time they'd made love. The cheeks of her rear jiggled as he gripped and released them, spreading them wider for his selfish penetration. She moaned like a cat in heat.

"Shhh. Shannon the walls are thin," he whispered.

She let out another moan.

The woman was out of control. He hoped to God the neighbors next door, two newbie SEALs, were out.

He thought perhaps he had pushed Shannon over when she lurched forward, grabbing his pillows and then squeezing them with her arms, pushing onto him deeper. She screamed into the pillows.

Good idea, Shannon.

"You like that, baby?"

"Yes. More, T.J."

"Glad to give you what you want, baby." He thrust inside her so deep he thought she'd split in two.

She jumped a bit at first, and he thought he'd hurt her or the baby. But then he felt her clamp down on him as her orgasm came with terrifying speed. She plunged her face into the pillow and wailed as he pumped her deep and slow.

He arched over her and finished, holding her breasts through the heavy cotton fabric of the bra that seemed more of a BDSM torture device. He made a mental note next time to get that thing off her first. He sure wouldn't be thinking of it later on.

CHAPTER 16

Shannon helped T.J. move his meager things into the house. She was surprised it all fit into half his trunk, and recalled how Frankie's things had been reduced to just a box as well. T.J. had more equipment than anything else. His kitchen things he'd agreed to give to whatever young SEAL would eventually take over his apartment. He had no furniture to speak of. She liked the fact that it was the man who was moving into her home with her and the baby, not the stuff he had. The man was who she wanted, not his stuff.

It moved her to see where he had spent his single days, where he and Frankie had stayed before Frankie moved in with her. The simplicity of his lifestyle and the private side of him that wasn't displayed to anyone else turned her on. He was embarrassed about his lack of decorating skill, and yet he had shown such tenderness with the flowers he'd planted around Courtney's playhouse and the beautiful words on the poster in her bedroom. She liked that he'd chosen to share intimate moments with her, intimate things about himself that no one else, and perhaps even none of his SEAL buddies, knew. All he showed the outside world was his equipment and the posters of naked women. She didn't even mind that he liked to look at them before he fell asleep. Even that was sexy to her. The man was a tight package, bound up in that hard body of his. He kept his personal life guarded, not public. No trappings to weigh him down. Everything he needed was inside *him*.

She'd cleared out Frankie's clothes two weeks into her mourning, knowing that it would help her heal. She'd held each one of his shirts up to her nose and inhaled his unique man scent, crying while she refolded the shirts and laid them in the box for donation. Though his clothes had been washed many times, she recalled how his scent remained, even after the man was gone.

What surprised her, as she laid T.J.'s shirts in the same drawer Frankie had used, was how comforting it was having him watch her do this little activity. She smoothed over the American flag-splashed boxers he wore, rolled up his socks in the same direction, and refolded his jeans to fit inside the shallow dresser. He let her position his clothes, ever careful to not intrude. She knew he was taking his lead from her. If she wanted it fast, he'd go fast. And fast or slow, he appeared to enjoy just watching her work out the details. She felt his respect for her private thoughts.

He took her hand, leading her to the kitchen, where he obviously felt most comfortable.

"T.J., I love watching you cook," she said.

"I'm not cooking, I'm making you a salad." His dazzling white smile sent a tickle to the top of her spine. His long fingers stroked the lettuce and caressed the tomatoes he was slicing. "You have to eat. You've exerted yourself this morning." He didn't look up at her, but maintained a Cheshire cat smile as he watched the sharp knife do its job.

"I still like watching you," she whispered.

"I know," he said, grinning down at the countertop, his cheeks slightly pink from a touch of shyness. "I kind of like it." He backed up a bit so she could see the tent in his pants.

"Wonder what we're going to do after the baby comes. We won't be able to be so selfish with our desires, will we?"

He nodded to the bowl he was preparing for her. "I'll definitely let you sleep a little more, Shannon. But honey, you can let me handle everything else but sleeping and feeding the baby. I want to cook for you." That's when she saw the deep blue of his soul. He passed the bowl across the countertop, handing her a fork.

"And here, I never pegged you for any of those domestic talents. Your kitchen couldn't have been sparser. Where did you learn to cook so well?" she asked.

"One of my foster mothers owned a restaurant. We learned how to do all sorts of things in there."

"Where's your lunch?" she asked.

"I'm going to fix something after you go down for a nap."

"What if I want you to nap with me?"

"I have a little research to do on the computer for work—which I can't tell you about, so don't ask, okay?"

She was hungrier than she'd thought. The crisp lettuce and fresh multicolored heirloom tomatoes looked like they'd come from a farmer's market.

"You get these at the Friday market?"

"Glad you noticed."

"I can't believe you know that about me too."

"You forget, Frankie used to talk about you all the time. We know more about you than I think even your parents do." He shrugged. "Guys talk to pass the time. You were his favorite topic of conversation. Shit, it was much better listening to him talk about you than his sorry life. I'm sure there wasn't a guy in the squad who minded his descriptions of all the things you liked, and the way they…" He hesitated, and then continued, "the things that turned you on, baby. Most of us had yet to find that. A woman who would love us like you loved Frankie. We could tell just by the way he described you."

Sadness crept over her like an old shawl. She took in a deep breath and found it helped when she let out all the air.

"This okay to talk about, honey? Don't want to upset you."

"No. I have to get used to it."

"Yeah. Helps me too, in a way. My promise to Frankie was to make sure his little girl knows him as her daddy. I intend to tell her lots of things about Frankie, the censored things, of course," he said with a warm smile.

She nodded and searched the remnants of her salad. "I'm moving forward, just not always easy."

"Roger that, Shannon. I'm right there with you."

She loved looking into his cool blue eyes, experiencing his passion and his pain. He was a package containing two powerful forces. *What does he see when he looks at me?*

"I'm grateful that I have you to walk me through this. Unfortunately, I suppose you have been through this before—I mean, losing a Team guy."

"Yes, but this time is different, sweetheart." He came over to where she sat atop the stool and smoothed a lock of hair back behind her ear. "You being here is helping me too. And in a strange kind of way, the promise I made to Frankie is helping too. Maybe he knew that, Shannon. Maybe that's why he made me promise him."

She gripped his forearm, feeling the corded veins covering powerful muscles. She let her palm glide over the dark hairs, then travel over his bicep and slip around his neck. "Thank you. Thank you for loving me, and loving our baby."

He massaged the top of her spine the way she loved. "My pleasure, sweetheart. My mission in life. Always will be. I'm never going to leave you, Shannon. I promise."

It caught her up short, tears spilling over her cheeks at the complex mixture of pain and the pleasure. She had a past she still mourned, but also a bright future. Remembering the past and anticipating the future was making her tired. Or perhaps it was the pregnancy.

Little Courtney kicked, a stunning reminder of her baby's demands to have a future more compelling than her past. Shannon smiled, and patted T.J.'s broad hand against her belly, disregarding the shadows that lurked. Courtney's coming was slowly stretching her, expanding her capacity to feel. Her love for her baby, and now the new love for this fine warrior were helping her heal the pain of Frankie's absence.

He pointed to her nearly finished salad, and she nodded, yes, she was done.

After he rinsed her bowl, he washed his hands and came around the counter to take her hand in his, leading her to the bedroom. "Cinderella has left the ball. She is going to go take a nap," he said to the spirits in the walls of the bungalow.

She followed behind him, loving that he towed her, drew her to the bed, like he was drawing her to the rest of her life. With T.J. she felt secure. Unafraid of whatever was coming next.

She slipped off her shoes and undid her drawstring pants so she could sleep loose inside her clothes. He'd pulled back the covers, and after she crawled in, he rested on top of the covers, holding her body through the comforter. He kissed the back of her neck, and tangled his fingers in hers. She found herself matching his breathing.

"What was it like for you growing up in all those foster homes?"

"Frankie never told you?"

"No. He said you never talked about it."

"He lied, Shannon. It was nothing like the life Courtney will have, I can assure you that. Made me a man at fourteen. You don't want to know all the details. Boring, really."

"I want to know. Tell me." She felt him tense behind her. "When you're ready to tell me. I want to know everything about you, T.J. I need to know."

"Well my parents, they say, weren't married and were young. I suppose I could feel grateful they placed me for adoption rather than, you know, the other choice."

"Did you go looking for them?"

"Nope. All I know is they lived somewhere in the South. And from then on, my foster caretakers—whatever they felt like telling me, told me stories. I don't think anybody really knew. I was told my mother was beautiful, a lady, but they were very poor. My dad was a war hero they said. Who really knows? What kind of hero abandons his child?"

"Maybe he didn't know. Happens."

"Like I said, the stories I was told are contradictory. As a kid I used to wonder what it would be like if they came, together, a couple, you know. It's every orphan's dream. I would lie there on my bed, look out at the stars and wonder if they were looking at the stars too, wondered if they ever thought about me. Ever."

Shannon was moved to tears again, but let them travel silently down her cheeks so T.J. wouldn't see them. Her life had been so different, but there was some toughness that had developed in her that matched T.J.

"I knew it was folly. Knew at the time it was just what I told myself to keep from crying at night, acting like a girl. It would take a while before I liked girls." The rumble of his chuckle rolled over her and nested in her heart.

"I can just see you lying on that bed looking up at the stars, T.J. I used to stare out at the lights and wonder whom I would fall in love with. Who would I marry? I didn't have your kind of childhood, but I still wanted a handsome prince to come whisk me away, take my vanilla life and ignite it. Take me away from the organized and ordinary and make it sparkle."

"I'm gonna work on that, babe. I'm gonna perfect that."

"You already have done a pretty good job, T.J."

She fell asleep dreaming of what it would be like when the baby was born, when she'd get to meet her little Courtney, hold her, and pass her into T.J.'s waiting arms.

She awoke to the sounds of T.J. tapping on his computer keys. The nap had freshened her. She cinched her pants up, brushed her hair and put it up in a clip. Examining her face in the mirror, she saw her skin was pinker, and perhaps a little fuller, but she looked good. She looked rested, and for the first time in many weeks, content.

The T.J. effect was definitely good for her. She tiptoed to the hallway and watched him work on the computer, intent, focused. The man could do anything and it looked sexy.

Little Courtney kicked as if she agreed.

Shhh, Courtney. You're way too young to have such thoughts.

The baby kicked again.

CHAPTER 17

T.J. took Shannon to a dance recital held by the wife of one of his Team buddies. Italian-American Sophia Beale was married to one of T.J.'s best friends, Mark. They'd met in Italy, where Sophia was living, before the two happened to find themselves on the same cruise ship. Their one night stand in Italy bloomed into a happily ever after while crossing the Atlantic, even surviving an attempted terrorist takeover.

The dance space was located adjacent Gunny's Gym, now owned and operated by the widow of the newly deceased Gunnery Sergeant. Amornpan had come all the way from Thailand to care for the aging Marine in his final days.

"Amornpan is Thai, a really beautiful woman," T.J. explained to Shannon. "Sanouk told us she never stopped loving old crusty Gunny, who used to describe her as an angel of the jungle."

"Who is Sanouk?" Shannon asked.

"He's the son Gunny didn't get to meet until his last year here. He got Amornpan pregnant when he was a young man in Thailand, but he never knew it."

Shannon nodded, frowning.

"Sort of a fact of life, really. Military guys do this all the time, litter the world with babies. I have friends that have four or five kids with like three different women, never marrying any of them."

Shannon's eyes were round with disapproval.

"Not me, Shannon. Never me."

"That you know of."

"Well, there is that." T.J. wondered why he'd even brought it up. Then he remembered. "Sophia has hired a bunch of instructors, from ballroom to belly dancing and everything in between. Sophia of course does all the Latin jazz, tango and most of the ballroom instruction. Amornpan teaches Eastern and some Middle Eastern dances and gives traditional Thai performances."

Shannon clutched his hand, weaving her fingers through his as they walked to the studio doors. Exotic reed, flute and drum music echoed out into the street.

"They're all going to perform today, along with some of their best students."

"You're going to get up there and shake your fanny if I call you to the floor, T.J."

He stopped so quickly, Shannon's huge belly rammed into his backside. "Sorry," he murmured.

"I've seen your moves. I'll bet you are a good dancer," she said to him, lips quirking into a smile.

This did please him. "As a matter of fact, I am rather good at it."

"I'm going to make you prove it."

He rolled his eyes and bent down to kiss her delicately, which got them both so distracted a skateboarder nearly hit them. The softness of her lips, sucking his, the placement of her hand at the buttons of his jeans were two of the little things he loved the most about how she loved him. She was never afraid to show affection for him. It filled a huge hole in his soul that someone so fine would find him so continually attractive. Made him want to think of dark corners and long nights with the crickets chirping in one of those no-name towns he grew up in.

He felt so lucky to be alive, and ached that it was his place to be with her now, not Frankie. That sadness never went away.

The music got loud when someone opened the doors.

"T.J. get your hands off that woman and get your butt in here," Timmons' gravely voice boomed just like T.J. remembered. "Glad to see you dressed proper, at least. Why, hello, Shannon."

Their old Chief, now retired, had taken an extra interest in the gym, and in Amornpan in particular. TJ opened the door wider to allow space for Shannon's large frame to get through.

"Timmons, you dressed up, too," she said to the older SEAL.

"I've been told I clean up real good. Sort of a special day for us here at the studio."

Shannon hesitated, like she was going to ask him about the "us" but T.J. gently pushed on her, and they brushed past his former liaison officer.

"Git yer butt over there by Mark and Nick," Timmons said, pointing.

T.J. had wanted to say something to Timmons about his new passion for working out, but was feeling so lighthearted, he didn't want to embarrass the man and ruin the mood for himself. He showed Shannon to a wooden folding chair next to Nick. Mark sat on the other side.

"Nick, how long are you down here for?"

"Just for the jump school course. Then back up to Sonoma County. We're in the middle of harvest. I shouldn't even be here."

"Glad to see you decided to stay in, my friend. We need guys like you," T.J. answered.

"Can you tell my intended?"

That caught Shannon's attention. "Good job, Nick," she said as she winked at him.

"Not like it's any secret. We've been living together for over six months now. This next workup will be our first real separation. We'd like to get married before that happens."

"What's your date?" Shannon asked.

"How about three weeks from today?"

T.J. whistled involuntarily. He leaned into Mark. "We have some serious planning to do, my web-foot friend."

Mark nodded with his arms crossed and shot T.J. with his imaginary forefinger shooter. When he turned back to Shannon it surprised him that she was frowning and staring into space, her face in profile. But T.J. could see the grimace and knew there were some unhappy memories. For his part, he'd never seen Shannon as lovely as she had been as a bride, and could now admit that was the day he fell in love with her. But he knew her memories of him were much different than that.

With an arm around her shoulder, he still managed to get his lips close to her ear. "Honey, I've changed."

The look she gave him, her doe eyes tearing up slightly but unwavering, told him he was going to have to work a lot harder at the convincing thing.

"I have," he insisted again and followed it up with a kiss to her cheek. He didn't notice the room had gotten silent, and someone had cut the house lights. A heavy-set woman in the row in front of them turned around and squinted.

"Shush," she said, reading him up and down.

T.J. rolled his neck and avoided Shannon's glare as the music began with a romantic ballad for a tango. Mark's girl-friend, Sophia, began a sultry number in her red form-fitting dress that left nothing to the imagination. Her dark hair was neatly gathered in a tight bun to the side of her face, adorned with a large bright red poppy matching the color of her full lips. The crowd was hushed. Mark sat with his eyebrows raised, and T.J. could see the beginnings of a crooked grin forming in spite of his tense jaw muscles. T.J. smiled too, and just as their eyes met, Shannon gave him another jab in the ribs.

Well, of course Shannon would be a little sensitive about her less than flat tummy. In her near-term condition, she couldn't move about the dance floor with such ease and grace. T.J. wrapped his long arm over her thin shoulder and squeezed her to him. "You're the most beautiful woman in here, babe," he whispered.

"Not that," she whispered, as the woman in front of them sighed and fidgeted. "Look." She pointed to a cluster of red-ruffled young girls with black low-heeled shoes similar to Sophia's. The oldest among them appeared not to be beyond six years, and two of them were barely out of diapers. When the music ended, Sophia took her bow to a standing ovation, and the cloud of red chiffon raced to take positions encircling her legs.

With arms raised above their heads, waiting for the music to begin, the young girls surveyed the crowd with wide dark eyes, glitter spray sparkling in their hair and over their young cherubic faces. As the Latin beat began, they twirled and strutted with remarkable skill, with only an occasional mishap. The audience spontaneously clapped in rhythm to the music, which seemed to foster enthusiasm among the young dancers eager to perform.

At last, the youngsters and their teacher were given a standing ovation. The group performed another routine and the girls were released to sit with their parents in the audience.

T.J. could see the excitement in Shannon's eyes, and he knew their little Courtney would someday take lessons here. "I can just imagine how cute she'll be," T.J. said, as he pulled several flowing curls back behind Shannon's ear. "She'll probably be the tallest, too!" Shannon nodded with a smile on her lips.

Sophia directed a series of partnered dances with the older children. There being a lack of boys in the class, most of the "couples" were two girls dancing together.

A modern jazz troupe with ragged clothing performed a difficult choreographed set of numbers, ending in a swing-fest the audience loved.

At last the music turned distinctly Eastern, and the house lights were turned down low. With the audience dark, a spotlight flashed on the golden vision of Amornpan, encrusted in a costume that looked like exotic chainmail. Atop her head was a headdress, over a foot tall. Her heavily painted features made her look like a china doll, T.J. thought. Just as with Sophia's performance, Amornpan moved with the grace and skill of a world-class dancer, her arms forming graceful angles, her head tilting horizontally as her fingers twisted backward, playing small bells and finger cymbals.

Nothing about the costume, the sounds or the dancing were familiar. T.J. found himself holding his breath in spite of the fact that this woman was old enough to be his mother. Her grace and beauty rivaled any twenty year old's. He found Timmons standing in the shadows in the back corner transfixed, arms crossed, and his face unreadable. T.J. knew the man's private thoughts were deep. He was happy for him.

After the performance, several of the SEALs and their wives and girlfriends went to a local microbrewery that also played sports on big screen TVs. Mark and Sophia were talkative, chattering and kissing, while feeding each other finger food. Timmons dropped by with Sanouk. Kyle and Christie were there, as were several others, including Fredo and Mia.

They all stopped and observed a news bulletin that interrupted the ball game announcing a terrorist beheading of another male American journalist, along with a female aid worker.

The American journalist was captured over a year ago and several attempts to locate and free the man and two others, were unsuccessful. Another aid worker from the U.K was executed a month ago.

The Team guys shook their heads, taking short looks at each other as they shared their private thoughts in mixed company. Team business was never discussed in front of the wives unless absolutely necessary. Since there was little chance they'd be deployed sooner than three months, all they could do was register their disgust, but T.J. knew everyone was thinking the same thing. The groups were getting bolder and bolder. It wouldn't take long before some of these actions would take place on American soil. And that meant innocents would be targeted.

The announcer came on and showed a scratchy sign written in Arabic. Jones squinted and swore, being the most fluent in Pashto. T.J. could recognize some characters and saw the distinctive "U.S" letters on the sign.

"The threat is considered credible. Members of the military and their families are being targeted. No one is safe, no matter where they live. No one.

The announcer signed off, and the news station made a brief statement T.J. couldn't make out, and then the ball game went back on. Most everyone was looking into their water glasses and beers, but as if on cue they looked over to Kyle.

"Well, there's no fuckin' thing we can do about it right now, so let's toast to Sophia and Mark. Hooya!" Kyle boomed.

Glasses were raised and the chant was repeated, adding Mark and Sophia's names.

"Where's your mom, Sanouk?" T.J. asked the gangly kid, in the silence that followed.

"She's cooking something special. A dessert for…" Sanouk threw a thumb in Timmons' direction. T.J. had never seen the man blush before, but he was bright red.

"Oh, this is serious shit, man," Fredo began. "When the woman starts making desserts, you got yourself trapped, man. They break out all the stuff they do really well, and then later, it's all TV dinners and—"

"What the fuck you talking about?" Kyle blurted. "You've never been fuckin' married, Fredo."

Jones added his opinion to the mix. "As a matter of fact, I don't think any woman has been brave enough to cohabitate."

The crowd laughed at Fredo's expense.

"So you gonna just sit there and take that, or you gonna tell them?" Mia said to Fredo, who was the second man T.J. had seen blush tonight.

"I proposed to Mia last Saturday night, and she said yes." Fredo could hardly look at anyone, and ducked his head like a beer had been poured on him.

"I hope Armando's okay with this. Mister *don't mess with my sister,*" Kyle added.

Christy stood, leaned into Fredo's back, and gave him a bear hug from behind with a kiss on the cheek. The cat-calls were long and loud.

"You done good, Fredo. Congrats you two," Christy said as she winked at Mia.

"Thanks."

T.J. felt Shannon stiffen at the early talk of Fredo's engagement, but he gave her a warm smile and a kiss, and she leaned into him with a sigh.

"So that's two weddings," Nick said as he drilled a look at T.J. and Shannon.

"We're doing it backwards, guys," T.J. said softly. "Having the baby first, and then if I do well enough in the delivery room, perhaps Shannon will marry me afterwards. But she needs to know I can handle myself in childbirth."

"Oh T.J., that's not what I said." Shannon had slapped his arm, but she was smiling in spite of herself.

"Wasn't what you said, honey. I read your mind." T.J. pointed to his temple and got another arm slap for his troubles.

"When's the funeral, Fredo?" Sanouk asked. Mia scowled.

Fredo cracked a smile that completely bisected his face and spread his already wide nose. "Going to Vegas this weekend. Who wants to give me away?"

CHAPTER 18

S hannon had felt slightly sick to her stomach at the brewery, so T.J. took her home early. She noticed her fingers and ankles were swollen, and they hurt from the pressure.

"Gotta get you off those feet," T.J. said. "You going to be able to sleep, honey?"

"Not with this nausea."

"If you're not feeling better by later this evening, I'm calling the doctor."

"I agree." Shannon had to admit, she was a little concerned by how quickly her mood changed with her upset stomach.

She took a cool shower and donned a big shirt, readying herself for bed.

It was usually comfortable in San Diego, since the temperature never varied by more than a few degrees all year round, but today there was no breeze coming off the ocean. She got up and turned on the window air conditioner that looked nearly as old as she was, but nothing happened. T.J. was working on his computer in the living room with a head-set so he could listen to his warrior music and not bother her. He had been obsessed with news accounts from North Africa, and although he never said so, Shannon suspected that was where they were headed on their next deployment.

Standing in the doorway, she watched him hunch over the blue light from his laptop. His enormous shoulders tapered down to an impossibly thin waist, which she noticed now more than ever, due to her condition. The baby had been lazy all day, but as she ran her hand over her over eight-months-pregnant tummy, she whispered to Courtney. "Won't be long now, sweetheart. Can't wait to hold you in my arms." She rubbed back and forth and hummed a little tune she'd been sung as a child, and eventually Courtney started moving slowly, almost in rhythm to the music.

She knew she should try to get her rest, because she'd been advised these quiet nights wouldn't always be here. And then she'd be nursing a young baby with T.J. overseas. Knowing how she'd worried about Frankie, as it turned out for good reason, she wouldn't be getting any sleep even if the baby didn't keep her up all night. There were still so many unsettled things.

T.J. sensed her presence and came over to her, kneeled and spoke to Courtney. "You keeping your mama up all night, darlin? Gotta let her get her rest so she can be strong to handle you."

He stood up and she buried her head into his shoulder and wept.

"Hey, what's wrong?"

"I feel like it's the quiet before the storm, T.J. I feel like I need to be prepared, like something's going to happen that will rip me from this peace."

T.J.'s hands were all over her back, her neck. He knew just where to knead her upper spine so as to work out the kinks and make her feel rubbery. "Good that you recognize that. We have down time overseas, too, but we know better than to let our guard down." His breathing was heavy as he shook his head.

"What is it? What aren't you telling me, T.J.?"

"You saw that report on the news tonight, babe?"

Shannon nodded, but stayed wrapped in the safety of his arms.

"You gotta be vigilant, watch everything and everyone around you. Especially when I'm gone, but even now. Things are changing out there, and some of the arena we've been working in is coming home to the U.S. We'll get them, that's for certain. We're hoping to minimize the threat, but we can't be everywhere."

"You really believe that guy?"

"They went after the World Trade Center twice before they got it right. These zealots are different from us because they don't value human life, so their own death means nothing. What we don't understand is how someone who is raised here and given so much could turn and want to destroy us. Those are the ones we probably can't stop, until the entire movement is crushed or some cooler heads prevail. Contrary to what some media centers say, we didn't cause this. It's because of who we are that they come for us. And if they can't get us on the battlefield, they'll try to pick off some of our non-combatants, our families."

"I hate to even think about that."

"I know, sweetie. But you have to. Your instincts are good. Stay alert. Know where that loaded gun is at all times. Never be without it when I'm gone, understand?"

His warm hands cupped her cheeks as he savored her lips slowly. She felt his heat coming on, mingling with hers, and allowed it to deliciously subside. She was ready to not be pregnant and could hardly wait.

T.J. escorted her back to the bedroom. "Couldn't get the air to work. Can you?"

"I'll go get one tomorrow, but lemme look at it."

Shannon got into bed, covered herself with just one sheet and lay back to watch T.J. fiddle with the knobs and then finally pound the top of the machine with his fist. The unit slowly sputtered to life.

"You're so masterful!" She extended her arms to the sides to invite him into her bed.

"Not really, I just knew where to hit it. You heard about the guy who was hired to fix some big machine in a factory and insisted he be paid up front?"

"No. Who was he?"

"It's a story, babe. He gets paid ten thousand dollars, walks into the plant and hits a pipe with his wrench and the machine starts working. The factory owner cries foul."

T.J. pointed to the air conditioner.

"The fixit man said, *Hey, I did my job. It's fixed.* The factory manager said, *But all you had to do was bang on one pipe. That's not worth ten thousand dollars.* The man said, *One dollar for hitting the pipe and nine thousand nine hundred nine-nine dollars for knowing where to hit it.*

"I don't care. You're still amazing."

"I think it was frozen up, and a chunk of ice fell outside. That's all."

"But you knew where to hit it."

"Nope. I guessed."

CHAPTER 19

T.J. got a call from his liaison during breakfast. Shannon had finally fallen asleep and he preferred to leave her that way.

"What's up, Chief?"

"T.J., I got a collect call from Tennessee, and I didn't accept the charges at first. They never called back, but left a number. I could hear a man's voice on the other end, and he kept shouting out your name over the operator."

T.J. closed their bedroom door shut before answering. "Who was this guy?"

"He says he's your father, T.J."

He'd always known that someday something would surface about his family. He expected to be contacted by a sister or brother, or perhaps his mother, but not his dad. T.J. had always envisioned a beautiful woman who had given him birth, remembering one of his foster parents' words about how she'd been a beauty queen in Arkansas. So, perhaps his father was from Tennessee. That *could* be possible.

"Can I have that number, Chief?" he asked. Even as he blurted the words, he wasn't sure he really wanted to talk to the man. But reflex made him ask anyway.

"Well, son, I'm afraid I have some bad news on that front."

"I don't understand, Chief Collins."

"The call came from Riverbend Maximum Security Prison."

It was as if he'd run into the end of a telephone pole they'd trained with in his BUD/S class. A wave of nausea consumed him. Black blotchy spots formed before his eyes, and he fought back dizziness.

Fuck me. My dad's a serial killer or child molester. If it was a maximum security prison, he wasn't there for stealing a car or writing too many bad checks, not that that would have been okay with T.J., either.

He didn't remember much of what Collins had to say after that, but he did have his wits about him to at least write down the phone number. After he hung up, he saw that a similar number was showing on his phone without voicemail. Could these be from two different family members? Maybe his mother? He wasn't sure how he felt about that, judging from how well he'd scored with the last scenario.

He hit re-dial, and it was answered by a message.

"*You've reached the office of inmate special services Travis Banks of the Riverbend Correctional Facility in Nashville. I'm not available to take your call…*"

Before he knew it, a beep indicated he was to leave a message. *What the fuck do I say?* He hung up and cursed.

What am I, in grammar school?

T.J. stomped around the kitchen, opening cupboards, looking for something to eat. He grabbed an apple from a fruit bowl and took a bite out of it. The interior of the apple was soft and a little mushy and contained the remnants of a worm, probably less than half of what he had in his mouth. He opened the front door, spit out the fruit onto the shrubbery, and threw the apple like he was throwing a grenade, past the next street at least, over the tops of red tiled roofs, until it was out of sight. He knew he could throw it far enough to make it to the estuary. He thought he had enough on it to send the red fruit all the way to heaven, but after a few seconds he heard the unmistakable sound of a car alarm going off.

Son of a bitch.

Walking inside, he slammed the front door shut, rattling the walls, and then he remembered Shannon.

Her face was white as she ran to him, bolting from the bedroom like it was on fire. "What is it, T.J.? What's happened?"

"Nothing."

"Stop that. You tell me right now what's going on. I'm getting really freaked here. I haven't seen this side of you. Ever."

He tried to take her in his arms, but she slipped away, hugging herself, twisting from side to side.

"Tell me first," she whispered.

T.J. lumbered over to the couch and collapsed, his face in his hands, his elbows propped on his knees. He mumbled, hoping she wouldn't hear, "I found my dad."

"What? I can't hear you."

He really didn't want to tell her, but he would have to. This was going to ruin everything.

"T.J. I want to know what's gotten into you? I *need* to know what you're—"

T.J. stood tall, and for a moment he saw fear on Shannon's face. At the same instant, the nausea in his stomach increased. He held his forefinger up to her. "Be right back," he said as he ran for the bathroom and deposited his coffee, breakfast cereal and what must have been left of the worm in the toilet.

After washing up, he came back to the living room to face Shannon, who hadn't moved. It was painful to see tears welling up in her eyes. He gripped the rounded doorway trim, inhaling, and said,

"I think I found my dad."

At first Shannon had a broad smile on her face as her eyes widened, her forehead creased in happy anticipation of a reunion he knew wasn't going to happen. She angled her head, frowning, but her voice was hopeful. "That's great, T.J. You've always wanted to find them."

"No. I did not."

"Yes you did, sweetheart."

"I fucking did not! And I fucking wish they were dead, or at least my dad. No wonder they never reached out to me. He couldn't."

"Why not?"

"Because I think he's been in prison my whole life!"

"You don't know that, T.J. Did you talk to him?"

"Fuck, no."

Shannon stepped back. "You need to lower that tone. You're starting to scare me."

At this, his knees nearly gave way. He was mucking up everything. One royal fuckup after another. "You suppose he's known about me all along?"

"Beats me. You have a number to call him?"

"I've already—" Then he remembered he hadn't left a message for the guy from the prison. He pushed the red redial button and got voicemail. "Sir, my name is T.J. Talbot and you called me today. Someone also talked to my liaison. I'm in the Navy, sir. The person my Chief overheard said he was my father. I spent my whole life in foster care, so I have no clue if my name rings a bell at all. Fact is, I don't really know who I am."

He left his cell number.

He held up the piece of paper, "I'm going to call this one now."

The phone rang and rang and rang without anyone picking it up. He was going to have to wait for the prison official to call him back. If his father was in prison, he was guessing this was a payphone in a prison common area used by inmates.

Shannon was drinking a glass of water. Her complexion was still pale. T.J. looked at her fingers and noticed her rings were tight. She filled up another glass and sat in the living room to drink it.

"How're you feeling?"

"Not very good, T.J. I think I should go back to bed. Can you come?"

"I'm going to let you rest. I've got some Team stuff to do, to read over. Don't want to disturb you."

"You don't disturb me. I like it when you're there."

"Should I call the doc?"

"If I can't sleep, might as well call him. Come to bed when you can, okay? I like having you next to me. I'm a little stressed for some reason."

T.J. registered that now Shannon was feeling some stress, which might mean her blood pressure was rising. None of these signs were encouraging, but if Shannon wasn't in pain and could sleep, he figured that would give her the most benefit. He decided to stay up in case someone from Tennessee tried to call him back.

CHAPTER 20

T.J. finally came to bed close to midnight and Shannon was engulfed in a deep sleep. He said a little prayer of thanks for this. He snuggled next to her, spooning to her backside, like he often did.

As the sun was peeking through the curtains, T.J. woke up and found the bed soaked. The baby wasn't due for nearly another month, but the doctor had said it could happen any day and the baby would be fine. So he figured Shannon's water had broken. But when he looked over at her, her skin was pale and clammy. She woke up slowly, more slowly than usual.

Something was seriously wrong.

When he turned on the nightstand light and drew back the sheets he saw the brownish stain everywhere, not clear like he'd seen in his Corpsman training. And Shannon's lack of energy told him she was in real trouble.

He cursed himself for not checking on her earlier. *Damn, I should have paid attention.*

He dialed their doctor.

"Doc, she's pale and has cold sweats. The bed is wet, but the water is light brown, Doc." He was near hysterics.

"She needs to be admitted. Can you get her here fast, because if not, I'm sending an ambulance."

"Shit, Doc. She going to be okay? Is the baby okay?" He watched as Shannon nearly fainted, coming from the bathroom where he'd heard her vomit.

"Can't tell, son. But the longer we're on the phone the worse it's gonna get. You get her to the hospital STAT, understood?"

"Understood."

He hung up and ran to assist Shannon. He got out her favorite pair of drawstring pajama bottoms, and a big shirt. The SEAL wives had made a quilt for Courtney, and he wrapped it around her shoulders, which made her burst out crying. Her emotional reaction sent him into the stratosphere with worry.

"You need anything, honey?"

"I couldn't keep anything down, even if." She inhaled and then let her tears burst forth, grabbing him and pounding her fists to his chest. "This wasn't supposed to happen this way."

"No worries. Please, Shannon. I'm here. We're going to meet the doc at the hospital. He'll have everything ready."

She'd been complaining of her feet hurting, and her fingers swelling. Now he saw her ankles swollen, almost bulging over her feet. He knew if they were this way right now, after a night lying down, it was a horrible sign.

He raced to the hospital and got there within fifteen minutes. Shannon was in pain, and had been consumed with heavy contractions. He was supposed to encourage her, thank her for enduring the pain. But he wasn't sure the pain was normal, since something was seriously wrong with the delivery. And he knew Shannon was sick. He hoped little Courtney would be tough enough to survive.

Doc Peters met them already dressed in scrubs.

"I want to be there. I have medic training," T.J. whispered to him, trying to calm Shannon's frowns as another contraction hit her. They were coming more frequently.

"They'll get you prepped, but right now I gotta get her examined and then into surgery. We're set up for a STAT C-Section."

T.J. didn't want to let loose of Shannon's hand, but finally allowed the heavyset nurse to lead him through a side door after they entered the double swinging doors of the surgery unit.

Scrubbed and prepped, armed with a mask, the operation was well underway when T.J. and the operating nurse entered the cold, sterile room. The sight of Shannon's blood on the table was not something he was prepared for, though it was normal and he had seen blood hundreds of times and had it spill or spray all over him many times in battle. She had been put under a general anesthetic, a breathing mask over her mouth. Sounds of her heartbeat were strong, but irregular. He recognized a very faint secondary heartbeat and realized the baby was in serious distress.

A sensor rang out as T.J. stepped next to the doctor, just far enough away so as not to interfere. The belly incision was completed, and he could see the bluish webbing of skin that was the uterus. A quick slice revealed an unmoving baby with a sickening blue cast to the skin. T.J. caught his breath.

There was no crying as little Courtney was lifted from her mother's womb. She was carried over to the lighted crib, the pediatrician rubbing her skin roughly with towels under the warm lights, and working to suction her nose and mouth quickly before starting CPR. A monitor was placed on the baby's chest but there was no heartbeat. T.J. was grateful Shannon wasn't awake to experience the pain of knowing the baby was stillborn.

More sensors were going off as they worked on Shannon's body as it went into convulsions. Orders were shouted over the din of beeping. He might have recognized what was being said, but he was in a state of shock.

Come on, Shannon. You can't leave me now. Being drawn between two horrible scenes, T.J. didn't know where he belonged, and he felt ripped apart.

He almost missed the little bit of good news as the pediatrician shouted, "And folks, we have a live birth." The baby still looked a light shade of pale blue, but had some pink to the chest and upper thighs, the face going from a light shade of purple to pink in the stretch of thirty seconds.

Doc Peters barked at him, "Go be with your baby. Nothing for you to do here, T.J." He immediately obeyed.

My baby. No, this is Frankie's baby. And I'm not going to let anything fuckin' happen to her.

The pediatrician's eyes showed a smile as T.J. touched little Courtney with his gloved hand. "Hey there, little Courtney. You're all right now. Mom's a little busy, honey, but you are just as sweet as can be. Love you, sweet thing." Hot tears coursed down his cheeks, blotting in his mask. He felt the reassurance of a tap to his back by one of the nurses as the doctor placed a breathing mask over the baby's mouth. Another nurse stuck a needle into her foot to extract blood, which drew a healthy reaction.

He was given a warm towel to continue to rub Courtney's feet, squeezing them, feeling the baby pull her toes back, raise her knees. At last he heard a raspy and tremulous cry through the mask. But it was one of the most wonderful sounds he'd ever heard.

"That's right, Courtney. You tell your mom you're here. Tell her you want her to get herself over here to hold you, Courtney, honey."

"She's a big girl," the doctor said. "Over eight pounds. That's good for her."

"Thank God, she's a girl."

"We're not out of the woods yet. She can't yet breathe on her own. But she's stabilizing. We'll know more in twenty four hours."

"Hear that, Courtney? Honey, you're gonna have to let them take care of you a little longer. You gotta breathe, sweetheart. We're all right here. You're beautiful, Courtney. My beautiful little girl."

Work on Shannon slowed as Doc Peters announced her vitals were improving.

"That a girl, Shannon. Hang in there. No more scares."

T.J. stopped rubbing Courtney's feet and looked over at Shannon's face, which had also pinked up. Trained to be even-keeled, to keep his emotions in check, he felt like he was going to explode. He didn't know if it was pain or delight. The mixture of fear and joy jumbled his insides. He wanted to rattle the walls and blow out the windows with a battle cry he knew would scare the entire ward. So he took a deep breath and swallowed. His hands were shaking and his guts were doing flip-flops.

One of the pretty nurses smiled up at him with her warm brown eyes, her long lashes glistening like she'd been crying too. "She's going to be fine. Everything will work out the way it's supposed to."

The comment didn't make him feel better.

She patted his shoulder again, like she had done before. "Relax," she whispered.

T.J. stepped back and almost lost his balance.

"He's done," Doc Peters said to one of the attendants, nodding in T.J.'s direction.

"No. I'm not leaving." He inhaled again and stepped to the table and took Shannon's hand, punctured with tubes held strapped in plastic tape. He rubbed her fingers and felt them warm to his touch. She was still way too cold, but her breathing was normal. "I'm here, Shannon. Courtney is in good hands now. I'm here, baby. Not leaving until you wake up."

The pediatrician wheeled baby Courtney from the operating room.

"She's beautiful, Shannon. Big strong girl, like you, sweetheart."

He felt her body stir. He looked up at the doctor, who had successfully stitched her belly up and was wiping her down with surgical wash. Peters nodded, so T.J. continued. "She's got Frankie's big jowls, fat cheeks. And her thighs, well, honey, those didn't come from you, sweetheart. Must have been on Frankie's side of the family because that one's going to be a high jumper. She's built like a rabbit."

A couple of the attendants giggled.

"I've seen lots of babies, Shannon, all wrinkled and mis-shapen. Little Courtney looks to be a beauty queen so far. Except for her—" He was going to say *coloring*, or something indicating she looked like a space alien, but thought better of it. "She's a blueblood all right. Not that she's blue or anything, just, just—" He wasn't having any luck recalling something appropriate, so he did something he was used to doing. "Fuck, honey, you sure gave me a scare. I'm here for the long haul, baby. Don't fuckin' leave me, Shannon. Don't ever leave me."

The pretty nurse's eyes sparkled. Dr. Peters grunted, but it was a grunt of approval. The gray-haired physician looked up at him and nodded. In muffled tones coming through the mask, he mumbled. "Go get yourself five or ten, T.J. She's not going to wake up for another hour or so. We'll come find you when she awakens so you can be there, okay? Go get yourself a quick nap."

"But I want to stay," he answered.

"If you don't leave, I'll make them get you, son. You've done all you can. Now leave us to do our jobs. You go do yours, which is buck up for the next round. I'll be out to see you in a bit."

With that, T.J. was led out of the operating room.

CHAPTER 21

Shannon felt as if she'd been run over by a girls' soccer team, cleats and all. Her head was pounding, her belly hurt, and when she moved her legs, it really hurt. She needed some pain medication, and right away. As she opened her eyes, for a second she wondered where she was, and then she remembered.

Courtney!

The white ceiling tiles moved back and forth as she started focusing on the sharp burning in her lower belly, intensifying until she heard a groan that sounded like it was from someone beside her, and then felt the last rumbles of it leaving her own chest. Instantly, there was someone peering over at her.

T.J.

She wanted to smile, but tears flooded her eyes at the intensity of the pain. She wanted to be happy to see him, but her body was in panic mode. If she didn't get something, she'd go mad with the sensations burning in her lower belly.

"You're okay, honey. I'm right here. Courtney's in the nursery," he whispered to her as he bent and kissed her forehead.

"Is she—" Shannon found she couldn't bring herself to say anything more.

"She's fine, sweetheart. She'll have to stay in the nursery for probably a few days, but she's fine."

"Oh God." A wave of nausea overcame her and she gagged, rolling her head back.

"Hold on a bit, Shannon. Honey, they're going to get you something. How do you feel?"

"I hurt."

"I know, sweetheart. It's coming."

An African-American nurse in white loomed over the bed. "Good morning, Shannon. How are you feeling?"

"I hurt. I'm sick."

"You sick to your stomach, too?"

"Yes."

"Okay, I'll get you something for the pain, and something for the nausea. You allergic to anything?"

"It should be in her chart," T.J. snipped back at her.

"I don't remember," Shannon interrupted.

"Why don't you let me do my job. I gotta ask, that's all, sir." She was stern with T.J., which bothered Shannon.

"Please hurry. It hurts."

"I know dear. I'm getting it right now. Just hang on for a minute."

T.J. talked to her, telling her how pretty Courtney was. She wanted to enjoy what he was saying, but she couldn't concentrate. Everything she was saw, felt and heard coursed through the hot excruciating pain in her lower belly. She felt like someone had punched her there so many times she'd surely be black and blue. She had a faint recollection of some pulling and tugging coming from her insides, and wondered if she'd started to come to during the caesarean.

At last the nurse injected the clear liquid into the IV tube above her head and patted her forehead. "That should make you feel better, sweetie. Just take some deep breaths, and relax into it."

She tried to inhale, but wound up in a coughing fit. T.J. held her head up, supporting her upper spine so she was half-way to a sitting position. His powerful arms felt good as he held her steady.

"Let me do all the work, honey. Don't use those muscles just yet."

A warm glow emanated from her belly to her heart, and she remembered the new love she had for him, the fresh new glow of a bright future deliciously brightening everything inside her.

She reached for his face with her free hand. "Love you, T.J." She couldn't find him, and didn't have the strength to search the space in front of her for him. Before her arm hit the bed, his fingers found hers and he squeezed and supported her hand, then rubbed up the surface of her forearm to her elbow, which felt heavenly.

"Not going anywhere, Shannon. Right here. Love you so much, honey."

"So Courtney's okay, then? I was sure that—"

"Shhh. She's a sick little one, but she's going to be okay. It was close, Shannon. Real close. They think she's out of danger now."

"What happened?"

"Something went wrong. They aren't sure, but I hope to God I didn't—"

"Don't be silly, T.J. You didn't have anything to do with this."

"Sure hope not. But she's a strong girl, and she has to fight an infection in her lungs. It's something they all go through when this happens. With antibiotics, she'll be okay, that's what the doctor told me. He'll be in later on to talk to us."

"Thank God, you were there, T.J. I felt you there the whole time."

"I was, honey. They had to kick me out."

"When can I see her?"

"Dunno. Let's just focus on you getting better. That's what I'm here for."

"No, I have to let Courtney know I'm here. I have to talk to her so she knows I didn't leave her."

When she looked at the expression on T.J.'s face, the full impact of her statement forced tears to her eyes. Neither one of them could speak. He bent and tenderly kissed her parched lips. In a low growl, he whispered, "And I'll never leave either of you two. Never. Never, never going to leave you."

The shiny dark hair at his temple and around the back of his head welcomed her fingers as they sifted, as she pulled him toward her again to claim another kiss. "I know that now, T.J. I won't ever doubt you or your loyalty."

"Or my love," he whispered and nibbled on her lips again.

"Or my own. I need you so much, T.J." She had to stop because the tears were coming again. The jumble of emotions was making her heart flutter. As her pain subsided, some of her desire for this man's body came rolling back like a favorite blanket to warm her. She wanted him close, to climb into bed with her right there in the hospital room, and comfort her.

He chuckled, as he must have picked up on her feelings. "Can't wait to get you home, honey."

Late in the morning, they were informed how sick Courtney really was. The fluid she had aspirated could cause a massive infection in her lungs. Blood work had come back with disturbing results, but they were reassured by the fact that the baby was responding to everything they were doing for her.

Shannon walked the halls with her IV, assisted by T.J., who chattered like a schoolgirl. He had more descriptions of Courtney than she'd ever heard before. It was as if he knew her whole personality. Knew what she would be like as an adult.

"She's got a cute face, and oh my God, her long fingers are so graceful."

He mentioned over and over again how perfect she looked, which told her he'd been concerned and perhaps she hadn't always looked that way. "How blue was she?

"Okay, Shannon. I'm not going to lie to you. She looked like a space alien." He was serious, and then broke into a warm smile filled with his bright white teeth. "Was beginning to wonder," he said as he bent down again and kissed her tenderly, "if you had done it with a guy from Pluto or something. But when I saw Frankie's big ears—"

"She has Frankie's ears? Oh. My. God. That's terrible." Then she realized his changing the subject from the baby's skin color had worked.

"Oh Courtney, honey, they look perfect," he whispered as he kissed her right ear. "Just like yours."

She was promised a visit with Courtney if she'd take a nap, but Shannon wasn't having any of it, insisting on seeing the baby. She'd agreed to follow the nurse's instructions about pumping her breasts since she couldn't feed Courtney yet, but there would be no real rest for Shannon until she could touch her baby. Even T.J. tried to talk her out of it, which made her wonder if there was something wrong with the baby he wasn't telling her. Something he didn't want her to see.

The neonatal nursery was filled with more equipment than a modern air traffic control tower. Several couples sat beside tiny babies hooked up to tubes and monitors that beeped. Courtney, at over eight pounds, looked like a giant. Although her color was good, she had difficulty breathing, her little chest moving up and down in raspy bursts of motion. It was clear the baby was fighting for her life.

Shannon took a chair at the side of the plastic tenting. A nurse helped her into Platex gloves and covered her hospital gown with another one, light turquoise in color. The instant she was allowed to rub her gloved fingers across Courtney's cheek and chest, she felt the connection between mother and daughter. As she had done while in the womb, the baby responded to the sound of Shannon's voice, even managing a squint that could almost be considered a smile. The forced little cry was sad and pathetic. Shannon spoke to her in a low voice.

"You're perfect, Courtney. You do have your daddy's ears, sorry to say, but you'll have beautiful brown hair that will cover anything you don't like about them. T.J. and I are right here."

T.J. squeezed her left hand, her fingers laced with his. He began massaging her neck and kissing the side of her face, which was just the encouragement she needed. He was such an instinctively tender and affectionate man, for all the warrior training he'd had. Knew just what to do to calm her down. She was so glad he was by her side, and couldn't imagine going through all this without him.

She closed her eyes and said a prayer. *Please, help Courtney to be strong so I can hold her, really hold her. I've lost Frankie. Don't take Courtney, too.*

T.J. must have seen the tear slipping down her cheek because he whispered, "It's going to be okay, honey. Everything's going to be okay." And that was the most wonderful thing he could have said.

"We're not going anywhere. We're here to keep you safe," she said to the baby. She looked up at T.J., kissed him and then turned back to Courtney.

"No one is ever going to leave you again. Ever."

CHAPTER 22

T.J. knew as long as he was in Shannon's room, she wouldn't sleep, but the bags under her eyes and hollow cheeks told him she really needed rest. He didn't want to leave, but it was better for her if he did. Best to not interfere with the nurses who were far better informed and equipped to handle their charge. T.J. had enough medical training to stop a man from bleeding to death in the arena, or do a quick stitch up or injection to stop an infection, but the fine tuning in the care Shannon required could only be done by a trained and loving nursing staff.

He was confident they were what she needed. He left the hospital on his way to the parking lot mulling over the situation with his father in prison. He'd always thought of himself as the guy who could solve anything, could "get 'er done," but this had completely blindsided him. He loved Shannon and Courtney, but the old friend Doubt and the evil twin Inadequacy had their hands all over him. It amazed him how quickly and almost comfortably he could go back to feeling like he was not good enough for anyone or anything.

He knew it was time to look up a Team Guy, but first he had to try to reach the numbers in Tennessee. He hit redial again, and got the same recording. This time, he didn't leave a message.

Tyler was happy to hear the news.

"That's just awesome, man. Congrats!"

"Thanks, Tyler."

"Anyone else know? Or you want it kept private for now? You know Christy, Kate and Sophia will all want to go see her. Is this a good time or should they wait a bit until things settle down?"

"I'll give Kyle a call, but no, go ahead and give everyone the news." T.J. reserved his communication with Kyle for himself, in case he needed that one on one with his LPO.

"Roger that. Kate's going to be ecstatic. I guess you won't be joining us this weekend in Vegas to give Fredo the ol' send off?"

"Nope. Besides, I got something else I got to do."

"This sounds serious. You okay, T.J.?"

"Naw, I'm feeling full of shit, man, and I should be hopping for joy right now. Timing's a bitch, but I just found out I *do* have a dad, and apparently he's alive."

"Well, he's a grandpa then. Makes no difference the baby isn't your blood. That child and Shannon are a part of you now just as if they were."

"I got that. But there's no fucking way that man is going to be anywhere close to the baby or Shannon. No way."

"Come again?"

"Found out yesterday my dad's apparently in prison. In Tennessee."

"Fuck no. That sucks. What for?"

"Does it fuckin' matter, Tyler? Really?"

"Probably not. Sorry, man. Simply selfish curiosity on my part."

T.J. could hear music in the background, and Kate singing to it. The sounds of Tyler's ordinary life only accentuated how misplaced he felt. He was torn apart by his love for his lady and the baby, and struck by the harsh reality that the plan hadn't started out that way, that this still was Frankie's life he was stepping into. And T.J.'s background left scars that might not ever heal. He found no compassion for a father who was now reaching out to him on, of all days, the day he was working up to his new role as father and, hopefully soon, husband. No matter how bright his future could be, and he'd been grateful for this new chance on life, his past just wouldn't leave him alone. Wouldn't leave him alone to enjoy Shannon and Courtney for one whole fucking day.

"You still there, Talbot?" Tyler's voice was laced with concern, and to T.J. it sounded almost condescending.

"Yeah, I'm still here. I'm not a fuckin' schoolgirl."

"No sir. You're one of the baddest, meanest motherfuckers out there, the guy who saved my life, and the guy who's going to save Shannon and the baby's lives now. *That* guy. Don't forget *that* guy. To hell with everyone else. Even me. Pay no attention. You're *that* guy and always were, T.J."

"Got it. So I'll quit my pity party now."

"You want some company?"

"Nah. Hate to ruin your day."

"Fuckin' no way, man. Kate's on an organizational whim. I'm about to have the cleanest and most organized underwear drawer on the planet. Can you fucking believe that? They teach these things on TV. Screw the Home Decorating channel, or whatever the hell it's called. Kate watches it practically twenty-four seven."

That was funny, but T.J. almost couldn't laugh. His feet were encased in weighted boots like in astronaut training. He was fuckin' walking on the moon.

"So, you'd be fuckin' putting me out of my misery."

"Okay. I'll give Kyle a call, and then meet you at the Scupper? Mind if Kyle joins us, if it comes to that?"

"He'll be babysitting if Christy goes over to visit Shannon, but yeah, no worries."

T.J. hung up, and called his LPO.

"Hey Talbot, how's it hanging?" Kyle picked up on the first ring. T.J. could hear Brandon's incessant jabbering and knew that Kyle was probably being overrun by the preschooler.

"Just wanted you to know Frankie's baby was born today."

Careful hesitation preceded Kyle's comment. "You mean *your* baby."

"That's right, LT."

"What's wrong? Everything go okay?"

"Not really. She was born with some problems, and we almost lost her."

"Why the hell did you go through all this on your own, man?"

"Hey Kyle, cut me some slack. I'll bet you weren't thinking much when Brandon was born."

"That's a fact. So, how's everyone doing?"

"Baby is improving. She was born C-section, and she aspirated the—"

"Spare the deets, T.J. But everyone's doing good?"

"I think so. Shannon's a trooper. The baby is going to have to stay in the hospital, but the doc thinks she'll be okay, and then we'll do the tests, you know."

"I do."

"But that's only partly why I'm calling. I'm giving Shannon a chance to catch up. Then she can have more company."

"I'll make sure Christy tells everyone. She's gonna want to tell the whole team, you know."

"Fine by me. Especially those that knew Frankie, they would want to know."

"You tell Tyler?"

"Yeah, just called him. We're meeting up for a couple of brews."

"Good. So quit pussy-footing. What's up?"

"I just got a strange call from Collins. Apparently my dad is trying to reach me."

"Your dad? Didn't know he was in the picture."

"He isn't. And he won't be."

"Okay, you wanna explain that to me?" Kyle was working to hide concern, but T.J. felt it anyhow.

"I guess he's an inmate at Riverbend prison in Nashville."

"Wow."

"That's a maximum security prison, Kyle. I haven't spoken to him, but there's an inmate services guy I've left a message for. He tried to call me during the recital."

"Gotcha. Timing sucks."

"Doesn't it, though?"

"And you've told Shannon?"

"Of course. Kyle, this was one of the hardest things I've had to do, tell her this." T.J. reeled himself in, but just barely. He wanted to protect Shannon and the baby from the reality that was his past. How he wished it was a different story that was unfolding, rather than one with dark unknowns he wasn't sure he wanted to reveal.

"Not like you knew anything about this beforehand. This is just the hand you've been dealt, T.J. It isn't who you are. But I'm reading between the lines—"

A loud scream came from the background on Kyle's phone. It sounded like Brandon.

"Sorry, gotta go. Brandon's just pulled a table over on himself. He's into everything now. Just wait, T.J. You can't leave them alone for a *second*."

"Roger that, LT. Catch you later."

The Scupper was cool and dark, which matched his mood and suited his needs. Tyler was dressed in cargo pants and a long-sleeved T-shirt with the SOC logos—skulls, tridents, and Latin phrases—covering up his tats. They'd been in the Scupper so many times with the Team, it wasn't as if any of the regulars wouldn't know who they were. Tyler could have worn a dress, and he wouldn't have fooled anyone.

He stood up and they embraced, his friend smacking him loudly on the back.

"You look like shit," Tyler said as he ordered his beer and searched the room. It was a habit they all had. Wasn't so much looking for people they knew as people they *didn't* know. That was the real problem. His scanning over with, Tyler glanced up. "Any more news?"

"Not a thing."

"Kyle coming?"

"You were right."

"Payback, I'd say."

"Double. Of course in my case, I doubt Courtney could ever do what I put my foster folks through. Like Rory, I burned down a woodshed."

"I know, because you could, right?" Tyler chuckled.

Images of being beaten bare-bottomed with a strap in that woodshed came flooding past, tugging on his gut and throwing his insides across the bar. He was so small then, and the evil foster dad he had at the time was huge with hands the size of basketballs. The guy could grip his upper arm with just one hand and swing that strap with the other so hard he had welts for a week afterward, and it hurt to go to the bathroom or even fart. He vowed he'd never be that small or helpless again.

"Something like that," he answered, and took a big sip of beer. He tried to remember when it was he received his first compliment or the assurance that he could trust someone, or that his little body wasn't going to be abused in some way.

All he could remember were the first days getting yelled at by his BUD/S instructors, by his Basic instructors at Great Lakes, and the odd feeling that he was home. He was *used* to it. He could *do* this. It was something he was made for. And that feeling grew every day he served, every day he packed and re-packed his parachute, every day he cleaned his equipment and stowed it away like fine pieces of china and crystal.

This was, after all, his *real* legacy. Everything else was pure fantasy.

"So here we are. Wanna talk about it?"

"Nope. Wanna forget about it."

"So what are your plans?"

T.J. shrugged. He hadn't thought about what his plans were, since it was a moot point anyhow. No way would he leave Shannon and the baby alone, not with nuts running around the country spouting their mouths off about getting revenge against innocent military men and women's families. He wasn't going to allow anyone else but himself to protect them.

But even if he could, he wasn't so sure he'd want to talk to his dear old dad, if it even was his dad.

His phone rang.

"T.J. Talbot?" said the burly voice he recognized as Travis Banks from Nashville.

"That's me."

"I'm—"

"I know who you are, so let's just cut the bullshit, and you tell me why you're calling me."

Banks let the line go silent a little longer than necessary. T.J. felt a reproach was coming.

"You're father is dying, son. He wants to see you before he passes on."

T.J. looked at Tyler, who was chewing on his lower lip and not making eye contact. He wasn't going to tell the man about Shannon and the baby, because he didn't think his father deserved to hear it. "I'm afraid that will take some time to arrange. See, I'm in the military."

"We know that, son, but your father has maybe a week tops on this planet. He's tried to escape twice from our hospital ward bare-assed in his gown, everyone chasing after him. He's hell-bent on seeing you. Our hospital is in the Riverbend Maximum Security Prison here in Nashville, so his attempts were pure folly, as are the years those attempts added to his sentence. He'll die here, son, and probably this week."

"Understood. I'd say he's your problem, not mine. Sonofabitch didn't even think to try to contact me until he was getting ready to check out. What do you think that makes him?"

"Like you said, Mr. Talbot, a sonofabitch. But he's your father."

"Sperm donor."

"I stand corrected." Banks sighed into the phone. T.J. heard a wooden chair squeak and could just picture the place. It probably would be a tiny office with old government-issue desks and gray file cabinets with inventory stickers on them, a window that didn't open, with bars on it. The employees of a prison were behind bars as much as the inmates were. Probably would smell like all the Juvenile Halls he'd been in from Texas to California.

Banks tried another olive branch. "Look Talbot, there's no good reason to say good-bye to the man who gave you life, except just to do it. Just because he wasn't there for you isn't a good enough reason to not be a decent human being."

"You're wrong, Banks. I owe him nothing. And I am an honorable human being. Of that I'm certain."

"So I hear. Thank you for serving your country."

T.J.'s internal alarm went off, hoping that his dad didn't know, or this man didn't know he was in the Special Forces. Now of all times, this sort of thing should be kept quiet.

"I've got some personal things going on at home now, and it will take time to get approved for leave. Not sure I can do this so last minute. So don't get your hopes up." He wasn't inclined to lift one single finger to request any time off, but it sounded better to say it.

"Well, I'll let him know we talked. You do the best you can, son. I'm sure that will be good enough." Banks hung up.

It would have settled things much easier for T.J. if the guy had yelled at him, shamed him in some way. That kind of direct challenge was something he could handle, and he'd win at that game. But when Banks used the phrase, "Do the best you can do," it irked him worse than if he'd sat on a rusty nail. Not a mortal wound, but it would fester, hurt like hell and eventually need to be addressed. It wouldn't heal on its own.

He set his phone down and then finished off his beer. "My dad's dying. Got maybe a week to live."

Tyler knew better than to say anything. They searched the bar, looked up at who came out of the men's room, where their hands were, and if they carried a backpack. Looked for someone lingering in the doorway to the outside and listened to all the traffic noise. The news program on one of several big screen TVs was turned up, and it had stopped the ball game.

"...we're just getting word now that at least two family members of a retired Marine have been injured: his wife and one of the couple's four children. Mrs. Cole was able to shoot the attackers with a loaded gun from the couple's kitchen, but was injured in the altercation. One child was spending the *night over at a friend's. Mrs. Cole and her child were taken to Scripps Mercy Hospital in San Diego. It's believed the attacker had been looking for Cole, who was not home at the time."*

The banner on the screen said Homegrown American Terrorist in bright red letters. It continued to scroll across the picture of the Emergency Room of the hospital.

Shannon's hospital.

CHAPTER 23

"**S**onofabitch." T.J. said as he and Tyler stood at the same time. He didn't even ask if Tyler wanted to go. In a minute they were both in T.J.'s four-door pickup, headed down the freeway, stuck in traffic.

Tyler spoke with Kate briefly on the phone, and then hung up. "She's going over to Christy's to help out. Kyle's been called in."

"No shit. That was Magnus Cole's wife on the screen. You know, he's the guy who has been organizing all those Warrior Runs? We've sponsored them at Gunny's."

Magnus had been another foster care product, although he had fared better. T.J. had spent time with him. Magnus was working with a lot of at-risk youths in his retirement and was quite high profile and in the media all the time.

"Yes. I've seen him. I knew you were friends. Sorry, man."

"He's gonna go off like a powder keg," T.J. said, and spit out the window.

They rode the rest of the way in silence. T.J. kept the radio off so he could think. They got to the hospital just as several large TV motorhomes blocked the entrance to the Emergency Room.

"Christ, wonder how anyone who really needed help could get in there. Where the hell are the cops? There are people all over this place, like ants. No way this is secure."

"I'm packing, just so you know," Tyler whispered.

"Always."

They parked in the reserved doctors' lot and were slipping in a side entrance, when someone exited wearing bloody scrubs. They expected to be stopped and questioned, but the orderly ignored them. T.J. opted to bypass the elevator and take the stairs. At the door to the second floor, a bloody handprint was framed ominously on the ivory painted metal door. The door handle was also covered in blood. Tyler and T.J. instinctively drew their weapons.

"Maternity and nursery are on floor four," T.J. barked.

Tyler grabbed his arm, holding him back. "You know what you're doing here, T.J.? Remember, we're in the U.S. of A. And we got permits, but if there's been violence the cops aren't going to know if we are good guys or bad guys, and they'll shoot us down like dogs if we're not careful."

"Yeah, well can you inform those assholes that it's illegal to kill innocent women and children? Do you suppose that would help, Tyler?"

"Fuck sake, T.J. I'm not worried about anything but you. You don't need trouble. Protection, yes. But trouble? We gotta stay calm."

"Roger that. No worries. We trained for this, remember?" T.J. yanked his arm out of Tyler's grip and dashed up the last flight of stairs to the white door marked *Floor 4.*

Stepping out into the hallway, it surprised them there was no chaos. No screaming. No unattended posts. They walked along the hall to one side, keeping their side arms down and behind them. Tyler frequently checked for anyone coming up from the rear. T.J. felt the familiar touch from Tyler's hand on his shoulder, like they'd been trained. "So far, so good. I got no one," Tyler whispered.

The vinyl flooring rippled unevenly under the light of the overhead fluorescents. A stacked meal tray cart was conveniently parked between two rooms on the left. T.J. held onto it while they both took cover behind.

"She's down four rooms, on the left."

The nurse's station was packed with hospital staff and what appeared to be a doctor. The heavyset charge nurse rounded the corner holding a clipboard, and stopped in her tracks when she saw T.J. peering around the cart.

"Mr. Talbot, what in the hell are you doing?" Her voice carried such that everyone within twenty feet looked first at her, and then over to the two SEALs. A quick assessment told T.J. that nothing out of the ordinary was happening, so he stuffed his SigSauer under his shirt and secured it with the Velcro strap he'd fashioned at the rear of his belt. Tyler stowed his in the lower pocket of his cargo pants.

He stood up and stepped away from the cart. "You do know there's a whole lot of commotion downstairs, don't you?"

"We haven't been notified. It would come over the speakers. No one's called. What kind of commotion?"

"There are victims in an attack. I think they've brought them in downstairs. This was an attack on a military family."

One of the young volunteers put her palm to her lips. The doctor picked up the floor phone and started calling, and several people looked at their cells.

"There are bloody handprints to the door on Floor Two, in the stairway." T.J. exchanged glances with Tyler. "Holy shit, the guy we passed at the side entrance—he was covered in blood."

The charge nurse ran for the desk and began dialing the phone. "I'm calling security. You two are gonna wait right here."

The doctor interrupted her. "Already got through. They've had an altercation but everything's quiet."

"What about Shannon?" T.J. asked.

The nurse kept the phone to her ear. "She's fine. Probably wide awake by now. Are you satisfied?"

"Not until I see her."

"You carrying—*yes*—this is Four South, are we anticipating a lockdown or emergency? I see. When did that happen?"

T.J. walked briskly toward Shannon's room, but the charge nurse raised her voice, cupping the phone. "Hey. Hey. You wait right here. You can just sit and wait." She hung up the phone.

"No can do, Ma'am," T.J. said as he walked backwards, holding his hands out to the sides, palms up. T.J. and Tyler were in the room before she could stop them.

Shannon was sitting up, looking a much better shade of pink. Even without makeup, she was beautiful.

"I knew when I heard all the shouting that somehow, my T.J. was involved." Almost as an aside she said, "Hi there, Tyler." She re-directed her focus to T.J. "What are you up to?"

"I'm just checking on you. That's all."

"So what's with the altercation with the nurses?"

Tyler poked his head out into the hallway, then stared back at T.J. and shrugged. "Security must be pretty busy. Don't see a soul."

"Security?" Her frown leveled on T.J. "What have you done?"

"Nothing. Look, there's been a terrorist attack on the family of a Marine. It's all over the news."

Shannon picked up the clicker, and all three of them watched the announcer give a special report as again pictures of the hospital emergency room filled the background of the screen.

"*…by the Middle Eastern America group, with sympathetic ties to certain radical elements in Iraq and Pakistan. In recent weeks, the government and local law enforcement teams have been stepping up their security measures following the threat of attacks against our military men and women. In this particular case, we understand Mr. Cole was in Washington working on a bill that would help military veterans and their families. He's been an outspoken advocate for at-risk youths in our community and helped to foster and sponsor many charity events here.*"

A photo of Magnus Cole in his Marine uniform was shown next.

"Shit!" Tyler blurted out. "Who gave them permission to give out all that information?"

"T.J., he's in the news all the time. It's what he's been doing," said Shannon. "Even I feel like I know him, and I've never met him."

T.J. was seething. He was fisting and unfisting his hands, grinding his jaw. He desperately wanted to throw something.

A passage from his least favorite book in school, a book he was forced to read in three different high schools that year, *A Tale of Two Cities*, came to mind:

It was the best of times. It was the worst of times.

CHAPTER 24

Kyle finished his briefing with most of the other LPOs of SEAL Team 3, some of the Senior Chiefs who were stateside from Team 3, several Lieutenant Commanders and the top three Naval Intelligence officers at Coronado. Kyle had never met those guys, as they tended to keep a very low profile.

What struck him was that the task force was preparing for this day, yet nothing special had drifted down to the SEAL teams not on deployment. They were focusing on methods of ensuring that military families were being protected. It was also discussed that perhaps the perps were a pair of unknown lone wolves with an axe to grind, a local disgruntled recruit or two who had been forcibly DOR'd or had some beef with the military. This idea was roundly rejected. The method of the second assailant's death and the claim of responsibility made it pretty clear there was a Middle Eastern connection.

Then he learned the details of the attack. The first assailant was in the process of going after the youngest of the three children with a knife, when Mrs. Cole fired point blank with one of the couple's five loaded handguns. The other assailant was run off the property and blew himself up in the middle of rush hour traffic on a busy neighborhood expressway, injuring multiple drivers but without further loss of life except his own. It didn't take a rocket scientist to figure out that the terrorist was looking to make a splash on the evening news, and he got his wish, although Kyle hoped he was enjoying his time in hell without the virgins and would never know the bitter fruit he had spawned.

He called Christy, hearing the screams of little children, Brandon the loudest amongst them, and several women conversing quietly so Christy could talk to her husband, their husbands' boss. There wasn't any laughter as would normally occur at such a gathering.

Upon hearing the children in the background, he thought of the Cole children he'd met at a Christmas fundraiser last year.

"How are you doing, Kyle?" That was his Christy. Always watching out for him. Right in his face, asking the tough question. God, he loved her strength. She was going to be a great help to the other wives and girlfriends.

"It's bad. You saw the news?"

"Well, of course, until the kids and others began to arrive. Phone's been going nonstop. Kyle, they put T.J.'s picture on the TV, right next to Magnus's."

"You're kidding."

"No. Remember that run they did last year for the Warrior Foundation? Someone dug up a photo of the two of them together."

Kyle knew it wouldn't take long for the facial recognition software to find T.J.'s name and publish that, too. He wondered if the news media had any idea how they had put his guys in jeopardy. On days like today, he felt like the war was being lost.

And then he adjusted his attitude. It wasn't lost, because he was still alive, and he'd die protecting the ones he loved. It was the same deal whether at home or overseas. They never left anyone behind, and they wouldn't hesitate to save the lives of others, even at great personal cost. It was what he signed on for.

"I'm coming home. I gotta get hold of T.J. first. I think Shannon is at that hospital."

"Oh my God. Should I go over there?"

"Absolutely not. Stay home. Keep everyone there. See if you can have the gals get hold of their husbands. I'm going to call a meeting for Charlie Company. No one else, though. No one is to talk to family, except to answer direct calls to their phones. No details. Just reassure people they're okay. Don't do anything to attract attention, and if the fucking news media arrives on our doorstep, make sure you call me right away and don't, whatever you do, answer the door."

"What's going on? Why is this happening?"

"Because they can't win. So they'll cause as much pain as they can. They can't get us, so they'll target the families."

Kyle let Christy absorb everything he'd said.

"Any questions?"

"No, I love you."

"Love you too, babe. Gotta be extra vigilant. Better to plan than not be prepared, right?"

"Roger that."

Kyle snickered. "Cute. I like it better when you say that in bed."

"Well come home at a decent hour, and I'll give you a repeat performance."

"Now that's worth living for, trust me. Okay, Christy, gotta go."

"Love you. And Kyle?"

"Yes?"

"You're right, they won't win. Maybe this was what we needed as a country to wake up to the real world. You guys do too good a job making it so we don't have to think about it. Only fair that we have to share in some of the risk. I signed on for that when I married you. I'm still solid with that decision."

CHAPTER 25

Shannon's concern over Courtney's condition had lessened, but she began to worry about the darkness that seemed to descend around T.J. involving his feelings towards his father. It worried her that he had no use for his own family. She wondered if love alone was enough to heal his pain, and how much of this pain would become part of her life.

She also knew he wasn't going to be able to come to her, that it would be her job to cross that ocean, prove to herself that she could handle T.J.'s intensity. Frankie had been easy to love, like her dad. But T.J.'s black mood was completely foreign to her, and she felt inadequate and more than a little afraid.

The meds they'd given her were really beginning to kick in. She wanted to talk to T.J. when she wasn't so distracted with the pain she could hardly think. She wanted him to go home, and come back rested so he could be fully present to her and Courtney. He needed to be able to feel her love

Tyler and T.J. had gone into the hallway to talk to security. She should have paid attention, but now she didn't want to meddle. She had to trust him. The emergency C-section had scared her. But the possibility of losing her man, again, scared her even more. She remembered the folly of thinking she wanted to raise her child on her own. What a stupid idiot she'd been. She was lucky T.J. was so insistent, that he'd made that promise to Frankie, that although Frankie wasn't perfect, he had the foresight to make T.J. make that promise. He knew perhaps better than anyone else did, that if T.J. promised, he would keep his word.

But that didn't mean T.J. would be able to make it smooth for her, despite what he might say. It was her job to toughen up, match him in every way. In grief and in joy. There would come a time when T.J. would need her as much as she needed him now, and she vowed to be there for him.

Just like the men on SEAL Team 3 he served with so honorably, the guys Frankie would rather spend time with than anyone else in the whole world, she'd never give up. She'd go to her grave trying to give T.J. what he so richly deserved. It wasn't about sex. It wasn't about being comfortable, staying out of trouble or any of the things she thought about that day when she married Frankie. It was all about being the best kind of woman she could be, rocking T.J.'s world and making sure he understood he was loved with every cell in her body. Was loved like he'd never been loved before, just like the words to her favorite song.

She would love the stuffing right out of him and heal all his sharp edges in the meantime.

Shannon wiped her cheeks just as T.J. and Tyler came into the room. "Everything go okay out there? I notice you didn't get carted away."

The joke fell flat. Tyler looked like he wanted to be anywhere but here.

"Tyler, can I have a word with my intended?" she asked. She liked that T.J. looked shocked. It wasn't joy, but she'd take it anyway.

Tyler wiggled his eyebrows. "You guys okay if I take a cab home? I'm kinda missing Kate right now."

"I'll drive you," T.J. said.

"No, he'll take a cab, because right now I need to talk to you, T.J. But we'll pay for it, right?" she said as she looked at T.J.'s puzzled expression.

"No worries, guys," Tyler said. "And congratulations! I think the ladies are arranging a visit tomorrow. Best to get some one-on-one time before the crowd arrives. Later, Talbots." He winked at the reference to a marriage that hadn't yet occurred.

"Sit here, hon." She patted the bed where she'd slid her legs to the side to give him room. The hospital springs squealed as he sat his frame down but avoided eye contact. "Tell me," she whispered, and then took his hand.

He allowed her to thread her fingers through his. She rubbed her thumb over his in a gentle massage. He watched in what appeared to be detached silence. The electric, erotic trance their touch usually created was missing. T.J. was in a deep freeze.

"Tell me," she said again, softly, this time touching his arm and gently rubbing up and down.

He stiffened, sat up straight, stuck his chest out and inhaled. Then he released her fingers and sat with his arms crossed, again not making any eye contact with her.

She was going to wait all night. It wasn't her place to speak up or ask him again. Twice was enough. She had to trust him. She watched the dark brown curls that were forming at his temples and behind his ears. His face in profile could have been the bust of an Native American Chief. She loved his broad nose and full lips, his leathered skin peppered with black stubble. She wanted to touch the dimple at the base of his chin, then kiss it softly as she'd done so many times. Shannon recalled what it felt like to lay her ear against his strong torso and marvel at his heart beating strong and true. He was a complicated package of strength and softness. He could be so fearless, like the day he'd hung those words on Courtney's bedroom wall, pulling his heart out and handing it over like an innocent trusting youth. Or, he could be shut down, like tonight.

The more he tried to be strong, the more she could see the soft, sensitive side of him. Why had she never seen these things before? Of course he would love her baby like his own. He was the kind of man who would love her more than he'd love his own life.

He'd been holding his breath, but this time he closed his eyes and let it all out. When he opened them again and looked down at her, some of the spark was back. Just a little, but enough for now.

"My dad is dying and wants me to come visit him."

"You talked to him?" She could feel his tension filling the room, and it scared her.

"No, I talked to the inmate liaison, or whatever he's called. The guy told me he has less than a week to live."

"Then you need to go see him."

T.J. stood, his hands in his jeans pocket. "I'm not doing that. I'm not letting that fucking man into my life. He didn't want me. Well, I sure as hell don't need him."

"Except that you would regret it your whole life, T.J."

"You have no idea what regret means, Shannon. Not like you ever had to worry about anything your whole life." He refused to have eye contact with her. She could see how hard he was working to hold in his anger.

The cruel statement had a ring of truth to it. She told herself he didn't really mean what he'd said. She was not going to let him see how much he'd hurt her with that comment. "I was scared today. We both were."

He said something under his breath she couldn't make out.

"I have regrets, T.J. I regret that I made Frankie wait two years to marry me. I regret that we didn't make love the night before he deployed. I regret I wasn't a more appreciative daughter growing up. I regret picking so many fights with you, when you were just trying to help Frankie grow up. I was jealous of how he loved you, T.J. You did for him what I would never be able to do."

T.J. was watching her hands folded neatly in her lap. She smoothed the pink blanket over her thighs until there wasn't a wrinkle or pucker anywhere.

It was her turn to take in a deep breath. "It would have been painful, but I regret not being there, to hold Frankie for his last breaths. That should have been me, not you. And he never should have made you promise what you had to promise him."

"No, Shannon, don't say that."

"Well, I didn't make it very easy for you, did I? I think you scared me to death, the way you looked at me. I was scared of the way you made me feel when I was around you. And I'm going to be scared when you go overseas, because now I don't know what I would do without you, T.J."

She didn't recall a time when they had honestly looked into each other's eyes the way they were right then. At the edges was the sexual tension, pulling them in that direction, but she wanted him to see that she could just as easily be his friend as his lover. For the first time, she just wanted to be there for him, without strings or expectations.

"You won't have to worry about that, honey," he said, as he held her right hand. "I may have to go places, but I'm not leaving you. Ever."

"Because you gave your word to a dying man. If you're reconsidering what you promised, just know that you don't have to—"

T.J. quickly knelt by the bed and put both her hands to his lips.

"Nonsense. Stop it," he said to her fingers.

"Would you have persisted if you hadn't promised?"

His eyes were watering when he answered, "That's an unfair question. That's not how it works."

"So you tell me how it works, T.J. How is all this going to work? How are you going to be a father to Courtney when you won't go see your own father, who's trying to reach out to you through time and space? I may not have a lot of things you have, but I do have love for my family. I know I could never live with myself if I let him die in a prison cell, knowing his son didn't want to see him before he went. You'd hate yourself too, I just know you would. I don't want that for you. I won't bring that hatred into our family."

He stood back up and turned his back to her. She could tell he was weeping. His shoulders slumped forward. She carefully got out of bed with the clattering of plastic tubing and the wheels of the IV squeaking, and he turned around just in time to pull her to his chest. His heavy breath was on her neck, his fingers digging into her back as he clutched her through the hospital gown.

She gently kissed the hair at his temple, whispering that she loved him while she allowed herself to melt into him, until the pain of her incision sharpened and she stiffened involuntarily and then stepped back slightly.

"Baby, did I hurt you? I didn't mean to—"

"Shhh. I'm fine. I got a little carried away is all. There will be time for that." She grabbed one hand and turned toward the door. "Right now I want to go see our baby, T.J. I want to watch as you touch her."

He brought his forehead to meet hers and nodded. "Okay. We'll do that."

With the assistance of the nurses, another chair was brought into the nursery, and T.J. was properly gloved and gowned. Shannon leaned into his side as he placed his hand through the plastic seam and gave Courtney a tickle to her cheek. The baby's complexion was a deep pink, but getting lighter almost before their eyes.

"Tomorrow I think maybe you can feed her," the head nurse said from the other side of the warming unit.

"Really?"

"Well, she needs your early milk as soon as you feel up to it. I'll help you pump a little so you'll be ready tomorrow."

"Oh, and I'd love a shower."

"Not for a couple of days. The doctor. has to inspect your incision tomorrow. Maybe day after. But I'll bring you some things to freshen up." She turned, and after giving T.J. a look that told him she didn't trust him to behave, left the room.

"I'm not letting that woman touch you. If there's going to be any washing up, I'm doing the washing."

Courtney was fussing, trying to push the mask off her face with flailing fingers and arms. T.J gave her his little finger and she grabbed it.

"Yeah. You're gonna play softball. You'll be a pitcher with that grip."

CHAPTER 26

T.J. had a hard time sleeping. The nurses made up a bed next to Shannon, and he'd fallen asleep off and on after watching her doze off, their fingers weaving together like they'd been doing it for fifty years. He'd tried several times to pull back his arm, which had fallen asleep from the elbow down, but each time, Shannon grabbed onto him harder, and he was unable to extricate himself without waking her. It made him smile and count his blessings.

Earlier, before he'd finished his private visit with Courtney, a young neonatal intern joined him. The young man patted him on the shoulder and took a careful look at the baby. He listened to chest sounds and nodded, raising his eyebrows.

"You've got a very strong little girl there."

"Tell me about it."

"Good thing she was so large. Hardly seems like she was, what, two weeks early?"

"Doc had told us just two days ago she could be born at any time. I'm guessing she figured she was ready."

"Under the circumstances, I'd say we got lucky." He repositioned his stethoscope around his neck. "I'm inclined to remove her mask and see how she does. Wanna do it?"

"You sure?"

"No, but I don't hear anything that disturbs me. I think she can breathe on her own."

"She's been fighting that thing ever since I got here tonight."

"Well, let's give it a go and see how she does."

Though T.J. had stitched salty combat vets up, the idea of pulling tape off little Courtney's fine light brown hair, ears and cheeks left him squeamish. "I think I'll let you do it, if you don't mind."

With the breathing mask removed, the baby eased into a deep sleep with regular up and down chest rhythms. He watched her for nearly a half hour, and then went in search of Shannon. There was a new crew at the nurses' station, so he informed them he was joining Shannon.

"We're gonna let her sleep tonight. She can have the baby tomorrow," he was told.

A young pretty volunteer brought him a set of turquoise scrubs to use as pajamas, blushing as she presented them. He didn't have the heart to tell her he never wore any, and thanked her with a wink.

Shannon was finishing up a sponge bath.

"You're gonna love this. Courtney is breathing on her own."

"You're kidding? That's awesome!"

"We just took the mask off, and the doc says she's breathing completely without difficulty. They've still got her monitors on and will check throughout the night, but that's a great sign, honey. Really remarkable, Shannon. I'm so proud of you both." He watched Shannon towel herself off.

"I can't wait to get a real shower," she said.

T.J. leaned over and kissed her. "And I can't wait to get you in the shower too."

He washed up in the private bath, but by the time he climbed into the hospital bed, Shannon was fast asleep. He extended her arm to his chest and held it there with both of his. Filtered light sliced into the room from the hallway. Outside, the sky was beginning to turn deep blue, and he willed himself to sleep. But as the early morning hours turned into real morning, the new sunlight was hard to sleep through.

He thought about the conversation with Travis Banks. He wondered what kind of man could do a job like that, and then figured it was some kind of calling, like the calling he had to become a SEAL. Not many people understood his motivation to jump in harm's way and not get any active recognition for it. The pay wasn't that hot, the life insurance was adequate, but then if that occurred, he'd not be around to enjoy it. It was a good way, though, to secure his family's future. Frankie's policy was going to pay down the mortgage on the house so they didn't have to pay PMI, and the rest would be saved. Courtney's education would be paid for, thanks to Uncle Sam. Shannon would get a new air conditioner for the back bedroom.

Voices in the hallway woke him several times. Each time, it got harder and harder to fall back asleep, so finally he got up, dressed and hung out at the nurses' station for some free coffee. He was informed the local donut shop would be making the rounds in an hour, mostly for the staff, but they told him a lot of the dads really enjoyed that service.

He was the only dad, of the several newly admitted couples, to spend the night, and he found that to be curious. How things had changed in his life. He wouldn't have thought he could enjoy sitting quietly by, watching Shannon or the baby sleep. It had all been about doing midnight HALO jumps, or training missions in the glaciers of Alaska.

T.J. decided to call Travis Banks.

"Maybe you can help me with some decisions, Mr. Banks."

"I thought you'd call back, son."

"No promises, yet. But I'd like for you to fill in the details, if you could. I don't know a thing about my dad." After he said it, he wondered if this was a good idea, but his curiosity was getting the better of him.

"I can't tell you anything without his permission. So much easier, son, if you'd just come out here, then ol' Bobbie Ray could decide for hisself what he wants to tell you."

"So his name is Bobbie Ray." Maybe it would be easier for Travis, but T.J. could see it would be more difficult for him.

"Yes, son. Bobbie Ray Stokes. He said he named you Bobbie Ray Junior, if you want to know."

"I could have gone a long time without knowing that." He felt the familiar lurch in his stomach from fear, followed by slight nausea.

"I understand." Travis' deep vocal tones ended on an even deeper, darker downturn.

"Is my mother alive?"

"I think that's what he wants to talk to you about. I think he wants to tell you where you can find her, if you're willing."

"I'm not sure I am."

"Well, it's your decision, of course. We're just here to help out."

"You enjoy your job?"

"Job? Oh, I see what you mean. No, son, this is not a paid position. I'm a volunteer. I have a little church about forty miles away. We do a lot of prison outreach. I'm only here three afternoons a week. The rest of my time, I'm tending to my other flock on the outside."

T.J. was pained with guilt he'd been so crusty to this man, who was obviously just trying to do something nice for the prison population. Guys like this were rare. He was glad that someone on the outside cared for these men, even if he couldn't go there himself.

"I'm sorry I got a little rough with you, Mr. Banks."

"You can call me Travis, and apology accepted. We all do the best we can do. You thought I was someone trying to insert hisself into your life without an invitation. A lot of people don't come 'round when a family member is in prison, and many don't have family to talk to. So we try to give them just a little lifeline. But they gotta do all the heavy lifting themselves. We're here to support that."

"I'll bet you've seen some drama."

"Oh, yes, I could tell you some stories. I work with many of the sick or hospice patients. They often want to clean up their lives as they prepare for their final destination. When you're livin' here, heaven looks like a lot better place."

"I can imagine."

"They might have messed up *this* life, but they can have a clean fresh *new* one, and that's what we focus on. Goin' home to rest."

T.J. couldn't speak, frozen by the man's story.

"Mr. Talbot, I *can* tell you this, your daddy has confessed his sins, of which he has many. I'm not goin' to lie to you. But give the man a chance to make his peace with you. He's told me it's the biggest regret of his life, and it has something to do with why he's here. That's all I'm going to say about *that*."

T.J. considered his choices. He was inclined to set up a visit, but mostly because he knew it would please Shannon. Wasn't going to be like welcoming dear old dad into his family circle. Courtney and Shannon would probably never know him. So what would it hurt? His dad would never live to meet anyone he cared about. So he reconsidered his decision, and found himself promising he'd work on it.

"And son, I'd hurry about that, if I were you. Hate to see you come all the way out here and not be able to talk to your dad. The sooner you can get here the better, if you want to connect at all."

He thought about Kyle's comments. "*This is just the hand you've been dealt. Not like you had any say in the matter.*" It was true, he was blaming his father for the abusive foster families he'd been so unfortunate to be placed with. He wanted to think his father would have chosen another trajectory for his son, but it wasn't within his power to do so. He'd have to be okay with that for now.

His plane touched down at Nashville International Airport two days later. He'd made sure Courtney was going to be completely healthy before he bought the tickets and called Banks, who agreed to pick him up at the airport and get him right over to the medical facility. The subliminal message was as clear as the orders barked at him from the instructors at BUD/S. His dad didn't have long to live.

Banks was younger than he'd imagined and much larger. He towered over T.J. by a good four inches and had a handshake that could crack walnuts. The African-American gentleman wore a black suit and quickly retrieved T.J.'s luggage from the carousel, then insisted he carry the bag to the car.

T.J. was concerned people would think Mr. Banks was in his employ, but it seemed to matter little to Banks, whose steady gait was damned hard to keep up with. He drove a dark-colored Chevy sedan that was old, but very well cared for.

"I'm afraid the air doesn't work too good. The heater does, not that we need that today."

T.J. was sweating before they hit the first right turn. "I left a reservation at the Rinwood Suites, and it's kind of on the way, I think. Mind if I check in?"

"Well sir, I'd be rude, wouldn't I, if I asked you to cancel your reservation? But I was planning on you staying with me at the parsonage so as not to be a financial hardship."

T.J. had to smile. Banks was a wily country preacher all right. He'd be a captive audience over dinner and breakfast, and that would give the minister two chances to save his soul. Well, that was okay. The man did save him some money on a rental car. The least he could do was listen to a couple of sermons. And who knew? Maybe some of it would take. Not like T.J. had much of a spiritual life.

"So you're a Navy guy, then. That right, Mr. Talbot?"

"Travis, if I'm not allowed to call you Mr. Banks, you sure as hell—sorry, you sure as heck can't call me Mr. Talbot. Can we get that straight, please?"

"Yessir, I get you plain. How long you been in the Navy?"

"Ten years."

"So you're gonna make a career out of it, then?"

"I haven't thought about that much. Playing it day by day. Had a rough tour last time over."

"I'm sorry about that."

"Wasn't your fault. Mine neither. War is messy."

"That it is, son."

"Travis, how old are you?"

"I'm almost thirty-six."

"So why you call me son? We're practically brothers as far as age. Not like I could be your son."

Banks was overcome by a deep belly laugh, letting go his straight demeanor and dropping his guard a bit. T.J. guessed he had some wild days behind him.

"Yeah, but we look alike. Gotta admit that."

They both laughed. T.J. liked Banks more and more as they drove to the outskirts of Nashville.

"How'd my dad find out about me?"

"I have no idea. He doesn't have access to anything on the internet, but he gets calls. Not many, but a few."

"My mother one of those calls?"

"Can't say, T.J. I really couldn't say. Remember, I'm only there three days a week." Banks hesitated and then he sighed. "I can tell you he only found out about where you lived recently, so I'm guessing it was a visitor or a phone call."

"So, who visits him?"

"Never seen a one. Not one."

"What's killing him, if I can ask that?"

"I don't suppose it would violate anything. Kidney failure. He's gone about as far as he can go. He's not a candidate for a transplant, unless you wanted to give him one of yours."

"You're not serious?"

"You mean would I expect you'd give your dad a kidney so he could die in a jail cell? No sir, I wouldn't bet on that one. Besides, he's way too sick now. If he knew about anyone he was a blood relative to, he'd have told the doctors at the hospital before now. But we hardly ever get those approved, even when we find a donor match."

"You're not considering one thing, though."

"What's that?" Banks had turned off the highway and was idling down a two-lane country road. The large prison facility was hard to miss, looking like a college campus.

"What if he wanted to die?"

"Well, I'll let you ask him yourself."

CHAPTER 27

Banks showed his prison ID at the external guard station. The heavy chain-link fence rolled shut behind them, temporarily sealing them in so the credentials could be verified before the second gate opened. After that, there was another perimeter fence around the prison hospital, this time with a guard shack, again denying them entry until their verification was run up the flagpole.

Travis parked in the staff parking lot, as opposed to the completely vacant visitor lot much closer to the front entrance.

"They're gonna check your person, so if you have anything you normally carry that could be construed to be as a weapon, you'd best leave it in my trunk."

T.J. removed his SigSauer and placed it in his canvas duffel before Banks slammed the lid closed.

"You got your wallet, right?"

T.J. nodded.

"They'll keep that with your I.D. until you turn in your visitor badge. Never leave any money in it, I always recommend.

"I got credit cards mainly. A few bucks."

"I think you're good. Staff here is all paid, no honor farm workers, so I think you're safe, but I don't mind opening the trunk if you feel uncomfortable."

"I wasn't until you started talking about all this."

"Fair enough. Forewarned is forearmed." Banks flashed him a bright white smile, and T.J. noticed for the first time he had one gold tooth in the front, one of his canines.

"That's an impressive crown you got there."

"Well, there's a story behind that, too. Stories. Everywhere we got stories, all *kinda* stories here." Banks waved his hands through the air like he was arranging a large flower display.

The two men mounted the four shallow concrete steps, and then T.J. remembered he needed to check in with his LPO. Most of the Team was in Las Vegas for Fredo and Mia's wedding.

"You get there okay? You okay?" Kyle asked.

"I'm fine. I'm at the hospital now. Looks like I'll be able to see him in a few. Give my best to Fredo and Mia."

"Will do. How're the little one and Shannon doing?"

"About as good as can be expected. I mean Shannon's doing great. Courtney is going in the right direction, they say. Shannon's mom and dad came down to be with her."

"Awesome. So I gotta tell you they posted a picture of Magnus on the local television station. Haven't seen it on the national stations, thank God. But it was that picture of the two of you at the Warrior's run, remember?"

"They posted my picture on TV?" T.J. felt powerless being so far away from Shannon and the baby. The thought that his face might bring them danger scared him.

"Yes, I'm afraid they did. I think it's only a matter of time before someone recognizes you, or uses that recognition software and they dig out your name. I need you to keep a low profile and be properly warned. Hoping these are a couple of nuts working on their own, but if not, you keep your eyes peeled for any signs someone recognizes you who shouldn't, okay?"

"Will do."

"Okay, be careful, and thanks for checking in."

"No problem. I'm going to stay over at this reverend's house. He works with the inmates." T.J. looked over at Travis, who tilted his head to him in acknowledgement. "I'll be coming back tomorrow. You staying over in Vegas after the wedding?"

"No. This isn't a good time for a couple of days R&R for me."

"Gotcha. Well, again, give my best—"

"T.J. you sound real good. Glad you're doing this. But don't linger there, okay?"

"No, I'm definitely coming home tomorrow."

After the call was over, T.J. thanked Travis for waiting. They continued their journey through a set of automatic doors that opened to a reception area. Unlike the hospital in San Diego, this one was completely devoid of female nurses or staff. He chuckled to himself that he was right about the smell too. Straight institutional eau de pee/vomit/bleach, just like juvenile hall, or at least the ones he'd "visited" in Texas and Nevada.

His guide brought them down a wide corridor with rubber bumpers as wainscoting, stopping at the first door on the right with a sign on it that read, *Chaplain*. Travis unlocked the solid core door with the brass handle, and inside T.J. actually felt like he was experiencing déjà vu. The room was filled with gray file cabinets along one short wall, a well-worn and stained leather couch on the other. The file cabinets had large red inventory stickers, just as he'd envisioned.

"You keep files on your flock?"

Travis chuckled. "No. Those would be death records. I guess they thought no one would want to break into the chaplain's office, and the chaplain, with a direct line to the man upstairs, wouldn't mind housing the last written evidence that these souls ever existed." He walked over to one cabinet with a large dent in the bottom file drawer as if it had been kicked in on purpose. His hand placed on top, he gently tapped with his palm to some imaginary rhythm. "These are my flock, in a way. The ones that flew the coop." His gold tooth gleamed in the morning sunlight filtering through the missing mini blinds like a spotlight.

He could have been the Grim Reaper himself.

Banks placed a call and informed someone on the other line they were headed down to see one Bobbie Ray Stokes. As he followed the large chaplain down the hallway and into the elevator, T.J. thought that he should have some kind of reaction to the sound of his real name, and found he did not. He was relieved to discover he didn't fit into Bobbie Ray's world, even though a tiny part of Stokes was imbedded in T.J.'s DNA.

Travis didn't say a word as the old elevator machinery groaned and slowly went from the first floor to the second. They could have walked the stairs faster.

As the doors opened, Travis examined the hallway, first right, then left, and then moved out of the way so T.J. could exit the tiny elevator car, much the same as T.J.'d blocked women and children behind him when he was on a rescue mission or was trying to get the injured to safety in a war zone. Well, he guessed sometimes this was a war zone. Despite his hardened heart, he found a little uptick in his right upper lip, the beginnings of a smile, at the vision of his father running down the hallway, or the stairs, or ducking into the elevator with his butt hanging out in all its glory.

The first bone-chilling scream came just as T.J. had turned the corner with Travis, on their way through a set of double swinging doors someone had the poor taste to paint in a blue sky and clouds motif. Only thing worse than that would be if someone had painted black wrought iron gates and labeled the outside *Hell*. Now that would have been funny. And it would have complemented the scream that came from a scrawny man in the first room to the right just past the doors. An attendant was attempting to calm him down, perhaps medicate him.

Travis was probably immune to it now, having been through these doors more times than T.J. wanted to think about. He kept walking, so T.J. followed quickly, shortening the gap Banks' long legs created when he wasn't paying attention. He had to admit, he was relieved the screamer wasn't his dad. He kept telling himself it would be all right, no matter what he saw, no matter how surprised or caught off guard he might be.

But that was before he entered the room. Travis stepped aside, and T.J. was face to face with his past. The graying man had sunken cheeks, his skin quite orange, and he had a feeding tube down his nose. They'd restrained him to the bed with 3" nylon straps like the TRX units they worked out on when they were deployed. One strap was pulled tight across his chest and under both arms, fastened to the bed frame underneath with special welded hooks probably designed for that purpose. What bothered T.J. most was that both the man's ankles were cuffed to the metal foot rail. The bottoms of his feet were blackened. Red welts had formed where he'd apparently tried to move. They were doing a good job keeping him in one place, in the same position. Probably the position he'd die in.

But that left his arms free, with one hooked up to an IV. With his unencumbered side, T.J. watched a bony finger rise from the bed and point at him.

Gray-white stubble covered the man's face, more than a few days', maybe even a week's growth. His liver-colored lips were spotted with dark stains that looked like droplets of blood, and there was a dark brown blood stain the size of a silver dollar on his gown, over his heart. The bony finger continued to rise as his lips pulled back into something that would have looked like a smile if he weighed more than eighty pounds. The man was tall, which made him look like death itself.

"That's him," he said with difficulty. "That's my boy. You takin' me home today, son?" The man's raspy voice was what T.J. had expected, but it still was uncomfortable to hear.

T.J. looked at Travis, who was focused on the dying man. "Bobbie Ray, he's come to visit with you. We've talked about this. You can go home anytime you're ready. You speak your peace now. I'll leave you two alone for a spell." Travis backed up and motioned for T.J. to sit by the bed in a metal chair that had chipped beige paint.

His father was able to follow along as T.J. sat, adjusting his focus a little slow and late, but winding up having full eye contact when T.J. sat. There were tears in the man's eyes. T.J. worked hard not to give him the satisfaction of seeing his own, but couldn't stop them from welling up and spilling over his lower lids. And fuck if his lower lip didn't start quivering too. He held his mouth shut, feeling the rush of emotion, the years of pain, the years of wonder and how he'd told himself every day of his life how he hated this man.

But he could not call upon that hate to control his tears. So, he just gave up and let them stream down his face.

CHAPTER 28

The wedding party clustered around the closed door of the wedding chapel in the Bellagio, which was decorated with flowers and had all the luxurious details of a much larger setting. Through the windows they could see another wedding in progress, the flowers and padded chairs drenched in the colorful hues of ambient light were worthy of any beautiful cathedral in Europe. The fact that it was small and intimate actually added to the festive mood. It wasn't like any Las Vegas venue Kyle had ever been to before. And he'd been to a lot of them. It was the favored destination for his Team guys, who often got married and divorced quickly.

That's just the way they are. He took Christy's hand and felt the searing heat that struck him every time he touched her. Married now five years, with two children, and if she'd let him, he'd have two more and love them all just like their first, Brandon. She worked like a son of a gun, and if it weren't for her income, they'd have a whole different life-style. And Christy would seriously have to alter her shopping habits.

Fredo and Mia arrived. Mia was stunning in a very low-cut bright white gown that she was practically poured into. With her bronzed skin and long black hair done up and cas-cading down over her shoulders, she was one of the most beautiful brides he'd ever seen. Several of the Team guys removed their dark glasses and bowed to her, clearing their throats. He'd never seen Mia blush before, but she was clearly moved by the experience.

And Fredo was in a tux. First time he'd ever seen his explosives expert dress up in anything but an ill-fitting bor-rowed suit. They wore their dress uniforms for funerals. His shimmery brocade vest in white was a perfect complement to his dark slacks and white shirt, but the white tie looked like it was going to garrote him. Or maybe it was just that Fredo looked nervous as hell. His man frowned and nodded to the door of the chapel, as if Kyle was in charge.

"They not letting anyone in?" he asked, his furry eyebrows tenting. Kyle chuckled to himself remembering the numerous discussions Christy had with him, along with a couple of the other wives, trying to convince Fredo to tweeze or at least thin out his unibrow. As with many things about Fredo, once he set his mind on something, there was no stopping him. Just like the way he pursued Mia, Armando's bad girl sister and troublemaker, who rejected him for nearly three years. Fredo kept after her until she finally came to her senses.

And that was why he was one of the best go-to guys around. Why he was so deadly with his explosive charges and gadgets in the arena. He was irreverent and careful, a rare combination.

"There's another wedding finishing up," Christy whispered to them. "Mia, you are just—" Christy could hardly continue. "You are a complete knockout, sweetheart."

Mia beamed. "I'm doing this all the way."

Fredo bent, whispered something to her lips and kissed her. Kyle was happy his man got the girl of his dreams, although he'd always thought he deserved someone with less baggage. But Fredo was a rock-solid warrior hell-bent on saving people, and he was going to be the best husband Mia could have ever chosen. And that's the role Fredo wanted to play.

Felicia Guzman, Mia and Armando's mother, held little Ricardo. The charcoal braid woven atop her head was laced with fresh flowers enhancing her handsome, dark features and her bright brown eyes. She and Sergeant Mayfield had gotten married this last spring, and Mayfield doted on his new adopted grandson like he was raising him as his own.

"Mrs. Guzman," Kyle nodded to Mia's mother. He shook Mayfield's hand. "Heard you're retiring, really retiring now?"

"Yup. Sent in the paperwork." He started to say something else when the doors to the chapel opened, and the crowd separated for the other bride and groom to exit the church. They were young and without family or friends. Surprise registered on the bride's face as she made her way through the crowd of SEALs, wives, girlfriends and other family.

An attractive older woman wearing a pink suit ushered them inside to their seats. She took Mia's hand and led her around to a doorway off the tiny vestibule, where they disappeared. Organ music flowed from a decent sound system.

He looked over his Team Guys. Cooper was there with Libby, holding hands with their son, Will, who was smartly dressed in a little short pants black suit and red bow tie. Jones was with a new girl, as he usually was. Nick and Devon were there, Armando and Gina, Kate and Tyler and Sophia and Mark. Rory and several of the other single SEALs on Team 3 were clustered in one powerful girl-chasing unit and would be engaged in that kind of activity as soon as the wedding was over. He'd already overheard plans to rent a limo and do the town and anyone who came their way who was willing.

But the new crop of SEALs was coming along, and Kyle was proud of the respect they showed their senior man by showing up. These new young additions to SEAL Team 3 hardly drank and stayed away from the ladies, unlike their older mentors. Some of the immoral or lewd behavior allowed among the teams in the past was coming under more scrutiny. They were even asked not to get full sleeve tats any longer, something that had been a time-honored tradition. These new guys had a dedication to country and perfecting their trade unlike what he'd seen before. Kyle knew the recent blowups in the Middle East were driving a whole new breed of fighting men into the arms of the Special Forces.

Several of these new men shook his hand and bowed gently to Christy with the brief, "Ma'am."

They'd left Brandon and little Camilla with a hired hotel sitter, and Kyle was happy for the alone time with Christy, even though he was surrounded by people. They were his people. It was about as safe as it could be. And he knew most all of them were packing, so heaven help the sorry asshole who might want to challenge them. There wasn't any need for the firepower, but he felt naked without it and knew everyone else felt the same way.

The music changed and winks and nods continued amongst the attendees. Fredo stood up front by the black-robed minister, and Kyle wished he'd insisted he stand up for him. He actually felt sorry for the man. Coop was in the front row whispering some encouragement, and then probably following it with some kind of verbal joust, as was Coop and Fredo's pattern. The first swear word he heard of the day came from Fredo's mouth, which caused the minister to take a step back and cough.

Mia made her way down the aisle to the Wedding March, standing next to Fredo. The short service was over in less than ten minutes. The rings were exchanged, and then Fredo kissed his glowing bride while the crowd whooped and shouted, "Hooya S.O. Chavez!"

Around the corner from the chapel was an Italian restaurant, Izzy's, where they'd agreed to meet for lunch. Izzy was the father of a Team guy on the East Coast, and it was nearly sacrilegious not to give him a visit when in town.

His heavy New Jersey accent fit right into the ambience that was Las Vegas, and Kyle had often wondered if he had "connections" somewhere. And he was known for sometimes paying for a wedding party out of his own pocket, if there was the need. They were all family, every one of them. Family takes care of family.

Coop raised his glass for a toast. Fredo looked uncomfortable, but Mia kissed him on the cheek which seemed to lighten his mood.

"So when I showed up for Indoc there was this guy they told me about. This little short asshole who thought he could be a SEAL. Everyone was laughing at him." Coop nodded to the bride and groom, winking at Mia. "We had to settle things, of course. I mean, boys will be boys, and everyone was nervous as hell about trying out for the Teams, knowing there was an eighty to ninety percent chance they'd wash out."

The nodding and verbal affirmations were lavishly strewn about the room.

"We had a couple of professional footballers trying out, and they definitely thought they had more of a shot than this little Mexican prick sitting over here."

Fredo gave him the finger, and the crowd loved it.

"So to settle things, someone suggested they wrestle." Coop stopped to properly apprise Fredo before he continued. "And that stopped just about all talk of whether or not Fredo could make it. Fredo, I don't think you lost one of those, did you?"

"Still haven't."

"And he cheats."

"Fuck you. I don't cheat," Fredo barked.

Those that knew Fredo well knew that he did put his hands inappropriately on the other guy's junk during wrestling matches. This usually caught them off guard, and Fredo would get the quick take-down. Kyle knew it was part of what made him such a good, innovative SEAL. Fredo had a plan and a strategy for everything.

"Here's to the guy who counts the number of dryer sheets I use when I used to do laundry at his house, and he calls *me* cheap."

The crowd loved it.

"The guy who thinks there is something unholy about tofu and green salads—"

"*Not* unholy, just not natural," Fredo quipped back.

"Who thinks that anything green, except green chili salsa is also unhealthy," Coop continued. Fredo shrugged, guilty as charged.

"To my best friend, and absolutely someone I would stand right next to and take the bullet for, to someone Mia will never have to worry about because he'll go through hell itself to come back to you every time, and heaven help the guy who tries to mess with you, darlin', I give you Mr. and Mrs. Alphonso Manuel Esquidido Chavez." Coop raised his glass. The room shouted, "Hooya Mr. and Mrs. Chavez!"

Gina Guzman, Mia's new sister-in-law, stood up next to toast for the bride.

"Mia, you were one wild child there, and I was thinkin' man, I don't know if I can keep up with her." Gina was referring to the fact that she had worked an undercover detail and had befriended Mia originally as a means to help take down a local San Diego gang she was hanging with.

"Then I met your brother." She bent down and gave Armando a kiss. She continued, fanning her face. "Who knows what would have happened if I'd not met him, huh? But I thank my lucky stars every day that I did, and that you and I became friends. You watched my back. You also gave me some fits, too."

The crowd laughed.

"But it is so nice to see you so happy, and with the best guy you could have picked. This guy is as solid as they come."

Armando stood up, and said, "Excuse me—"

Coop pulled him down to allow Gina to continue.

Kyle's phone went off, and he saw from the display it was from T.J. He whispered to Christy, "Gotta take this."

He exited the restaurant as Gina was finishing and heard the shouts of acknowledgement from the revelers.

CHAPTER 29

"**A**re you in any pain?" T.J. knew he should address this dying man as "Dad" but that was not something he could do. Not that he didn't feel anything. He felt a lot. He felt too much. He just couldn't make anything out of it. And that wasn't what he was used to.

The old man searched his face, back and forth, squinting in a smile of recognition.

"You grew up strong, son. I can tell. It was better that way. Better for you."

T.J. had to break away at that remark. *In your dreams, you old prick.* There wasn't any point to make him suffer even more than he already was, so he kept his mouth shut.

"They treating you good here?"

His father's laugh lines preceded the grimy grin he got back. T.J. noticed he was missing quite a few teeth. He tried to visualize him young and healthy, and just couldn't.

"I can't complain." His graying blue eyes were still bright, though his body seemed to be rotting away from them. "So I guess you want to know about your family then, T.J., or did your sister get hold of you?"

Well isn't that something choice. A sister. I have a sister. He was still feeling somewhat numb, but this news began a slow thaw.

"No one from 'the family' as you say, has ever contacted me, or if they tried, they gave up."

"Don't you want to know about your sister?"

"I'm here out of respect that you wanted to see me, and you haven't long for this world. I'm here so you can tell me whatever you want to tell me."

"Okay. First things first. I killed a man. I laid in wait for him, and I killed him. I shouldn't have, but I couldn't help myself." The old man didn't take his eyes off T.J. "I loved your mother. Loved her too much."

"Well, you're here. Where is my sister?"

"She lives about a hundred miles that way." He pointed west. "And your mother is buried nearby."

Bobbie Ray looked vacant, his eyes staring off at a distance, and at first, T.J. thought he'd passed away. He stood up to lean over and check, slightly alarmed, when his father lurched forward involuntarily, like he was coming back from the dead, which totally freaked T.J. out. He also smelled of death. He'd learned to recognize that smell over the past few years.

"You taking me home today? You got a nice car?"

"No, you're staying here. I'm going back home. This is your home now."

His father shook his head. "Did you drive or fly?"

T.J. was getting more impatient by the minute. He knew there wasn't anything he could do for his father, except listen to his stream of consciousness wanderings. He actually prayed that he'd go peacefully, and soon. And if he was in a dulled state, perhaps that would be better for everyone.

But T.J. did have questions. He just wasn't sure it was appropriate to ask them. Or, maybe he just wasn't sure he'd like the answers. His mother apparently was dead. But he had a sister, and that changed things for T.J.

"I met a real nice girl," his father started. "She looks a lot like you. Has your eyes. Beautiful girl. I'm going to ask her to marry me."

"That's nice." T.J. thought he might find out details by just listening and not asking. Perhaps there would be some pearls in the old man's words that would give him some of the clues he was seeking.

"I messed up. She loved him. She loved the man I kilt."

"My sister? What's *her* name?"

"Lois. Lois Foster. Old Mr. Foster died many years ago. Never did like me and when I got sent here, well, there wasn't any way for me to get in touch with her. I fucked up, son."

"So, my mother's name was Lois?"

"You know Lois? Did they introduce you to her? Don't you think she's pretty?"

T.J. wanted to get up, run away and never come back.

"I thought about this day for many years. What would I say to you if I ever found you."

"Have you talked to my sister?"

"Twice."

"What's her name?"

"She has a boyfriend. I met him once too."

"What's her last name?"

His father looked back at him like he was the crazy one in the bed. "*Who?*"

We're losing time.

"My *sister.* What's my sister's name?"

"You have a sister?" his dad asked. "Congratulations. Wonder why they never told me!"

He had that far away look again.

"Hey, son, you taking me home? I'm ready anytime you are."

He could see his father's body shutting down by the minute. His speech was starting to slur. T.J. reached out and touched the old man for the first time in his life, placing a gentle palm on his frail shoulder which felt like all bone and very little flesh. "Dad. You *are* home. Remember what Travis said? You can close your eyes and go there anytime you want."

His father seemed to get half of what he said. "They're really good here, you know. Take such good care of us. Really topnotch place. I'd come back here anytime."

Great. Dad thinks he's in a vacation resort or something. It was funny, if it wasn't so sad. His father didn't register in the slightest that he'd been physically touched by his own son for the first time ever. "Tell me her name, Dad," he asked softly. "Tell me my sister's last name."

But his dad had checked out of the resort and was on his new adventure.

"Glad you got to see him," Travis said as they traveled down the highway toward the town of Dover. The reverend managed to do a little digging and had found the address of one Connie Fallon through an ancestry.com account, checked the phone book and found she had a listed phone number as well as her address. Dover was only about twenty miles from Travis's church and parsonage, so he agreed to accompany T.J. on the trip. They'd tried to call ahead, without luck.

Next, T.J. called the hospital, reaching the nurse's station to check on Shannon.

"I don't want to talk to her if she's sleeping."

The nurse checked and confirmed she was asleep.

"Wonderful. How's she doing?"

The nurse was shuffling through some paperwork, probably checking the permission slips Shannon signed on admittance. "Everything's going in the right direction, sir. I'd let her sleep."

"How's little Courtney doing?"

"I understand there is an update, but not until the patient has been informed."

"Good news or bad news?"

"You're going to have to get that from your wife."

My wife. He liked the sound of that. He wanted to celebrate, but there were too many unknowns and he wouldn't let his heart go there. He told himself it would be easier when he had an update on Courtney. That was, if it was good news. Something in his gut told him it was.

"Would you ask her to give me a call when she awakens?" He gave his cell phone. "Tell her I will be coming home tomorrow, okay?"

"I'll do that. She's had a lot of visitors. She really needs to rest right now, so I'll give it to her when she awakens."

T.J. wondered who would be pestering her so much, when most of their platoon on Team 3 were in Las Vegas.

"Can we cut out the visitors?" he asked.

"Sure, but the police have been in several times. And a newspaper reporter. We got rid of *him*."

"Police?"

"We didn't know you knew the Marine whose wife was injured."

"Okay, I'm going to get someone to come stay with her. Her parents been by much?"

"Oh yes. Both sets, yours and hers."

T.J. didn't correct her. Frankie's parents had every right to see their new grandchild. He was going to make sure that always was allowed.

Next he called Shannon's parents and got her mother on the phone. T.J. and Mrs. Moore had a difficult relationship going back to Shannon and Frankie's wedding. He guessed his taking off for Tennessee was just another example to Mrs. Moore of a lack of good judgment. She was frosty, more so than usual.

"You kids are in the middle of all this media circus, and Shannon needs to get her rest while you're streaking all over the countryside searching after lost relatives."

"My father died this morning."

"Okay. You sound *devastated*," she said mockingly.

He was wondering if he'd ever have a normal relationship with her. Probably not. "I'll be home tomorrow. Turns out I have a sister I didn't know about, so I'll be stopping by to see her if I can, and then I'll come home."

"How nice for you."

"Look, the reason for the call, although I *always* enjoy our calls, Mrs. Moore, is that there have been some police and other people bothering Shannon. And there has been a reporter snooping around. I need her left alone as much as possible."

"Well, well, we finally agree."

T.J. was so glad Shannon hadn't gone through with her plans to raise little Courtney on her own in the Bay Area where her parents lived. Her whole life would have been changed by the proximity to this woman. But she was Shannon's mother, and he wasn't going to interfere, especially when he needed her keen eyes doing a stealth mission to order people around, which was exactly what she was well suited for. She could have run a whole platoon.

"We want to cooperate with the police. But in light of what happened to Magnus' wife, and that hospital area not being that secure—"

"Yes, we were told you actually saw one of the terrorists."

"One of the terrorists?"

"Apparently small cell, they've taken responsibility."

"All the more reason. I need you to stand guard over Shannon and be extremely picky about who she talks to. Be rude if you have to.

"I can do that."

T.J. knew she definitely could.

CHAPTER 30

Courtney was resting comfortably in Shannon's arms when Shannon's mother and father arrived. The baby had been transferred to a regular nursery crib, which was sitting nearby.

"Oh, hi, guys," Shannon called out to them. She hadn't expected them until this evening.

Her mom gave her a hug and kiss, and sat for a minute on the edge of the bed, brushing her fingers over her granddaughter's pink fuzzy head. "She's really beautiful, Shannon. Ears are a little big."

This tickled her. Long past caring about this little feature of her anatomy, Shannon was happy the baby was going to be allowed to go home with her today. When she told her mother, they were thrilled.

One of the nurses came in after Shannon buzzed her.

"Yes?"

"Say, I'm wondering how soon before we are allowed to leave?"

"Leave?"

"Well, the doctor said he was going to release me. My parents are here to help me. We're ready now if everything is okay."

"Let me check. Is she nursing or just sleeping?"

"Mostly sleeping."

"You want her to nurse, honey. She'll get comfortable and all warm and snuggly, but she needs to eat so you keep your milk in. You'll have problems when you get home if not."

"I think she's getting plenty. But this is my first."

"All right." The nurse came over to the bed and addressed Mrs. Moore, "Excuse me, honey." When Shannon's mother stood next to Mr. Moore, the nurse leaned in. "I'm gonna take the baby, get her weighed, take a final blood test and get her cleaned up for you. Then I'll bring her back. She'll be good and fussy when I get done poking around with her."

"That woman is rude," said Mrs. Moore.

Nothing could dampen her mood, except she hadn't heard from T.J. She'd gotten the message he'd landed safely while she was resting. But his call was overdue, and she needed to hear his voice, curious how the meeting with his dad went.

"I wish T.J. would call," she said to her mother.

"He didn't call you? That's why we came right over. He's coming home tomorrow, he said."

She wondered why he'd not called her directly, but instead called her mother. "Hope everything went well."

Mrs. Moore glanced at her husband, and then added, "Honey, I'm afraid his father passed away this morning."

"All the more reason—"

"He should be home with you and the baby," Mr. Moore asserted. "You are unprotected here and I don't like that. With that reporter yesterday and all the questions the police are asking. T.J. felt it too, asked your mother and me to come over and stand guard. We're not leaving until they release you, Shannon."

An attractive male intern in scrubs, a stethoscope draped across his neck, popped his head inside. "Can I have a word for a second?"

"They can stay here," she answered.

"Sorry, confidentiality rules. I'm really sorry." He smiled at her parents who looked at Shannon for direction and when she shrugged, they exited to the hall.

As the door to her room closed, he came over to Shannon's bedside and sat down, which alarmed her.

"So, where's your husband?"

"You guys know he's—" All of a sudden it began to dawn on her there was something wrong about this man. He had a faint accent, which normally wouldn't bother her, but the nametag on the scrubs identified him as being with house-keeping. Why would he need a stethoscope?

He was drawing something from his pocket. She saw the flash of a syringe containing a light yellow liquid. Adjusting her weight, she pushed back away from him just before he lunged forward attempting to inject something into her neck. She wanted to scream but his hand covered her mouth. With a quick kick to his hip, he was thrown off balance and fell to the floor, scattering her IV and several other items, including a plastic water pitcher on a nearby stainless steel tray, all over the ground.

But the kick had had also thrown off her balance, and she found herself reaching for anything to avoid falling from the hospital bed onto the other side. She clutched the air, knocking over a vase filled with flowers, sending it shattering to the floor as she fell hard. She tried to scream but found the air had been knocked out of her. Pain seared her abdominal area.

At last she found her voice and screamed.

The next instant, he was around the end of the bed and, reaching over her, attempted to grab her hair. Her hands swept the floor. She felt the wetness of the broken vase as well as the sting of a piece of broken glass that had gotten stuck in the palm of her hand.

In the meantime, something was happening outside the door. She could hear her mother shouting for help. Sounds of a struggle, with something heavy being thrown against the door. Was there someone else outside? She remembered the warning T.J. had given her mother.

Hopefully Courtney is safe. Please, let her be safe. She has to be safe.

She heard a definite gunshot sound and screaming. Her assailant yanked her hair, pulling her head up like a rag doll with a jerk. Now he wasn't holding a syringe any longer. He held a heavy knife like T.J.'s KA-BAR, the one she had looked at several times. She knew where his intended trajectory was. Her legs flopped and scraped on the wet, slippery floor as she tried to throw his balance off from the lethal crouch position, a tight tripod. His center of gravity was too low, she realized.

This is not acceptable. This is not going to happen. Never. Not at any time. She was not going to die, wind up another statistic on the evening news.

He was twisting her head to get a lethal angle at her neck. She knew what he was after. She remembered something T.J. had explained to her.

Sometimes when you're in a struggle, best to stop fighting. Go in the same direction as the attacker, because if you resist, you cause them to use deadly force to restrain you.

Instead of pulling back, trying to avoid his body and the knife that was gripped in his right hand, she leaned forward into him. He lost his balance for just a second, enough time for her to bring up her palm, drawing her arm over and outside his left. The glass wedged there hurt like a son of a gun, but as her fingers gripped it tightly, cutting her further, she drew strength from the pain. She hoped it was big enough to do what she needed it to do. Using her own fist as the hilt of the glass blade, she swung upward and rammed it into the assailant's neck, remembering to throw whatever weight she could muster from her own body following behind, and then pulled down.

She felt the satisfying crunch of cartilage and muscle tissue being sliced open, followed by a warm spray of his blood, covering her face and chest. He tried to adjust, dropping his knife in order to hold onto his neck, but his knees slipped in the pool of blood. Shannon seized another opportunity, drew one knee up to her chest and then pushed with everything she had, her bare foot landing square in the middle of his chest, sending his body backward.

He was skidding across the bloody floor when the heavy door swung open and knocked him solidly in his head.

Seeing her parents in the hallway, worried but apparently unharmed, the bevy of staffers behind them and the two uniformed guards hauling up the unconscious assailant by his armpits, she allowed herself to collapse and breathe. Other than the pain in her palm, and something intense burning in her lower belly, she felt pretty good, considering.

She looked at her bloody hands, the sloppiness of the mortal combat she'd just engaged in, her heart pounding so hard it nearly exploded her chest, and she discovered something.

It felt damn good to be alive.

CHAPTER 31

"You like living out here, don't you?" T.J. asked Travis.
"Yessir, I used to. It does me good to be in this beautiful part of the world. And the cost of living is a lot less than other places. I won't lie, part of the charm, part of the charm."

Travis' gold tooth was glinting in the sunlight. "So you gonna tell me about that tooth?"

This gave the big man a belly laugh. "You're gonna think me quite insane. Maybe a bit more eccentric than you like."

"But you forget. I'm in the military, and let me tell you, I see stuff all the time on deployment that is pretty fuckin'—sorry, man, just force of habit."

"It's all right. You're an all right dude, Mr. T.J. Talbot. I think you're one of God's warriors. And God's warriors get to take special liberties with they language." He smiled broadly and then swung his eyes back to the road.

He sucked in air as if he could create a vacuum in the old Chevy, then blew it out so hard T.J. thought the windshield might cave.

"Okay, here goes," Travis started.

T.J. could already tell he was going to dig the hell out of whatever the man was going to say.

"I met this lady when I was twenty-five, over a decade ago now. We didn't obey any of God's commandments, in fact, I think this woman was hell bent on breaking jus' about all of them."

Travis stopped and threw out a throaty laugh, his belly rubbing against the steering wheel of his car. If it involved a woman, now T.J. was even more sure he was going to like the story.

"I've known a few of those," he admitted to the preacher. "They don't interest me any longer either, but man. I haven't thought about those days for a while now, but that's all I used to think about."

"You was just finding your way, son."

"That's a fact. Not there though. It was never there."

"No, it never is. And that kind of relates to this story. See, she and I, we got married. The woman was one of those who would get something into her mind, and then she'd never let up, you know what I'm sayin'? She was one wild child. I thought at first it was cute. I mean, at twenty-five, she was the most exciting thing to ever come my way, and I wanted excitement."

T.J. remembered the hundreds of girls he'd slept with over the years. Luckily, most of his liaisons he couldn't remember.

He couldn't even remember their faces. Maybe that was a good thing.

"Well, Mr. Talbot, that woman wanted excitement too. And when I was no longer her drug of choice, she moved on. And when I say she moved on, I mean she took it upon herself to sleep with anything that would walk, know what I'm sayin'?"

"I do." T.J. felt sorry for the man.

"It cost me every penny I had, which wasn't much, just to complete the divorce."

"You married now?"

"Nope. Not looking yet, either. I'm still wearing off the effects of my last one. Some days, T.J., the sight of a woman scares me all the way down to my toes."

"I understand."

"When it was all said and done, I was left with two gold wedding bands. And that's where they is," he said as he tapped his gold tooth with his forefinger. "Right there so every time when I looks in the mirror I gets to remember I'm a survivor, and I'm never goin' down that rabbit hole again. I gets to smile and look back in the mirror at the face of a free man."

T.J. was smiling and he knew Travis was interested in hearing what he thought. He kept looking over at him as they turned off the highway and onto a small single lane country road. In the distance a small town took shape.

"You know, Travis. I think that some time soon you'll meet the right woman, and she'll want you to get that tooth fixed. I think the sight of her will light that golden path to heaven itself for you."

"You think so?"

"I know so. Yup. I know so." T.J. was feeling more comfortable with the preacher the more time they spent together. "I sure found the right gal." He told Travis about the baby, about Frankie.

"You're a good man, Mr. Talbot."

"You know, I almost didn't want to come here at all. It took a while to shed off all that dead skin. I was worried it would suck me right back into that angry place I grew up in. God, how I hated that man. And today, I just realized I didn't hate him at all. I hated myself. I was exorcising demons." He watched Travis' face in profile. "You've done that too. So now you can give that to someone else, or rather, let someone else give that to you. You help everyone else. You tend your flock. Time to let someone tend to you, my man."

"You could be right. I'd like to think you are."

"And speaking of which, I need to give my intended a call." T.J. dialed Shannon's number and got her message. He dialed his mother-in-law and got the same. He double checked to see if he'd missed anything and found he hadn't.

They drove into the little town with one stoplight.

"Kind of peaceful here. This a nice place to live?" T.J. asked.

Travis bobbed his head. "Yes and no. We got something strange goings on here. I notice it because I see the change in the prison population, which comes more from this area than any other. Lot of poor folks here. But a lot of angry folks coming in from other places. Big cities. I'm just one preacher at Riverbend. They's groups here that send their guys in every day."

T.J.'s attention was sparked. He had to ask, because they'd all been talking about it on the Teams. "Religious types?"

"Doing the conversions, yessir, but I don't take my flock out and do no target practice. They have a big communal camp right here in this little town. News media says there are known camps operating, dozens of them, and we got one right here. Can you explain to me why no one is asking questions? And I see men I grew up with changing, becoming hard. Mostly I see strangers in this area where I used to know everyone's name. So, if you ask me, T.J. I say no. Not any longer."

"I've seen the bloody effects of fanatical groups overseas. A lot of people are getting killed. A lot of innocent people, and that's just wrong."

"Sort of feels like it's all coming to this country, don't it?"

T.J. knew for a fact it was.

Connie drove up just as Travis and T.J. were getting back in their car. They'd been standing on the porch, knocking on the painted old screen door of a bungalow that could have been in any small town in America. The birds were chirping, and there wasn't any traffic noise or car horns blaring. A single airplane overhead made its way across the sky, leaving a white tail behind it.

She was holding a bag of groceries in one arm, shielding her eyes with her other palm. "Can I help you?"

T.J. figured she was about his age. He could definitely see a family resemblance to his own face.

"Holy Mother of God. Is that you?"

"I think so," T.J. started. "You're Connie?"

"Yes. Yes. I'm your sister. Your twin sister." She set her package on the hood of her car and ran up to him, but stopped just in front. They both took a tentative step toward each other and embraced safely. She had lighter brown hair than his, but the same light blue eyes.

This was another surprise in a day of surprises. His father hadn't mentioned anything about him being a twin, so T.J. was skeptical. "We came from the hospital, and I'm sorry to say, Dad has passed on."

He expected a different reaction than the one he got.

"Well, that's done, then." She returned to the car, closed the door and picked up her packages. "Come on in, and we'll toast to dear old Dad."

As T.J. passed Travis, the preacher's eyes got wide.

Over the next hour, Connie told him she'd been raised in Colorado and had been adopted into a good family. T.J. let her know his was quite a different path, but spared her the gory details.

"When my mother died last Spring I figured that would free me up to go looking for my birth parents. I got here just in time to see Mom before her passing, and I took care of her a bit in the end. She told me her father forced the adoption, and it was one of the biggest regrets of her life. I'm glad I got to tell her I had a good upbringing. Now I'm glad she never found out about yours."

T.J. remembered what Kyle told him, about living with the hand he was dealt. He realized that that was the life he was supposed to lead, just like he was supposed to be Courtney's father.

"She lived in this very house her whole adult life. Never married again. Never had any other children. And she never went to visit him, even though she was a couple of hours away all that time."

"Wonder why?" T.J. pondered.

"I don't think we'll ever know. They weren't married, you know." She brought out pictures to show him what his mother looked like, and she gave him a smiling photo of her that was his favorite. "Here, so you can show your little girl, someday."

"Funny how that happens. Now I have something physical to show of the past I never had. Thank you."

Connie then pressed a small envelope into his palm. "Keep this too. Open this after you've gone."

T.J.'s cell phone rang. It was Shannon.

CHAPTER 32

"Oh God, T.J. It's so good to hear your voice," Shannon said. She'd told herself she would be strong, but upon hearing him, she lost all her composure. He began firing questions at her, and she lost the ability to speak all of a sudden. "You have to come home. Please come home now."

"Is everything okay with you and the baby?"

"Yes. But almost no." She told him about the afternoon's events, explained that her parents took her home, and that Kyle had insisted a couple of Team Guys stay with her until T.J. could get home. "I know you said tomorrow. I need you here as fast as you can get here."

Shannon was relieved T.J. headed straight for the Nashville airport where they determined he could catch a flight back to San Diego that would get him home near midnight.

Just over an hour later, he texted:

Made the plane. Taking off soon. Coming home to you. Get ready. Love you more than I thought possible.

His text thrilled her. She ached for him, missed him now more than before. With giddy relief that he was finally going to be home tonight, she texted back:

Ready? All I can think about, sweetheart. Safe travels. I might never let you out of the bedroom. Ever. Love you too.

She got the little ping that told her she had a return message:

Hmmmm. That sounds yummy. I don't belong anywhere else. See you in a few. Kiss Courtney for me. All my love.

The Moore's settled in the third bedroom, while the two new SEAL Team 3 members were given pillows and blankets to sleep on the couch. Shannon had wanted to go to the airport to meet T.J., but knew it was not wise. Ollie, one of the young SEALs, would go while the other one would stay behind and keep watch.

She dashed into the shower, wrapping her stitched hand in a plastic bag, the plastic covering her abdominal stitches. Anticipation was boiling in her stomach as she carefully changed the sheets, placed fresh candles all around the bedroom. She tried to eat the food her parents had prepared, tried to make small talk with the young SEALs while they all waited, but in the end, she was so distracted by anticipation of T.J.'s homecoming, she couldn't focus on anything but what it would feel like to be wrapped in his strong arms. He was coming back home to her, and that made her feel giddy as a school girl. Seven hours was waaaaay too long to have to wait.

Courtney was demanding a feeding, and this eased her nerves. She lit a candle in the bedroom and leaned into the soft pillows of their bed, nursing her, telling her about her daddy.

"He's tall and handsome, and he loves you so much. He'll shower you with kisses and you'll love falling asleep in his arms."

She placed her little finger close to Courtney's waving hand and fingers. The baby grabbed it like the lifeline it was, and they rocked together on the bed by candlelight.

"Little strong Courtney," she said, and kissed her.

A few minutes later, she put the baby to sleep in the portable sleeper by her bed, covered herself up in the quilt the SEAL Ladies had made for her, and let herself fall asleep.

When Shannon's cell phone pinged with another text, she awoke to a darkened bedroom. The screen on her cell glowed on the night stand.

Just landed. Found Ollie. We're headed home, sweetheart.

She returned his text with hearts and flower images.

The baby began to fuss, so she changed her, nursed her again and then put her back down. Just as she stepped into the hallway she heard Ollie's truck, and knew he was home. Her heart was racing as she saw the front door open, and there he was. Her parents flocked to him immediately while his brothers stood nearby. Ollie leaned forward and peered down the hallway at Shannon and gave her a wink.

He hadn't taken his eyes off her since walking through the doorway. Dropping his bag, he ran to Shannon, pulled her inside the bedroom and slammed the door behind them. She could hear a generous serving of chuckling coming from the other side.

Alone in the darkened room with the candles lit, T.J.'s honest face danced in the glow of candlelight. He wrapped his arms around her waist and hoisted her up off the ground as she felt the urgency of his deep kiss. She could feel his chest expand as he inhaled her, gave her that gravely groan from deep inside.

"God how I missed you," he whispered through his kisses. "Shannon, I'm so sorry for all that's happened, and for not being here."

She placed her fingers over his mouth. "Shhh. No talking now."

"But seriously," he insisted. "Is everything okay? Are you both okay?"

She showed him her bandaged palm. "Just five stitches and maybe some surgery later on, but I was lucky."

He unwrapped the gauze outer wrapping and then peeled back the adhesive tape to examine the work. She watched as he calculated its adequacy and saw the slight nod, giving approval. He pressed the wrapping back down, securing the bandage and then carefully wrapped it back in the gauze, kissing her palm gently, kissing every layer of the wrapping. "Does it hurt?"

"Just a little."

"And here?" he placed his palm on her belly.

"Better now that you're here."

He smiled. "You need anything for the pain?"

"No, sweetheart. All I need is right here."

The baby stirred, so T.J. let Shannon slide down his frontside, drawing her over to the crib. "She's beautiful. God, I'm a lucky man."

"We're the lucky ones," she said. The tenderness she saw in his face for Courtney filled her heart to capacity. "We were so lucky they'd taken her away before the—"

"No," he said, stopping her with his kisses. "You were right. No more talking. Besides, we'll wake her." He took her hand, examined the room full of candles and brought her over to the bed. "Our time now."

"Yes," she said as she felt his hands slide up her front, squeezing her breasts. She helped him remove her clothes, and then took her time removing his shirt, kissing his warm flat stomach muscles, up the center of his chest to under his chin. She undid his belt and button fly carefully, one by one, slid her hands into his pants and then around to his butt cheeks and pulled the denim fabric down until his jeans fell. When he stepped out of them, they were completely naked together, his erection pressing into her belly.

Her hands massaged the full length of him, massaged his balls as they kissed. Their heat ignited, and he pulled her down into the bed. He kissed a trail under her ear, and whispered, "God, Shannon, I don't know what I would have done if anything—"

"I know, love."

"You were so brave. So very lucky," he said to her mouth. He kissed her neck, down to her breasts and then back up again. She held his head between her hands, and he leaned into her bandaged palm, kissing her again on the wound. "So strong. Do you know how incredible you are, Shannon?"

She rolled back into the pillow, placing her arms back above her head. "Show me."

His answer was swift, and with another guttural moan he was rooting for her opening. "Sorry, but I have to—"

"It's what I want too. I need you inside me, T.J."

"I don't want to hurt you, honey. You sure this is okay?"

"I need you."

He thrust deep, being careful not to press against her lower abdomen, but matching her urgency. The delicious feel of him made her arch back, raise her knees and press her pelvis into his. His long strokes were tentative and careful. Then he began a deliberate rhythm that was long and smooth enough to absorb every motion, but fast enough to heighten her arousal with each thrust. He kissed her eyes, whispered *I love you's* to her mouth over and over again.

He arched up, slid his knees under her thighs, bracing her back with his powerful arms and moved her down on his shaft, carefully grinding her down and then releasing her to writhe against him. He was so deep she was melting as her internal muscles milked him, as she felt him tense and then thrust several more times deep into her tender soft tissues that burned for him. On one final thrust he allowed himself to release into her, holding her pressed against him as she felt him lurch and begin to spill.

"Oh, God, T.J. I need this."

"Yes, baby." The sound of his voice triggered a slow rolling orgasm as her body exploded. She pressed her chest against his, grabbed the hair at his nape and let her pelvis ride down onto him, her legs balancing them as he pushed up and deeper inside her.

He held her firm, slowly pressing harder, then releasing, working her insides with deep, short movements as her spasms subsided and her bones turned to rubber. A forlorn moan sounded somewhere, and then she realized it came from her, so completely spent, and yet craving more.

At last they collapsed back into the bed, a tangle of arms and legs, kisses and caresses.

This is the life I've always wanted. This is the way it's supposed to be.

Turning to the man in her arms, her rock, his eyes searching her face, she realized that whatever came with the intensity of loving this man, whatever it was, she was in for it one hundred percent, and always would be. This was the life she was destined for.

The next morning Kyle came over, and the family held a strategy meeting.

"We have only a few choices," Kyle said. "The Navy is working hard with local media outlets, who have promised no more inappropriate posting of pictures of family or Team members. This has been a tradition going back many, many years, but oddly enough, we have to keep repeating it."

"Can't believe they didn't know that, Kyle," added T.J.

"Well, we have to be ever vigilant. You know that."

Everyone nodded. Shannon sat on the couch between T.J. and her mom, and she was holding hands with both of them.

"It's a double-edged sword. We can have you guys move, which in essence disrupts your life, changes your plans, maybe permanently, or we stay and fight." He lowered his eyes. "And we're not supposed to be fighting here on our soil. But everyone understands we need to be prepared and, if attacked, we defend."

Shannon felt T.J. tense up. "What does your Navy liaison suggest? Should we move?"

"We don't know what they know about you, Shannon. We know they are probably studying T.J., because the news put up his picture. It may be that T.J. being here poses more of a danger to all of you, which totally sucks, because he's the one that could defend you better than anyone else."

"But if we move together—" Shannon began.

Kyle shook his head. "Still no guarantees, Shannon. Should we house our families in a compound somewhere to keep them safe? Are we going to do that just to make sure they are? That's not what we're about. That's not how we live. We live free."

"Just that we have to root out the bad guys," Ollie added.

"How do we do that?" Shannon asked.

"Two schools of thought there. What we're not going to do is go on a search and destroy mission. We don't do that here. Ever. We hide in plain sight, or you move to a location that they don't know about. We don't know how long that would work. Will you have to be looking over your shoulder for months, years to come? No guarantees even if you do move, you will be safe."

Shannon could see the dilemma. She knew her answer, if T.J. would allow it.

"I can't take that chance," T.J. said. Shannon closed her eyes. She'd known he'd say that. "I'm the one who is exposing this family to more danger. You're right, Kyle."

Shannon knew she had to be careful with this next part. "But they came after me in the hospital. They found me somehow." The room remained quiet.

"It has to be your decision. I don't know how they got your information, Shannon. Maybe it was one of the hospital staff, someone who knew you were in labor, and knew what T.J. did for a living. Just hard to say. We don't talk about what we do. We were never supposed to. But especially now, we don't talk about it."

Everyone agreed with this.

T.J. squeezed her hand. "Honey, I am causing further danger by staying here. I say we move, or—"

Shannon stood up and addressed the seated circle. "I won't *be* safe, T.J. if you leave. We stay together. If we move, we move together. Or we stay here, and we keep our eyes and ears open. But I'm not running away."

Kyle smiled. "That's exactly what Christy would say. You gals are tough, I'll grant you that."

"Look at what she did yesterday. They'll be asking her further questions. Won't that trigger curiosity with the neighbors here?" Mrs. Moore asked.

"We can arrange for all interviews to be done at the jurisdictions. None here. I think that could be carried out," Kyle added.

"What about Frankie's parents? What if they stayed there?" Shannon's dad asked.

"That would be putting them in danger. I couldn't ask them to do that," Shannon answered.

"Come here, Shannon," T.J. said and stretched out his arms.

The group chuckled in response as Shannon sat on his lap, legs across his thighs. The protective shield of his arms warmed her and calmed her nerves.

"I say we ask them, honey."

Shannon couldn't believe he was actually proposing this.

"I think they'd want to help, in fact, I know they'd love to help. And they'd love spending time with Courtney."

Kyle nodded. Shannon could see he thought it was a good idea too. "I don't think they'd be on anyone's radar," he said.

"If they know I live here, or know anything about you, Shannon, they'll come here. But they may not know about Frankie's parents," T.J. followed up his statement with a kiss. He ducked his head to make direct eye contact, "Or, do you not want me to be there with you? You could stay there alone, if you want."

"Don't be silly." Shannon was beginning to warm to the idea.

"Shannon and the baby could come stay with us in Palo Alto," Mrs. Moore cut in cheerfully. She got an immediate reaction.

Kyle, T.J. and Shannon all answered with a resounding, "No."

CHAPTER 33

T.J. knew the Bensons would be happy with the arrangement, and he really didn't mind the fact that he'd be spending time with Joe Benson, one of the best dads ever. First day they stayed with the couple, Joe reached out to T.J.

"I was real sorry to hear about your father," he said, his warm eyes not following the smile on his lips. T.J. could see the death of his son still pained him, and probably always would.

"Thanks. That helps, Joe. We both lost someone. I lost a brother, and you a son. Although I also lost my dad, I didn't have what you guys had."

"Everyone does the best they can, son."

"I've heard that a lot lately. Too much, I'll admit." T.J. had thought he'd purged it all out of him, but some of the familiar loathing for his horrible childhood came roaring back.

"Well," Benson said as he removed his hand from the top of T.J.'s shoulder, "We just take it a day at a time. We celebrate when we can, and we cry when we must."

Nothing was ever discussed further. Shannon and T.J. moved several items in two trips from the old house, enlisting the help of a couple of the Team guys. The rush of every day life, with a newborn and with grandparents to dote on the child, started to make everything seem normal.

But that was a problem for T.J. He did not feel normal, and it was getting worse. He was filled with pain, and needed more and more time alone. He retreated to the back bedroom often and lay down while Courtney slept beside the bed. The sounds of the baby's breathing were healing, reminding him of new life and future miracles. But it was short-lived. He couldn't put his finger on it. This was not something he was used to, a family routine. Loving relatives who were gentle and civil to one another. The more he was around it, the more he began to feel out of place.

Today was an especially bad day. He'd tried to work it out down at Gunny's, overstaying the meter and getting a huge parking ticket. Fredo and Mia were back from their honeymoon in St. Thomas, and all of a sudden everyone on the Teams wanted to know when he and Shannon were getting married. The police interview today was especially hard, because they brought up his juvenile record.

Like I'm one of them? Do they really think that?

The FBI agent in charge of the questioning separated him and Tyler and kept harping on the fact that their stories didn't entirely match and kept grilling them for several hours. Even Tyler was upset by it, but took it a lot better than T.J. did.

"You getting along with your wife?" the heavyset agent asked him. The guy had a grease spot on his tie T.J wanted to cut off with scissors.

"Of course. Never better." He knew the man knew they weren't married and had said it on purpose to pick a fight.

"You're living with her in her dead husband's parents home. Why are you not living in your own place? You're not married, right, and have no plans to?"

"We have plans to."

"Yet nobody here seems to be able to give me a date. Have you set a date, Mr. Talbot?"

"What do these questions about my personal life have to do with this investigation?"

"You have a problem talking about your personal life?"

"Fuck no. Except it's personal."

"You've always been known as kind of a loose cannon, Mr. Talbot."

This one really got to him. He fisted his hand under the table and purposely didn't grind his teeth. "Who told you I was a loose cannon?"

"Your LPO, Lansdown. Said you had been kind of a party animal, and now you were more domesticated. Surprised him, he said."

"Then I'm sure he meant it as a compliment." T.J. didn't think Kyle would have said this, or at least didn't mean the implication.

"You like being domesticated? That idea appeal to you, or are you itching to get out there and do something wild and crazy?"

"We all do that. It's what we do. But no, I don't have any plans to go chase girls or go off on a stupid drunken bender. I don't do that anymore. Kyle's right."

The agent leaned back in his chair and took his time answering. "I'm wondering if all this bliss, without the ring and the date, has got you feeling like your balls are in a vice. Know what I mean?"

T.J. hated the man now. He looked back at him like he wished he could've looked at his father years ago growing up, not the kind of look he had to give him as he was dying in the hospital bed. He didn't care what the man thought of him now. He knew it was a danger sign, and he was powerless to stop it. He decided no response was the safest course of action. He was used to some professional jealousy, but this was over the top.

But the agent couldn't stop either. Something was growing between them, and it stunk up the little interview room.

"You ever get angry with your girlfriend? Strike her?"

That was enough. T.J. reached across the table and grabbed Agent Asshole by the greasy tie and yanked his face close. "You fuckin' prick. Get off my back. I don't ever raise my voice or my hand to Shannon. I'm not the one you're looking for. I was clear across the country paying my respects to my dying father, you asshole."

T.J. released the agent before the door burst open and two other agents poured in. They were sent outside immediately. Agent Asshole straightened his tie and smirked. "I don't like you, Talbot. We can do this hard or soft. But something tells me you like it hard, so I'm not going to play that game with you. We got us some homegrown terrorists with special knowledge of your particular family's whereabouts. We've got stories of bloody handprints in places where you were, conflicting witness descriptions, and an assault on your girlfriend while you are in Tennessee visiting a man you hated your whole life. It just doesn't all add up.

He worked at adjusting his mood before he got home. It did feel restricting, trying to play nice when he was angry at so many things. He was angry Shannon had gotten injured. Angry that she was naturally so understanding and compassionate towards his family, when he found it difficult to even think about them. Shannon was consumed by the baby, and although he expected this, he didn't expect that it would pick a scab with him. He felt invisible.

In the old days, before Shannon, a good old night of doing all kinds of things he'd regret the next morning was the call to order. But it was out of the question, and up until now, that had not appealed to him.

He told the Bensons he was going to take a short nap before dinner, retreating to the back bedroom where Courtney was sleeping. Looking down on the baby, he asked himself again why circumstances had taken Frankie, who was loved, cherished and honored by this family and by Shannon, and left him behind in the man's place. A reject. A raging war still brewing inside him. Full of flaws. He was unfamiliar with not being in control, worried about being good enough, deserving enough to be able to protect Shannon and his new daughter. Did Shannon deserve better? Was it right for him to reap the rewards someone else had sowed? Was this stealing?

He moved to the high-backed reading chair and let the mood wash over him. *We celebrate when we can, and we cry when we must.* It was just like the arena. The waiting was the worst.

Shannon entered the room with a basket of laundry.

"Whoa, T.J." She set the basket at her feet and knelt in front of him. "Where did you go?"

"Sorry, Shannon. I'm not doing this very well, am I?"

"Doing what?"

"I feel Frankie—" He had to stop because he didn't want to show her the depth of his darkness.

Shannon slipped onto his lap. Her easy demeanor usually lessened the burden, but tonight it annoyed him. He didn't want her pity.

"I feel Frankie all over this house too. His pictures from his Little League teams are still on their dresser. Our wedding pictures are in the hallway, did you notice?"

T.J. nodded. One of the first things he noticed was that. He remembered how he felt that day. He was focusing on trying to get laid, and still knew that Frankie was one of the luckiest men alive. And now she was *here* with *him*.

"I think your mom was right. I never should have gone to Nashville. I should have been here. Maybe we could have caught all those guys, and we wouldn't have to move or impose on the Bensons."

Shannon held his face between her palms. "Hey. T.J. This isn't you. Where is all this coming from? No one is saying those things except you. We don't know why things happen. You were honoring the request of a dying man, your father."

"Who was a prick and an asshole."

"But the important thing is that you did the honorable thing. I can't believe I'm hearing this." She stood, hands on her hips. "Is this the way you're going to be? Because if so—"

"Don't say it, Shannon.

"What? You mean I can't tell you the truth? After what we've all been through in these past two months? We have to start couching our communications around each other? We're not strong enough to face the facts?"

"That's unkind, and you know it." He was seething. He felt his anger was becoming directed at her. He felt as hopeless as the child he was in the woodshed. He couldn't solve the problem. He had to wait to do anything, and waiting was totally the pits. He hoped Shannon had the control to stop, because he wasn't sure he did.

"I'm not buying this, T.J. I'm not going to spend my whole life walking around on eggshells, pretending things are one way, when reality says it's another."

"Whose reality? Yours? Mine? The Bensons? Those assholes? My dear old dad?"

"You're confused."

"I'm *not* confused. I fuckin' know who I am and don't need you fuckin' telling me otherwise." His voice boomed and bounced off the walls, waking Courtney.

"Well, I hope you're satisfied." She turned her back to him and picked up the baby. On her way out of the room she delivered the kill shot. "You're not the only one who's lost someone, T.J. Man up."

He grabbed his car keys and stormed out of the Benson's house without saying a word. He got in his pickup, wanting to make a public display, to squeal down the road, but at the last minute remembered who he was and what he was really fighting.

And then he knew what he had to do.

CHAPTER 34

The Bensons were understanding after hearing the argument, but clearly didn't know what to do. Shannon and T.J. hadn't really settled in. This loving couple had been delighted to spend so much time around the baby, and now T.J. was going to mess this all up.

She'd been telling herself she had to be strong, and all this nightmare would be over soon, but now she had serious doubts. Perhaps the attack in the hospital was the easy part. Maybe she and T.J. were not going to work out, and she'd go back to considering raising a child alone, back full circle from where she'd started a couple of months ago right after Frankie's death.

Mrs. Benson brought her a hot cup of herbal tea, which was a lifesaver. As soon as she took a sip, she felt her milk let down and Courtney nearly choked on the stream that came towards her.

"Thank you," she said to the kind woman.

"Used to work for me every time with Frankie. As a baby, he'd get so hungry and frustrated. The more he fussed, the tenser I became. Then of course the milk didn't come. It's always touch and go with your first, they say. You start worrying about everything."

"You're right. The little argument with T.J. didn't help either."

"It happens. You know, Joe even asked me after Frankie was about a month old if I still loved him. Can you imagine? Here I was trying to be the best mom, thinking I was doing all the right things, and I'd forgotten to let him know how special he was to me."

Shannon thought that was very good advice.

"He's probably trying to work out his grief at losing his father. It comes on in strange ways. We've certainly learned a bit about that. When you least expect it, something will—" She abruptly stopped and gave her a warm smile. "I'm sure everything will work out just fine."

Shannon wished she could feel as assured.

Courtney went down again, and the three of them ate dinner together without talking about T.J. Shannon was mulling their earlier words and grew more and more concerned again that she'd done irreparable damage to their relationship. She wanted to call him, but thought he'd feel chased. She decided she needed to trust him to come home soon.

Ollie and Rory stopped by the house looking for T.J.

"He left about an hour ago," she told them.

"That's when he tried calling us. You know where he went?"

"No. Sorry. He needed to do something. I'm not exactly sure what it was."

After the boys left, Shannon decided she would turn in early. She took a long hot shower and settled in to bed, reading herself to sleep.

Two hours later, T.J. awakened her, kneeling at her bedside. "Wake up, Shannon," he whispered.

She could smell alcohol on his breath as he tenderly kissed her.

"Come on honey, we have to talk." He picked her up out of the bed and sat with her across his lap in the reading chair. She found the shelter of that spot just below his chin where her head fit so well, the warmth radiating from his body along with the sound of his heart and the ebb and flow of his breathing.

She spoke to the top of his shirt, her forefinger tracing over his lower lip. "Where did you go?"

"I went over to the house. I got out Frankie's 30-year old whiskey we brought back from one of our cross-country trips and opened it. We were saving it for some special occasion."

"What's the special occasion?"

"Well, maybe I got ahead of myself." His fingers worked over the tension he felt in her shoulders, her upper spine. Hear me out, Shannon. And then you tell me."

She lay back against his chest as he began again. His raspy voice was something she could listen to forever.

"I was thinking about what was wrong with me. I have you. I have beautiful Courtney. My past is, well, behind me now. I have a sister. All the right parts are so right, and the wrong parts are gone. Except for this homegrown threat, which is real and considerable, everything about my life, our lives, is going well."

She snuggled closer to him and sighed. "Yes, T.J. we have it all."

"What happened in the hospital made me realize that anything can happen at anytime. We can't control it all. Ever. We try, we pay attention, but it's an illusion to think we can. We have to live with it."

She wasn't sure where he was going with this.

"And I've been fighting it, Shannon. I've been holding my breath and resisting this."

"Resisting what?"

"Taking life on life's terms." He squeezed her tightly. "I was waiting until the baby was born. Then waiting until we were settled here. And honey, I don't want to wait any longer. What if we all die tomorrow? I mean, Frankie taught us that."

She sat up and searched his face. She could see his full lips in the light of the moon and the reflection of light in his eyes. But she felt the warm arms that held her, the words that soothed her soul.

He fumbled through his pockets until she heard paper rustle. He brought out a small brown envelope not any larger than a couple of inches long. He slipped his fingers inside, and she saw him draw out a plain gold band and hold it to the moonlight. "This belonged to my mother, and is all I have, all I can give you from my family, from my past. But if you'll marry me, Shannon, it and everything else I am, everything else I own, is yours. Forever, honey."

She didn't have to think about it. She placed her finger into the ring opening, allowing him to slide it on. Then clasping his hand, she said, "It would be my honor."

He took his time with her. The careful, gentle nourishment he gave her in bed was more than sex. She let him start slow, matching his actions with her own. Her touch mirrored his. As he kissed and caressed her delicate places, sending her on a mind-bending journey of passion, her fingers traveled over the scars and wounds of this warrior, tracing the tats she could not feel but knew were there. She kissed the invisible scars in his heart, loved the little abused boy and the brave man who never gave up hope even in the face of tragedy. She could give him everything he needed. Frankie's parents could be his parents. She and Courtney would be his family in every sense of the word, a better family, a family that would mirror the joy he brought to them.

She pushed on his shoulders and guided him to lie on his back. Mounting him, she lowered herself on to him slowly. Her hands braced against his upper torso, she ground her pelvis down slowly, watching his face in the moonlight, and feeling the delicious sensations of their joining. She rocked and angled her body back and forth on him, squeezing her muscles, enjoying every inch of him deep inside her. She watched his eyes sparkle and non-verbally let him know how much she loved and cherished him.

Their lovemaking was a sacrament. She felt her heart would forever be the sanctuary of his soul.

His lips on fire muffled her cries. He waited for her explosion, before he plundered her deep, lodging himself until he began to spill, holding her so close she could barely breathe. He loved her with everything he had, and she knew that she would willingly take all the intensity, even the pain sometimes, and claim it for her own.

She asked him for more lovemaking during the night, not able to get enough of him. She held up her hand with the ring shining in the midnight light and he kissed it, as he kissed the palm of her other hand where she'd been cut.

"You are my warrior princess. Nobody should mess with you," he whispered.

"Except you. I want you to mess with me. Promise it will be like this every night?"

He chuckled. "I'm not Superman."

"Yes, you are. We'll train together."

"I like that kind of training."

Early in the morning, before the sun rose, Courtney needed another feeding. T.J. changed her very wet diaper and brought her into bed with them. He watched as the little mouth latched onto Shannon's breast, while his fingers laced through her hair. He rubbed her temples.

"So beautiful. I am the luckiest man in the world," he said.

"To me, you are the *only* man in the world."

CHAPTER 35

T.J. got up at sunrise, slipped on some pajama bottoms and tiptoed quietly into the kitchen to brew some coffee. Movement outside got his attention, and he saw two men dart into the yard of the neighbors across the street. They were holding semi-automatics.

He grabbed the landline and dialed Kyle.

"I got two men outside the Benson house, I think with AKs."

"Shit. I'll see who I can get on the way. Be there in ten. Hang on."

"Roger that one, big time."

He woke the Bensons from the master bedroom, who quickly made it into Shannon's room. T.J. threw her a pair of his pajamas while she grabbed his shirt from last night from the floor.

"I only saw two, but there could be more. You guys stay in here and wait." He pulled a SigSauer from his duty bag, pulled the hammer back and handed it to Joe Benson. "If you have to. You got twenty-one chances."

"Right," he answered.

"This door is no cover, so move the chair in front of you, or use the mattress if you have to. Do not let anyone in here unless they knock four times, got it?"

"Got it." Benson said.

"That means shoot them through the door if it starts to open without it."

"Got it." But T.J. could see Joe's hands shake and hoped the man wouldn't shoot himself first.

He grabbed his H&K and kissed Shannon. "Try to keep her quiet. She's gonna freak if she hears gunfire."

He closed the bedroom door and wondered why they hadn't come in the middle of the night, when the element of surprise would have helped them.

Hiding just inside the second bedroom, which would be out of the line of fire if they came from either front or back, he texted Kyle:

Family, closed door. Your ETA?
Here. Got 3 more.
!!

Just then, he heard glass breaking and knew they were already in the house.

Glass broken in kitchen.

At the sound of movement in the kitchen, he knew they'd come in through the garage. Checking the windows in the bedroom, he did not see movement. He heard the staccato of a Middle Eastern tongue and decided the two were together in the kitchen.

Conf 2 Cajuns.
We're coming from the rear. Armani front.

He stored his phone, adjusted his grip on the H&K short barrel he'd brought with him, and readied himself. A dark shadow crossed the end of the hallway, just as he saw Armando on the outside run forward. If he was planning on a front door breach, T.J. would not have the shot he wanted or he'd hit his own guy. He'd have to wait for instructions.

One gunman dressed in a black headdress but wearing sneakers and blue jeans came down the hallway, causing one of the floorboards in the old house to groan, and he stopped. T.J. saw the shadow form outside his door and couldn't risk a peek. The door moved slightly so he blasted through it chest-height and heard the drop of a body and retreating footsteps.

Courtney screamed, revealing the family location.

Hearing glass crunch in the kitchen he guessed the gunman was headed back to the garage area but he couldn't risk a shot. Nothing was moving on the other side of the door. Just then, the front door shattered in an explosive charge. Mere seconds later he heard the staccato of gunfire and a few seconds later heard the word, *"Clear!"*

He was never so happy in his life to hear that word. Opening the door, he checked the body in front of him and confirmed he was shot through the heart.

"Not so fast, you dog," a voice said from the master bed-room behind T.J. "You will drop your weapon."

T.J. tried to turn.

"Now! You will drop your weapon now!" And then the gunman addressed whoever was in the kitchen. "I have your man. You will surrender, or I put a bullet in his brain."

T.J. was still crouching, and he knew the gunman's sole interest was to carry out the mission and probably not to take prisoners. He didn't buy the stall. As the seconds ticked by, and he heard the man back down the hallway toward the closed door of his family's hiding place, T.J. inhaled and yelled as loud as he could, "High."

Armando's kill shot hit him in the middle of his nose, and his head exploded. T.J. scrambled to the back room to make sure there weren't any others.

"Clear," he shouted.

Armando's smiling face appeared in the hallway.

"Way to lie low, Talbot."

"Roger that. Knew you could make that shot."

"With my eyes closed."

T.J. stood up, knocked four times on the door and then stepped in.

Joe Benson had been holding the gun out in front of him and was so rigid with fear that when T.J. entered he kept the gun aimed at him.

"Whoa, there, Joe. I'm one of the good guys, remember?"

Joe sighed, dropped his arms and his shoulders, and nearly collapsed. T.J. took the Sig away from him, and uncocked the hammer so he wouldn't shoot himself in the leg.

Police and rescue squads descended all over the house. Kyle and the others retreated and disappeared. Armando had to stay, as did T.J. Their liaison, Collins, as well as other Navy personnel showed up to run interference and guarantee neither of the two SEALs were exposed to the public. It was decided the attack would be classified a robbery stopped at gunpoint by a sharp-thinking retired carpenter who happened to be pretty good with a gun.

Lined with tears, Shannon looked exhausted. Of course, Courtney was nursing and didn't seem to be affected by the sea of activity around her. Mrs. Benson attempted to bring coffee and water to the investigators and crew who had shown up. She tried to engage the services of her husband, but Joe appeared to be in shock still. T.J. sat him down.

"Joe, you did real good, there."

"Man, I'm sure glad I didn't have to shoot that thing. I'm not sure I would have."

"Trust me, you would have. The way you looked at me and pointed it right at my chest, you would have. Just took you awhile to register who I was, but you were ready."

"I could never do what you do, T.J."

"You would if you had to, and you would have tonight. But you didn't have to, and that's what we're all about." He draped his arm around the man he would forevermore consider his father. "Frankie was right there with you. He's jumping up and down in heaven, Joe. Believe me, he is."

That brought a smile to Benson's face.

The local police were able to control the two news vans that showed up at the scene and worked to keep a wide perimeter of neighbors.

Collins brought T.J. two yellow ponchos so they could exit as part of the rescue squad. They concluded their questioning, Collins observing everything. "I'm afraid I can't have you leave with the family. It just would draw too many questions. They'll be here awhile and I'm going to sit in on Benson's interview, make sure the story goes the way it should."

"Only guy I'm worried about is that prick from the FBI who interviewed me yesterday."

"May not be able to keep you away from him, but I'll try. Now you and Armando go crash at his place and get some rest. I'll get the family over there as soon as I can, okay?"

T.J. put on his yellow rubber slicker and looked for Shannon, who was changing Courtney.

"You did great, sweetheart," he said as he wrapped his arm around her waist. Shannon collapsed into his chest. With one hand on Courtney and the other arm squeezing the love of his life, he propped her up until her sobs ended.

"I'm so grateful, T.J. I'm—"

"You guys were troopers. You got nerves of steel, Shannon. I'm gonna need that in the months and years to come, honey. You're my rock.

"Dad was—"

"Awesome," he interrupted. "He was freakin' awesome."

She chuckled. "He was kind of, wasn't he? I thought he was going to shoot you." That brought a smile to her face.

"I think you would have jumped him, rather than let that happen," he joked. "You're tough, babe. Really tough. You guys kept your wits about you. That's what it takes."

"And training."

"There is that."

"Do you think this will end it?" She picked up Courtney and held her against her shoulder, patting her back.

T.J. didn't want to answer, but he had to be honest with her. "No. Unfortunately, no. But I think this group is done, for now. I think we can expect more. I'm going to have to wait to see. Might be they relocate me to an East Coast team, but the Navy's got their work cut out for them. Getting this close to our families is going to be something they're going to have to look at."

She smoothed his cheek with her right hand. "Thank you, T.J. for coming into our lives. You kept your promise to Frankie. You protected me and Courtney. I love you."

Armani and Collins interrupted their long kiss at the doorway.

"Gotta go, Talbot," Collins' voice was curt and efficient.

T.J. kissed Shannon one more time quickly and then addressed her, "I'm going to slip out with Armani, and we'll meet up later at his house. Collins here is the man you want if you have any questions. He'll be here when they formally interview Joe and Gloria. He'll make sure you get to where you're supposed to be without the news media or nosey neighbors getting in the way.

"Right."

"Okay, then."

It was hard to leave them behind, but for their best interests and for the circumstances, it was their only option. As he made his way toward a waiting unmarked van, next to the Puerto Rican sharpshooter, he discovered something else about himself.

The anger and anguish he'd been feeling before he'd gone over to the house, before he'd given the ring to Shannon, before the gunfight, was completely gone. He knew it was something he'd be dealing with his whole life, but one huge problem had been solved.

Shannon said it earlier.

You kept your promise to Frankie.

CHAPTER 36

T.J. was dressed in a tux and felt like a stuffed penguin. Kyle, Armando, Tyler and Fredo were beside him as they watched the last of the attendees filter into the little chapel. Green leafy vines covered the side of the building, with a large terrace at the back where the reception was going to be held. Sounds of birds echoed throughout the mostly stucco surface of the Spanish-style complex.

It wasn't the grand, lavish wedding Shannon had the first time, but it was what she wanted, and T.J. was grateful for that.

Cindy, Shannon's former maid of honor, flounced by wearing a bright blue dress, on the arm of another SEAL T.J. recognized from one of the other Teams. She twiddled her fingers at him with a sultry smirk.

And I'm not even slightly interested. But he winked for her benefit, and gave her a warm smile anyway. Fredo, Kyle,

Armando and Tyler followed the two women until they disappeared into the church. It was just what they always did. No one said a word.

Mrs. Moore was to be escorted to the front row, and that was T.J.'s responsibility. Though it would normally be his best man's duty, T.J. had insisted it be his job. She appeared before him, looking wound up tight but gorgeous. He noticed she smiled at him a lot more, which gladdened his heart. Maybe the truce they'd called during the wedding planning would work after all.

"Why, Mrs. Moore, you look absolutely divine," he said as he bowed in her direction.

"Glad to see you haven't taken off for Alaska," she said and winked at him. T.J. could clearly see where Shannon got her fiery spirit.

"Never. I messed up Shannon's first wedding. I won't mess up the second. I promise."

She dazzled him with her smile, her eyes filling with tears, just the way Shannon's did when she was overwhelmed by emotion. "I know I can count on that promise."

The groomsmen each punched T.J. in the arm and went ahead to stand at their places in the front of the chapel. Organ music wafted through the hallways and mixed with the sounds of the birds. He would always remember this as a perfect day. He was going to be stepping into a role he had never had before, to complete a mission he was made for.

He took Mrs. Moore's arm and accompanied her toward the entrance to the chapel. Mr. Moore appeared out of nowhere and stood behind him. T.J. turned, and they shook hands.

"Son," he said, "I'm very proud you're marrying my daughter. Nothing could please me more."

As he escorted Shannon's mom down the aisle, he looked at his side of the church. They'd talked about someone else standing in for his parents, but T.J. told everyone to leave those seats vacant. Joe and Gloria Benson defied his edict and stood tall in the front row anyway, next to his sister Connie. He brought Mrs. Moore to her seat and stopped to give her a warm kiss on the cheek. "You're beautiful, just like your daughter," he whispered.

Mrs. Moore straightened for a second, her eyes darting up to his face, unsure about the compliment, but then he could see her insides melt. Something else was on the tip of her tongue, but she tempered it. "Thank you," she breathed back to him softly.

T.J. took his place next to Tyler, held his hands together and winked at his sister.

The audience began rustling as the music changed and everyone turned to see the vision of Shannon, standing in the same wedding dress she'd worn before. He was surprised and wondered about the protocol of this. He remembered that day, how Frankie had fallen and her bodice had been pulled down. He blushed and cleared his throat as he relived that memory.

Whatever possessed her to wear the same dress?

Looking at Mrs. Moore, he caught her wink at him. This had been her suggestion, he realized.

But as he watched her lightly drift down the burgundy carpet towards him, a proud Mr. Moore on her arm, he saw that yes, this was the perfect choice. He was stepping into the role that had been created for him. He was on a path that had been blazed for him, part of the tradition he'd always shunned, veered away from. As a SEAL, he was following the brotherhood of those who had fought before him, some of whom had perished. He wasn't independent of them, he was *part* of them. The living and the ones who had passed on.

As it should be.

Shannon stood before him as Mr. Moore gave him her hand. He kissed her palm, the one with the now-healed scar in the center. Her eyes were glistening, her breathing ragged. "I am the luckiest man in the world."

She slipped her fingers into his hair and shook her head. "I wish you could kiss me right now."

"Very well." He pulled up her veil, and, completely without regard to protocol, pulled her to him and kissed her, as she exploded in his arms. They listened to the crowd titter, but he didn't care. He could see she didn't care either. He kept his hands around the small of her back and no lower, but damn, he wanted to.

Just as he had the day of Frankie's wedding, though it was so inconvenient, he was getting a hard on. *It's the dress.* Something about all the flouncy, crinkling material flowing everywhere. It brought out the familiar wild side of him.

The minister cleared his throat, and again a ripple of laughter waved through the audience.

"I guess I should get you properly wed before I get you out of this dress," he whispered. She remained in his arms, waiting for him to take the lead. She'd have stood there half a day if he wanted, and he loved that about her.

"You can take your time, I understand you're a special operator, and I'm going to let you special me all you want."

"Let's get you mine, legally. I don't want you slipping away on me."

"Never going to happen, T.J."

The crowd was laughing now heartily. Several Hooyas enthusiastically gave him encouragement. He turned to the audience and gave them a thumbs up, and several returned his gesture.

"I'm ready now," he said to the minister, whose face showed a mixture of concern and amusement.

"Good. Okay, ladies and gentlemen…"

But T.J. had kept his arms around Shannon as she leaned in all her perfumed glory against him, her breasts pressing against his biceps. He matched her breathing, as they stared into each others eyes at several places during the reading of the canon. The minister had to interrupt their gazing for the presentation of the rings.

For the second time in his life, he slipped his mother's ring on Shannon's finger, looking over at his sister. Connie immediately lowered her chin and could not look back at him. Shannon was now his for all eternity with the pronouncement. Her veil was already tucked back from her head. He lifted his hands to cup her face and spoke, "If you can find it in your heart to love me a tenth of the amount I love you, you'll make me a happy man, eternally."

Their kiss was brief. Shannon wanted to say something, "T.J. you are the man I was always destined to be with. My heart is filled to bursting. I'll be here for you forever."

T.J. picked her up and whispered, "Honey, I hope you don't mind, but I've got the biggest hard-on I've ever had, and I need some cover."

She threw her head back and laughed. "Perfect. Don't ever change, T.J."

"Not to worry, baby."

He carried her down the aisle, as he winked and she waved to faces in the audience. He continued carrying her down the brown tiled floor to the minister's office, which was locked. Still with Shannon in his arms, he found a Sunday school room open and slipped inside.

His hands were all over her, first pulling down the bodice to expose her breasts. He knelt and suckled them, at the same time reached under her white skirts and found she was not wearing underwear.

"How did you know?"

"I was hoping. And I liked the feel of walking down the aisle without them on."

"You're a wicked bride."

"I am that. So wickedly in love with you."

He sat her on a countertop, brushing the contents aside.

"Hurry," she whispered as he began unzipping his pants.

All he could do was fumble. He'd never had so much trouble with his zipper in his life. Then it got stuck in the fabric of the front closure.

"Fuck!" he said.

"Please, yes."

"No, I mean, the zipper is stuck."

"Let me." She squeezed his package, massaging lower, pushing his hands away. Her fingers deftly found the zipper, untangled the fabric from the teeth as she pulled the device down slowly and her hands found his shaft. "Ah, there we are, T.J." She slipped his trousers over his thighs.

She guided him to her entrance, and he at last felt her moist folds around him as he squeezed her buttocks, pulling her onto him.

Shannon was not going to leave his side. She didn't want to dance with anyone else, but in the end she caved and socialized. She watched him from behind as he talked to his Teammates. She watched how delicately he treated her mother. He even danced with his sister.

She was happy that at last they would be able to move forward together.

Joe Benson asked her for a dance. "I think I am just as happy today."

Shannon's eyes filled with tears. "He would be happy for me, for all of us, Dad."

Benson looked down and lost his timing for a second, stepping on her gown, and apologized. "I think he would. Gloria and I have no regrets, Shannon. None."

At last she was able to dance with her handsome groom. T.J. swung her around the room with the practiced composure of a professional dancer, and it surprised her.

"You've been practicing," she said.

"Sophia's dance lessons. Secret stealth mission."

"Ah, I see. And what else have you been practicing?"

"You'll just have to wait, Mrs. Talbot. That has taken a lifetime of planning. I may have to do a lot of practice, but I plan on becoming absolute master and commander."

"Counting on it. And I'll be your second in command."

The End

SEAL BROTHERHOOD SERIES
Accidental SEAL (Book 1)
Fallen SEAL Legacy (Book 2)
SEAL Under Covers (Book 3)
SEAL The Deal (Book 4)
Cruisin' For A SEAL (Book 5)
SEAL My Destiny (Book 6)
SEAL Of My Heart (Book 7)

BAD BOYS OF SEAL TEAM 3
SEAL's Promise (Book 1)
SEAL My Home (Book 2)
SEAL's Code (Book 3)

BAND OF BACHELORS
Lucas (Book 1)
Alex (Book 2)

TRUE BLUE SEALS
True Navy Blue (prequel to Zak)
Zak (Book 1)

NOVELLAS
SEAL Encounter
SEAL Endeavor
True Navy Blue (prequel to Zak)
Fredo's Secret
Nashville SEAL

OTHER BOOKS BY SHARON HAMILTON

SEAL BROTHERHOOD SERIES

BOOK 1   BOOK 2

BOOK 3   BOOK 4   BOOK 5

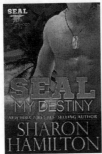 

BOOK 6   BOOK 7

BAD BOYS
OF SEAL TEAM 3

BOOK 1

BOOK 2

BOOK 3

BAND OF BACHELORS

BOOK 1

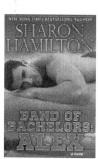

BOOK 2

  **TRUE BLUE SEALS**

PREQUEL TO ZAK   BOOK 1

SEAL NOVELLAS

Golden Vampires
OF TUSCANY

BOOK 1   BOOK 2

THE GUARDIANS

BOOK 1   BOOK 2   BOOK 3

ABOUT THE AUTHOR

Sharon's award-winning spicy Navy SEAL stories in the SEAL Brotherhood series, have consistently made best sellers lists and review sites. Her characters follow a sometimes rocky road to redemption through passion and true love.

Her Golden Vampires of Tuscany are not like any vamps you've read before, since they don't go to ground and can walk around in the full light of the sun.

Her Guardian Angels struggle with the human charges they are sent to save, often escaping their vanilla world of Heaven for the brief human one. You won't find any of these beings in any Sunday school class.

She lives in Sonoma County, California with her husband, and two Dobermans. A lifelong organic gardener, when she's not writing, she's getting verra verra dirty in the mud, or wandering Farmer's Markets looking for new Heirloom varieties of vegetables and flowers.